Born in the east end of London, grew up in Essex, Rosi Morgan-Barry now lives in Berkshire. Married with five children; she has worked as a speech and language therapist. Now retired, she crams her diary with Methodist local preaching, and spends her time in gardening, singing in two choirs and writing.

To my husband Bill, always quietly encouraging.

Rosi Morgan-Barry

THE BITTER AND THE SWEET

AUSTIN MACAULEY PUBLISHERS™

LONDON • CAMBRIDGE • NEW YORK • SHARJAH

A CIP catalogue record for this title is available from the British Library.

ISBN 9781528983280 (Paperback)
ISBN 9781528983297 (ePub e-book)

www.austinmacauley.com

First Published (2020)
Austin Macauley Publishers Ltd
25 Canada Square
Canary Wharf
London
E14 5LQ

Introduction

In all great novels, the main characters shine with a brilliance that adds lustre to the whole work. Jane Austen's *Pride and Prejudice* is no exception: Elizabeth Bennet was her author's favourite heroine; Mr Darcy every woman's favourite hero. Other characters weave through the story to delight, exasperate, amuse or annoy in various proportions. But what of those minor characters who remain in the shadows and seem to exist only to pull a few threads of the story into place?

Miss Anne de Bourgh is one such. She is described as: "'such a little creature!' 'Sickly and cross', 'thin and small', her features, though not plain, were insignificant and she spoke very little except in a low voice."

Yet, she was the grand-daughter of an earl, the daughter of a baronet and of an over-bearing, arrogant and at times, ill-mannered mother. She was also heiress to a great estate and a considerable fortune.

So, why is she so described? What of her father, Sir Lewis? Who were the other members of her family? What was her childhood? And what became of her?

This is her story.

*** \
** \
*

Book One
Mistress of Rosings

Chapter One

"Death surprises us in the midst of our hopes."
Thomas Fuller: Gnomologia (1752)

Anne regarded her mother's face gravely and with attention. She knew it so well in all its expressions. The lift of the chin in hauteur; the lift of the eyebrow in disdain; the set of the mouth when issuing an order, the thinning of the lips into a straight and uncompromising line after making a pronouncement. Lady Catherine did not converse: she made pronouncements which brooked no disagreement. Rarely did the mouth lift into any semblance of a smile; frequently would a frown-line appear between the fine brows, signalling extreme displeasure.

The most that could ever be said of Lady Catherine's range of positive expressions was that a look of smoothness and satisfaction would settle on her features when, for example, she contemplated the first sight of Rosings Park from the carriage, or received a particularly fine (and extremely expensive) article of apparel from her modiste. The family emeralds brought that sleek look on her face, as did any particularly obsequious courtesy extended to her by her retainers, particularly Mr Collins. Her own daughter never called up that look. Her ladyship's nephews might have evoked it in their younger days and before a certain fall from grace. But not Anne. Whether Sir Lewis de Bourgh had ever called forth his wife's look of aloof pleasure, Anne had no means of knowing. He had died while she was still too young to have known him well, but not before she had learned to love him above all others.

But now, the aristocratic face was devoid of all expression. The body of Lady Catherine de Bourgh lay straight and still in the ornately canopied bed where she had slept since she was a young bride. Her hands were folded devoutly over her bosom, her eyelids closed. Under her lace cap a thin white ribbon passed tightly under her chin. Her skin had the colour and texture of candle wax. Tentatively, and with curiosity as to how it would feel, Anne stretched out a hand and laid it against her mother's cheek. At this simple gesture, her companion and former governess, the ever-present Mrs Jenkinson, began to sob aloud.

"Oh my poor dear Miss Anne! To be thus orphaned at such a tender age! To think that never again will your mother's hand caress you as gently as you now touch her cheek…"

Anne turned and silenced Mrs Jenkinson with a gesture.

"Please. I wish to be alone with my mother. To—to say a prayer. For her soul."

Mrs Jenkinson, apparently now totally overcome, could only press Anne's hand in mute sympathy before leaving the room. She left the door the tiniest bit ajar and lingered. Old habits and Lady Catherine's instructions die hard, and Mrs Jenkinson's eyes and ears were accustomed to door-cracks and keyholes.

Anne knelt down and rested her head on her clasped hands in an attitude of piety. She did indeed pray, but not as her watchful companion might have expected.

"Lord God," whispered Anne. "Almighty and Everlasting. Receive my mother's soul. And thank you. Thank you. Thank you."

The vigilant eye applied to the crack of the door noted with approval Anne's shaking shoulders. But the owner of the eye could not have guessed that they shook in silent but exultant laughter.

*

Over the next few days, the servants behind the thick oak door that separated their world from that of their betters, were busy telling and re-telling the gruesomely exciting account of Lady Catherine's demise. Roberts, the butler, had, of course, seen it all, and the housekeeper and her ladyship's maid were also in the know, having been hastily summoned to the morning room.

Roberts had taken the daily letters to Lady Catherine on his salver: one from her man of business; one with a London frank—that would be from her sister, Lady Cecilia Gould, whose husband was a Member of Parliament who could frank her letters. Lady Cecilia was, therefore, profligate in correspondence and wrote regularly, but seldom received a reply; Lady Catherine having been greatly displeased at Cecilia's first marriage to a city man. The fact that he had been engaged in respectable foreign trade, and that when he died, he left her a very wealthy widow, had not greatly softened her sister's heart. Neither had Cecilia's subsequent marriage to the eminent Sir Thomas Gould. Lady Catherine had thought her sister could have done better for her second attempt at matrimony than a mere knight.

There was one more letter on the salver, written in a firm, clear hand and with the Pemberley crest clearly visible. Roberts knew that hand well and could guess the contents of the single sheet, which, when Lady Catherine perused it, caused her to utter a loud shriek and fall prostrate on the floor. The butler immediately rang the bell for Martha Dawson and Mrs Rowlands, instructing the one to run for hartshorn and water and the other for feathers to burn. But neither the acrid smell of burnt feathers, nor the attempt to administer the hartshorn had an effect. Lady Catherine's heart, which had been filled with an icy rage ever since her nephew's, Fitzwilliam Darcy's marriage to the totally unsuitable

Elizabeth Bennet, the previous year, had finally burst. Anger and chagrin had coursed along her veins and she died as she had lived, in disappointed fury.

"But whatever was in the letter to cause her ladyship such grief?" wondered the upper housemaid. Everyone turned to the butler.

"Now, do you think I would abuse my position as to read it?" he demanded. "That were her ladyship's private correspondence. But I did note..." he dropped his lofty tone and became conspiratorial, "...as how it came from Pemberley. And was in Mr Darcy's handwriting."

The women looked at each other and nodded wisely. This, they surmised, was women's business.

"You think Mrs Darcy...?" began Cook.

"Has been safely delivered of a fine son. Yes. Both mother and child doing well. A strong, healthy boy," Roberts affirmed, not of course having actually read the letter, merely having ascertained its contents when he retrieved it from Lady Catherine's dead fingers.

"God be praised!" exclaimed Cook devoutly. "And God bless dear Mrs Elizabeth!"

The others endorsed this view with nods and smiles. They had all taken a fancy to the delightful Miss Eliza Bennet on her only visit to her friend, Mrs Collins at the parsonage. Indeed Charley, the second footman had been heard to remark she had right rum ogles, and had been severely reprimanded for this remark by Roberts, who nonetheless did not check him when he gleefully recounted Miss Elizabeth's lively repartee with Lady Catherine, below stairs. The servants had gawped and gossiped at the news of her marriage to Mr Darcy.

"A fine strong son!" said the second housemaid. "That's one in the eye for..." she faltered and bit her lip. Her eyes were on Roberts who, not infrequently, had to remind her not to bibble-babble and to mind her tongue. But he was looking as sleek as the kitchen cat.

"Quite!" he said now. "Though I don't think as you should have said it Betty. That's what caused it I reckon. It was a shock, you see. Lady Catherine de Bourgh always had her eye on Pemberley, which would have come her way if Mr Darcy had married Miss Anne as he was supposed to. And then I reckon her, Lady Catherine that is, still went on hoping and planning, that there'd be no heir p'raps, or that Mrs Elizabeth would die in childbirth like..."

"That's a wicked thing to say!" exclaimed Cook.

"Wicked thing for her to think," responded Roberts, "if, of course, she did think it, which we have no means of actually knowing. I know we should never speak ill of the dead, as Parson Collins is always telling us, but the truth of it is, she was a proper harridan."

"A bracket-faced mort," added Charley.

"A right Friday-faced, weasel-gutted..." said Abel, the first footman.

"Now, now, now!" Roberts admonished. "Give your red-rags a rest or you'll be out of here without a feather to fly with."

"And I'll not have that thieves' cant in my nice clean kitchen. Thank you very much," put in Cook. "What would Mrs Jenkinson say if she heard you?"

"That ol' fussock? She's nobbut a toad-eater…"

A bell pealed, making them all jump guiltily. Up on the wall hung rows of pulls, each connected to a room in the upper part of the house, an innovation installed by Lady Catherine but a few years ago. The one that was wagging now, and Betty always thought they looked like little tongues - was that of Miss Anne's sitting-room. Roberts nodded to Anne's personal maid.

"Up you go Sarah," he commanded. "See what her young ladyship wants." Sarah Smallbone realised with a start of astonishment that her position in the servants' hierarchy had risen above that of Martha Dawson, Lady Catherine's maid. Martha tossed her head.

"Mind your manners now," she said. "No taking liberties."

"Wouldn't dream of it," retorted Sarah. She sped away.

*

Miss Anne de Bourgh was seated at her writing bureau. Her slenderness and natural pallor were accentuated by the unrelieved black of her mourning, but Sarah noted that the narrow back was held a little straighter than usual and there was a hint of determination in the pale face. Mrs Jenkinson, who seemed to feel that a continuing excess of grief was a necessary part of her duties, was seated in the window seat, faintly moaning, clutching a damp handkerchief and watching Anne out of the corner of her eye. Sarah bobbed a curtsey.

"You rang Miss Anne?"

"Several things, Sarah. Will you inform Roberts that I require the key to my mother's bureau, and will you instruct Dawson to bring me Lady Catherine's jewel case?"

Mrs Jenkinson was moved to protest.

"My dear! Poor dear Lady Catherine is not yet in her grave…!"

Anne motioned her to be quiet with a gesture—so like her mother's that the astonished Mrs Jenkinson closed up like a clam. Sarah too clamped her lips so as not to be seen to smile.

"And I will need to see Mrs Rowlands to ensure that all the servants have acceptable blacks before the funeral. You have all that, Sarah?"

"Yes'm. Mr Roberts for the key, Martha for the jewels and Mrs Rowlands for the blacks."

"Good. Then return to me with a dish of tea. You will take tea, Mrs Jenkinson?" That lady moaned a little louder.

"My dear! How can you think of tea at a time like this?"

"Very easily. Sarah, ask Cook if she has any of her delicious honey biscuits. If so, I would like some of them too."

"Miss Anne! Is that wise my dear? Your poor dear mother was always so careful of your delicate digestion."

She ended on a quavery note but Anne ignored it, nodding a dismissal at Sarah.

The maid curtsied again and scurried away, fleet with importance.

Back below stairs, she delivered her messages. Roberts and Mrs Rowlands departed with dignity; Martha tossed her head again and Cook eyed Sarah with a grin.

"Don't go getting above yourself, now."

"Wouldn't dream of it," Sarah said again, departing with the tray of tea and honey biscuits.

*

The week between Lady Catherine de Bourgh's death and her funeral was one of intense activity for the servants of Rosings Park. The estate carpenters had already fashioned a carved and ornate coffin in seasoned oak, which needed only the addition of brass handles and fittings. In this her ladyship lay in state until the morning of the funeral. Tall silver candlesticks stood at her head and feet. The trunks containing the family mourning had been opened and the servants had all been provided with their blacks, Mrs Rowlands ensuring that stains were removed with boiled fig leaves. The sewing women were busy altering and mending, and quantities of black crepe had been issued to the villagers for armbands, gloves and bonnet trimmings. The kitchen was a-swirl with steam and a-scurry with activity, while the housemaids skittered up and down stairs with brooms and mops, aired sheets and cans of hot water in readiness for the assembling guests. *"Aunts and cousins,"* thought Anne, *"and uncles I have not seen since I was young enough to be chucked under the chin."*

Of her father's family, these uncles consisted of the baronet's brothers: John de Bourgh, Dean of the cathedral in Belmingham and Captain William de Bourgh, serving in His Majesty's navy and just home from a spell of duty in the West Indies. Both these gentlemen had been determined chin-chuckers. But of the youngest of Sir Lewis's three brothers, Percy, Anne had but the faintest memory. She had seen him only once, when she was very small and retained but the haziest memory of one who had been considered the handsomest of all the good-looking de Bourgh brothers. Nothing was ever said of him—at least above stairs. The only girl in the de Bourgh family was Anne's favourite aunt, the Lady Harriet Claydon, Dowager Countess of Brentshire. She brought apologies from her son, the third Earl, and the prettily expressed condolences of her daughter Harry, busy with her own young family.

Her mother's family was represented by her three nephews: Charles, fifth Earl of Matlock with his shy little wife Mary; his brother Colonel James Fitzwilliam, and Mr Darcy of course, whose communication, unbeknown to him, had caused his absence from Pemberley during his wife's lying-in. Of the female members of Lady Catherine's family, there was but her one surviving sister Lady Cecilia Gould with her pretty daughter—another Catherine, but known as Kit. They were accompanied by the gruff but amiable Sir Thomas Gould.

The competent Mrs Rowlands organised this influx of relations and their servants with deferential reference to Anne, whose only modest request was that, if Sir Thomas and Lady Cecilia had no objection, the small drawing-room adjoining the Blue Room could be made over completely for their use, thus allowing Miss Kit Gould to be accommodated away from her parents' watchful gaze. This damsel, having just turned seventeen, was looking forward to her first London Season, and indeed considered herself quite a grown-up young lady. Her only regret was that her first adult outing should be in black gloves.

Mrs Rowlands hesitated over Anne's proposal, then pointed out that the schoolroom was still swept and furnished, and Miss Gould only just being out, she might have no objection to being placed there.

"Perhaps," Anne acknowledged, "but maybe her just being out has given her a dignity that would object to being returned to a schoolroom so soon after having quitted it. I on the other hand, having been some years out, would have no objection at all to returning to my old room, and she could have my room."

"Indeed no Miss Anne! That is not to be thought of! Rosings has rooms enough and to spare; Mr Darcy and Colonel Fitzwilliam bringing but their one man each and Lady Gould but the one maid for herself and Miss Kit. Dawson is of course available to serve their ladyships should the need arise. No, no, Miss Kit Gould can be accommodated in the small Chinese room that adjoins Mrs Jenkinson's sitting room. Lady Gould can have no objection to that."

Anne nodded, and asked whether Mr Clements, the family's man of business, had yet arrived.

"Indeed yes, Miss Anne. He is to be put in the ground floor suite of the East Wing, below the gentlemen's gentlemen."

Thus, noted Anne with wry amusement, preserving the social niceties. Mr Clements, being in business, could not claim accommodation with the family in the West Wing, nonetheless ranked higher than the gentlemen's gentlemen by having both a dressing room and a sitting room allocated to his use.

*

Down at the Parsonage, Mr Collins was polishing his prose in some anxiety, hoping that his sonorous hyperbole would do justice to his deceased patroness, and ensure the continuance of his possession of the living of Hunsford under her daughter, the heiress of Rosings. Mrs Charlotte Collins, only slightly less anxious than her husband, was taking pains to ensure his cassock and shovel hat were well-brushed and his clerical bands snowy white. She had let out her own black dress, made for her uncle's funeral a few years ago, on account of her expectation of another happy event, and was busy supervising the dressing of her two-year-old son so that he should appear tidily and respectfully attired and as clean in his small person as a lively toddler could be expected to remain.

She did not fear for her husband's living: as a clergyman resident and serving Rosings Park, the village of Hunsford, the hamlets of Upper and Lower Broughton and the farms of the estate, he had always looked down on a goodly congregation assembled under Lady Catherine's stern eye each Sunday; it remained to be seen whether there would be back-slidings and absenteeism under Miss Anne. He also conducted Thursday Prayers for the Rosings family and servants, and extra services on Christmas Day and Good Friday. In this he was more zealous than many other churchmen. He oversaw the cleanliness of the church and the tidiness of the churchyard; ensured the clerk and the members of the band were neat and punctual and did not clatter their way down from the gallery and out of the church before the nobility had left their pew - a tendency in those who thought their scrapings and blowings led them to deserve immediate refreshment at the village hostelry. He performed weddings, christenings and funerals promptly to order, and always wrote and practised his own sermons; indeed, thought Charlotte, he laboured over them to the extent that his lengthy periods and artificial inflexions of voice went completely over the heads of most of his listeners. The hard-working servants, farmers and village folk took the opportunity to doze, more or less quietly. Lady Catherine, in her high-backed pew remained watchful, and if Mr Collins preached more about deference and obedience to one's earthly masters than to God, she had no fault to find with that. Mrs Jenkinson did her best to appear interested, but Miss Anne, with her eyes ever demurely cast down, could scarcely be seen under the high poke of her Sunday bonnet.

The time arrived; the congregation assembled and were seated according to rank; Mr Collins preceded the coffin, intoning the time-honoured words:

'I am the Resurrection and the Life, saith the Lord'.

Lady Catherine was borne on the shoulders of six sturdy footmen, with her brother-in-law and three nephews as pall-bearers. The bugle, clarinet, trumpet, trombone and bass viol muted their usually exuberant noise, and Mr Collins' sermon was heard with more attention than usual. Finally the coffin was carried to the family vault; the parson proclaimed the final words of the funeral service:

'Dust thou art and unto dust thou shalt return'

- a sentiment he privately thought ought not to apply to such an august personage, and the family emerged into the clear air, leaving Lady Catherine to her final rest beside her husband.

The villagers dispersed; the servants scattered hastily back to their various duties in the house—there were the 'funeral baked meats' to be 'coldly furnished forth', Cook has truly done justice to the occasion. Among those left in the churchyard, there was a sudden release of tension. Whether this was due to a burst of spring sunshine, mocking their black apparel, a cheerful trill of birdsong or the solemnity of the occasion being over, could not be said, but it was marked by young Master Collins, hitherto a model of quiet behaviour suddenly breaking away from his nurse and running helter-skelter across the grass. Away went the nurse after him, her bonnet ribbons flying, and Charlotte hastily excused herself from conversation with Mr Darcy over her friend Elizabeth's state of health and went after them. A chatter and a laughter broke out, but Mr Collins, scandalised, began to utter profuse apologies to Miss de Bourgh. She however, merely said:

"Please do not think ill, Mr Collins. He has been so good and we cannot surely expect small children not to respond to the call of spring. They are perhaps closer to Nature than we are. And can we not say 'In the midst of death we are also in life?"

"Miss Anne, you are all graciousness..." began Mr Collins, but Anne nodded and smiled and moved away to talk to Lady Matlock, leaving him to the mercy of the Dean, who, first congratulating him on his sermon, then wished to debate the vexed question of diminishing congregations in the present age, and to ask whether he was troubled in his parish by those poxy Methodists.

***
**
*

Chapter Two

Within a few weeks Rosings Park was almost returned to its normal state of inhabitants, namely: two elderly ladies and a young one. The young lady was, of course, Miss Anne de Bourgh, now mistress of the house, with the ubiquitous Mrs Jenkinson continuing to shadow her as she had done for the past nine years. The remaining lady was the Dowager Countess Harriet, who being widowed and whose family were following their own pursuits, had fewer calls on her time than other family members. She had agreed to remain to help her niece over the first few months of her bereavement and new responsibilities. Of the former, Lady Claydon noted, there seemed to be less sign than of the latter; Anne appearing to spend little time in displays of grief, and a great deal of time considering her new duties.

Almost returned to its normal state it was said, because Mr Clements was still a resident in his suite in the East Wing and had spent several hours each day with the new mistress of Rosings. It would seem from his earnest discourse, and the presentation of facts, figures and estate papers that while Rosings could still expect a healthy revenue from land-lets and the tithes on farm produce (Sir Lewis and his father before him having authorised a number of innovations in husbandry), nonetheless, since the baronet's death nearly ten years ago, little had been done to further such agricultural innovations.

There had of course been sales: Sir Lewis' hunters, the hounds and Anne's first pony, but set against these, there had been the purchase of two new carriages: an elegant landau and a town coach with the coat of arms emblazoned on the doors, together with a pair of high-stepping matched bays, new livery for the coachman and postillions and the low pony-phaeton which had been bought for Anne's particular use. In the eyes of Mr Clements, a serious minded business-man, Rosings had become a byword for extravagance and faulty domestic economy. True, the closed stove recently installed in the kitchen may have proved a saving of Cook's time and temper, but the marble chimney-piece in the Diningroom, designed by Robert Adam and costing more than eight hundred pounds; the wall-hangings and drapes for the morning-room and the large Drawingroom; the collection of porcelain, pictures and chinoiserie, seemed to him an unnecessary drain on the estate. Had these expenses continued—and it seemed her ladyship had entertained the notion of remodelling a number of rooms completely: the Red Saloon to become an Oriental Room in the grand manner, with silken swathes festooning the walls to resemble a Sultan's tent; the Large Drawing Room to be embellished with paintings by Mr Reynolds and Mr Gainsborough and the park landscaped by Mr Repton—then such improvements would have diminished the resources of the estate still further. Not that Mr Clements said a word of these plans and ideas, but Anne was well aware of them and of their implications. All she said, however, was that she regretted the complete refurbishment of the London House, which Lady Catherine had carried out three years ago:

"It seems now to have been so unnecessary; our use of the London House was never more than a few weeks a year, my mother being averse to the London Season."

"I understand," Mr Clements coughed gently, "That you yourself have never been presented at Court?"

"That expense we have at least been spared," said Anne dryly. "What information can you give me as to the farms of the estate?"

"Most of the tenant farms are well managed, but for two or three, the land is in poor heart. Your bailiff, Mr Castleton, can supply further details; he has ideas for a number of agricultural improvement schemes which I gather, Lady Catherine was reluctant to countenance. You will want to discuss these with him I am sure."

Anne agreed and requested Mr Clements to summarise her position. He shuffled his papers and began to make clear to her both her assets and her responsibilities.

At present, said Mr Clements, Miss Anne de Bourgh was in possession of Rosings: the house, the park, the Home Farm and some further hundred acres of farmland let to tenant farmers; she owned the house in fashionable Bedford Square; a further smaller house in Bath, and, of course, a bevy of servants, carriages, horses, dresses, jewellery and all the accoutrements of fashion. But Mr Clements' indications were that instead of the twenty-five thousand a year which was Anne's expected worth, she could probably not reckon an annual income of more than fifteen thousand, perhaps, less. Anne's perusal of these figures, coupled with an innate dislike of ostentation, firmed into a resolve. At the end of a se'nnight, Mr Clements received clear instructions with which he was happy to comply: the Bath house to be sold, with all its contents; the London house to be let, with such appurtenances as seemed reasonable; four of the six Rosings carriages to be sold along with several of the horses and the pony-phaeton. To Mr Clements' look of inquiry as to how she would travel the park and the estate, Anne told him firmly she intended to ride. Her cousin, James, as good a judge of horseflesh as anyone she knew, had told her of a friend wishing to sell a pretty little mare, no more than two years old, and already equipped with all that was necessary for a lady to ride. Mr Clements had a sudden memory of one of his early visits to Rosings, and Sir Lewis cantering across the park closely followed by a bright-eyed little girl on a small but gallant pony. Since Sir Lewis' death by a fall from his horse, Lady Catherine had forbidden her daughter to ride.

"I doubt," said Anne, amusedly catching his thought, "That I have forgotten the way of it."

Mr Clements hastily denied any such ideas.

It was not to be expected that the Countess and Mrs Jenkinson would give unqualified agreement to these financial reductions, although Lady Claydon approved the loss of the house in Bath.

"An ugly awkward place, my dear, and certainly not situated in the better part of the town! Why Lewis bought it I cannot imagine! But to let the London house! Surely you cannot think of it! I had such hopes of you doing the Season. As you may know, I begged your mother every year to let me present you, or to let Cecilia do it, but she would not. She always said you were not robust enough. She regarded Anne critically. Although I must say you seem to be looking remarkably well for one who has suffered so much - to be thus orphaned and to have to shoulder such responsibilities! And you scarcely more than eighteen years of age!"

"Aunt! I shall be twenty in two months!"

"Do not admit to it! Eighteen is the age at which we should always strive to remain! I was married at eighteen, and I'm sure at your age I had not a thought in my head but whether I should wear the family diamonds at my next ball, or how high my head feathers should be. Such a fashion that was! My Lady of Buckingham and the Duchess of Devonshire vied with each other for the tallest heads, and there were cartoons in the press of their head-dresses catching on fire from the candelabras! But as to letting the London house—well, if you will not change your mind, I suppose you could always stay with me in Cavendish Square, or with the Goulds, or even with the Darcys, although no doubt people will think it a trifle shabby that you do not have a house of your own."

Mrs Jenkinson was more inclined to bewail the loss of the little pony phaeton, and on hearing that Miss Anne intended to ride once more, gave a little scream. Lady Catherine, she moaned, had always been so careful of poor dear Miss Anne's health and safety, and had instructed her to be sure that she was always well wrapped up whenever she took an airing, and that now she was no more, she felt sure she should continue to be as careful of her now as ever she had been in her lifetime. Anne, disentangling her companion's "hers" and "shes" with the ease of long practice, and smiling inwardly at her aunt's bemused face, made yet another resolve. Mrs Jenkinson must go.

This, however, was not so easily achieved. Mr Clements could supervise without difficulty the dismissal of the servants at the house in Bath, ensuring, on Anne's instructions, that each received a suitable reference and a gift of between one and five guineas according to status. Anne herself would do all in her power to assist Martha Dawson, her mother's personal maid, to find a good position.

Since the departure of Lady Cecilia and Miss Kit Gould, Martha had had little to do. Lady Harriet Claydon had her own maid; a pert young thing who had been with the Countess not quite a year. Martha considered her much too young for such an elevated position; she seemed insensible of the honour attached and Martha had been shocked at some of her comments on the Dowager Countess in the servants' hall. Sarah of course, jealously guarded her rights over her own mistress, and, thought Martha sourly, was getting too uppity for her own good. It was partly that Miss de Bourgh always referred to her maid by her first name—a modern habit which the elderly Martha deplored. She was, therefore, grateful to receive Miss Anne's request to sort, brush, mend and lay out Lady Catherine's gowns, petticoats, mantles, bonnets, caps and shawls etc. until such time as it should be decided what should be done with them.

She was joined in this task by Harriet, Lady Caydon and Miss de Bourgh. Harriet gazed with unconcealed delight at the display reverently laid out. Lady Catherine's gowns spanned nearly thirty years of fashion: from the trained robes worn as full court dress and supported on wide side hoops, to quilted and embroidered petticoats, lace ruffles on the sleeves and the looped silk and cotton styles known as the polonaise. There were high-waisted dresses fashionable in the 1770s and 80s with the back-gathers held on pads and bustles, and wide hats adorned with voile, lace and feathers. Lady Harriet was in transports.

"My dear! Everything in the first style of fashion and of the finest textures! Oh do look! Here's a polonaise jacket and brocade gown of the kind much favoured by the Queen. It's said this was a fashion started by Mrs Margaret Caroline Rudd while in Newgate prison, for fraud you know. Such a scandal that was! The two men who were implicated in the scandal were both hanged, although I was convinced they were innocent of any crime. And she managed to get off scot-free! All the papers carried articles and letters for weeks afterwards, until we all got quite tired of hearing about her. But in spite of all, she was quite a fashion setter!" Lady Harriet stroked the gown gently.

"I never knew my mother had such a gown."

"Ah, Miss Anne," Martha put in, "If I may make so bold: this was one of her gowns when she did her London Season. In 1773 that would have been. She was much admired. And this," holding up a sacque gown of pink flower embroidered Spitalfields silk, "she wore to the Drury Lane Theatre to see Mr Garrick perform Ranger in 'The Suspicious Husband'."

"How well you remember it!" marvelled Anne.

"Well Miss, that's as how her ladyship was invited to go with Mrs Whytton, as was cousin to the Lady Elizabeth—that's Lady Catherine's mother and your grandmother, Miss Anne, and I was asked by Lady Elizabeth to go along as well, Mrs Whytton being but new-married and still not up to snuff as 'twere. If you'll pardon me. And I remember Mr Garrick well, striding about the stage and giving out his lines in that wonderful voice he had. Oh yes, Miss Anne, I'll never forget it. That was the night when Sir Lewis first set eyes on your dear mother. Though they didn't meet up - well, not then exactly."

The Countess, who had been sorting through an array of Indian shawls of the silk, looked up.

"So when did they meet? Exactly?"

"Well ma'am, it was at a masked ball, at Ranelagh?"

"My mother went to a masked ball at Ranelagh?" Anne could not imagine her mother doing any such thing.

Martha now had both ladies' full attention.

"Indeed yes Miss, my lady. It was a beautiful spring evening and my lady Catherine wore a simple gown of pink lustring and over it a black calash and domino lined with pink and shot with silver. This one in fact," and Martha's gnarled fingers smoothed the silk over the wire frame of the hood with reverence.

"Ah yes," sighed Lady Harriet. "We all wore pink that season. It was so fashionable."

"Did you attend on that occasion, Dawson?"

"No, Miss, not that time, Lady Catherine having her mother with her. But I heard all about it, later. She danced the first two dances with your father, Miss, but not knowing who he was as everyone was masked you know, and he paid her many pretty compliments but said as how he couldn't ask to pay his addresses to her as he was only a half-pay officer and it was obvious she was a great lady."

"Nonsense!" cried Harriet. "He had come into his inheritance at that time."

"Yes ma'am, but he had got it into his head that all young ladies like a bit of mystery and romance, and also he was tired of so many of them setting their caps at him you know. So, he wanted to find a lady who would love him for himself. Or so I was told."

The countess burst out laughing.

"How very absurd of Lewis!"

"As you say, ma'am. But well, anyway, the outcome was that by the end of the evening, when he had taken Lady Catherine in to tea, and then round the garden walks with her…"

"No! Did he?" exclaimed Harriet, delighted. "How very naughty of him!"

"…and danced several more dances with her and talked a lot of sweet nothings in her ear- or so she reported to me later, ma'am, well then at the end when everyone had to take their masks off, he was nowhere to be seen!"

"Oh the nonsense of the man!"

"Well but the next day, there came flowers and notes and a beautiful little pearl pin, all signed from her 'ardent but penniless masked admirer'."

"How romantic!" sighed her ladyship.

"If he was penniless, how could he afford a pearl pin and flowers?" demanded the practical Anne.

"I don't think her ladyship thought of that, Miss, her head being fairly turned with it all. And here I'm afraid, Ma'am I was put in a quandary, what with her wanting me to carry secret notes to him, and him wanting me to arrange secret meetings."

"Oh Dawson! Did you really?" Lady Harriet was shocked.

"Well yes, Ma'am, but there! I was all taken up with the romance of it myself. Although I did think as how I should of told Lady Elizabeth, but I never did. You see, she and the Earl had a rich old gentleman in their eye for Lady Catherine, and he wasn't a patch on your father Miss Anne, if you'll pardon me, for looks, or wit or pretty speeches, as well as him, Sir Lewis I mean, being bang up to the mark."

"True," sighed the countess, "He did cut a dash!"

"Well and then, Miss, Ma'am, after a few weeks of smelling of April and May, but in secret so to speak, my lady comes to me and says as how they were planning to elope."

"No!" both ladies exclaimed together.

"I cannot believe it of my mother!" cried Anne, "Surely she would never do anything so-so rackety!"

"Except that somehow the Earl got wind of it and set out to find Sir Lewis and wring his neck or somesuch. A crusty old gentleman was your grandfather, the Earl, begging your pardon, Miss. Well then, he found out the young upstart, as he thought, wasn't a half-pay officer at all, but Sir Lewis de Bourgh, Baronet, of Rosings Park and worth twenty-five thousand a year. So then, he apparently went home to Lady Elizabeth, chuckling, and said they ought to let the young people run off together and let Lady Catherine find out afterwards. But Lady Elizabeth wouldn't hear of it…"

"Shame!" cried Harriet.

"…and she stormed in to my lady and gave her a real dressing down. Saying how could she ever think of disgracing herself by eloping, or of marrying to disoblige the family, and begging her to consider her Rank and the Importance of The Name, and a lot more besides about ingratitude and unkindness, so as my poor lady was reduced to tears. So then, Lady Elizabeth ups and says as how Lady Catherine could marry Sir Lewis de Bourgh, but, of course, the poor young lady didn't know it was the same man as she'd fallen for. So, she was still more tearful, and Lady Elizabeth says as how she'd lost all patience with her and she would have to stay shut up in her room until she got herself some sense."

"I know!" exclaimed the Countess Harriet, suddenly much struck. "This is exactly like that play by Mr Richard Sheridan! What is it called? With the girl with that silly aunt and lots of secret meetings and messages. And the aunt pretends to be the girl and carry on with an Irish peer—O'Trigger or some such name. They all have such funny names in Mr Sheridan's plays. What was it called?"

"*The Rivals*, Ma'am," said Martha, placidly. "Mr Sheridan and Sir Lewis were in the same set you know, and Mr Sheridan did run off with his young lady, and he put his adventures and Sir Lewis' together to make the play, like. Except my Lady Catherine was not at all as silly as that Miss Lydia Languish. And I'm no Lucy either! Scheming little minx of a maid! I would never betray my lady's confidence, get what I might for it," she added with spirit, thus betraying considerable knowledge of the play, due to another visit to Drury Lane theatre.

"Indeed no, you are a queen among ladies' maids," soothed Lady Claydon. "But how and when did Catherine discover the truth?"

"Do not you know the story, Aunt?" asked Anne.

"Me? No! The Earl and I were abroad for three years. He had diplomatic missions in France and Holland. We came home for the wedding—in the spring of '74, I believe. I have not heard a word of this until now." She turned inquiringly to Martha, who took up the tale.

"It was a week or more before the truth came out. My poor dear young mistress was confined to her room all that time, and Sir Lewis sent up notes bidding her to be brave and patient—and still signing himself 'your secret admirer' or something like. Then he wrote that he had obtained her parents' permission to pay his addresses all official, like, and she was allowed down to the morning room to see him. And he must have said then as how the deception was all to do with her being the only woman he could ever marry, because seeing as she was willing to take him with no money, could she not take him with twenty-five thousand a year?"

"Oh my word!" Harriet was quite overcome. "How could she possibly resist?"

"Well no, Ma'am, she couldn't. Could she? And they were married at Easter, like you said, in '74 that was."

"I remember," said Harriet. "Catherine was dressed all in white and silver. Very pretty."

"And she wore the little pearl pin Sir Lewis had sent for her first gift."

"How little one knows of one's relations after all!" mused the countess. Anne could not but agree.

"Dawson!" the lady went on, suddenly struck with yet another idea. "Did I not say you were a queen among ladies' maids? Is it possible you might consider coming to me? You may not know it but I lost my dear Mary Hill to the smallpox last year; since when I have been training up Ellen Penn. But she is too young for me and would prefer it I think if I sent her to my daughter, Harry. Her daughter will soon be needing a maid now she is coming out of the nursery, and I'm sure Penn would find that a much livelier situation. But Dawson, do not you think we should suit?"

A slow blush spread over Martha's placid face.

"If Miss Anne agrees." She ducked her head deferentially.

"Oh! Of course, My dear. I was forgetting! It is for you to say."

"I think," said Anne fervently, "That it would be an ideal situation."

Thus, a few weeks later, departed the Countess Harriet with two maids, both well pleased with their prospects. Martha Dawson felt herself amply rewarded with a choice of three of Lady Catherine's morning gowns, several caps, petticoats, handkerchiefs, shawls… and the little pearl pin that had featured so largely in the story she had spun.

***
**
*

Chapter Three

"Parting is such sweet sorrow…"
William Shakespeare: Romeo and Juliet (circa 1597)

Following her aunt's departure, Anne sent a note down to the Parsonage requesting the pleasure of the company of Mr and Mrs Collins for dinner and insisting on sending the carriage for them due to Charlotte's condition. The note was a little more apologetic in tone than those her mother used to send, but Anne had not yet become as peremptory as her new position might allow her to be. Neither was she used to commanding attendance as her whim dictated. She was also aware that Mr and Mrs Collins had dined at Rosings but the once since Lady Catherine's funeral, and that after that occasion, Lady Claydon had declared she would not sit through another dinner listening to Mr Collins and his obsequious ramblings.

"If you feel you must invite them again while I am here my dear, I beg you will excuse me to them and say I have one of my heads. I vow I would rather have my dinner sent up on a tray."

"But you did not object to Mr Clements dining with us, did not you, Aunt?"

"Indeed no! He is a man of good conversation and with sensible ideas, which, I was thankful to note did not confine themselves to the enclosure laws, or the new agricultural policies. And he knew when to keep silence. Unlike Mr Collins! My dear, you must develop your mother's aptitude for simply riding over his words with some of your own."

Anne, who had disliked this particular gift of Lady Catherine's almost more than anything, had merely nodded and kept silent. But now she realised she must manage the evening herself, and in her own way find a means of stopping Mr Collins over-reaching himself in empty compliments.

In the event, the evening produced an unusual occurrence, although it began as such evenings usually did: the conversation as to the excellence of the dinner being provided solely by Mr Collins, while the three ladies said little. Mrs Jenkinson was as always, wholly concerned with watching Anne's plate, and murmuring every now and then:

"Are you sure you can manage a second gooseberry tartlet, Miss Anne? I am never sure of the bottled gooseberries at this time of year. Allow me to help you to just a very small slice of the beef. Remember your poor dear mother was always so careful of your delicate constitution."

Anne thanked her in her polite fashion, and turned to ask Charlotte how she did.

"Thank you I am very well. Only a little tired I think."

She was looking somewhat pale and had eaten little, but as she was in almost daily expectation of being confined, Anne could not wonder at this, and quietly said:

"If you wish for the carriage to be ordered early, please do not hesitate to say so. I would not have you tire yourself on my account."

Mr Collins, overhearing this, was moved to cry out a remark on Miss Anne's kindness, etc, so like her dear mother's, but added that he would undertake his wife's being quite capable of spending the evening at Rosings. However, when the ladies rose from dinner, Anne begged him not to linger over his solitary port, but to join them in the drawing room as soon as was convenient.

The three ladies had not long been seated in the drawing room, and Mrs Jenkinson was fussing over whether or not there should have been a bigger fire:

"- as these late April evenings can be so chilly, you know and I would not have you catch a chill, my dear Miss Anne on any account," when Charlotte, biting her lip, failed to suppress a little cry of distress.

"I am so sorry Miss Anne," she began, "but I fear my pains have come upon me, and rather more suddenly than I was prepared or."

Mrs Jenkinson started up in in some alarm.

"Oh my poor dear Mrs Collins! Dear me, that such a happening ... er ·... so very sudden is not it? Should I order the carriage Miss Anne?"

"Indeed no," said Anne calmly. "I would not have Mrs Collins subjected to waiting for the horses to be put to, and then to suffer a jolting ride even as far as the parsonage. Instruct Mrs Rowlands to prepare a room, if you please, and to send for the midwife. I do hope," she added, turning to Charlotte, "that you do not object to the possibility of your child being born at Rosings?"

Charlotte was torn between the increasing pain of her labour, laughter and protestation. What her husband would say, she did not dare to think. Indeed it would be a great surprise if he ever ceased to talk of it.

The inestimable Mrs Rowlings ably assisted by two housemaids and the midwife, soon had Charlotte as comfortably installed in the Blue Room as her situation allowed, and before the night was out, all was happily over. The Collinses had a daughter. Mr Collins applied to his patroness to name her Anne Catherine. To this Miss de Bourgh made some demur, saying that instead of 'Anne' she should carry 'Charlotte' as her first name, and that being so, she would stand sponsor to the child. Mr Collins felt, and indeed said: truly the cup of happiness runneth over.

Anne now found herself in the happy position of enjoying the company of children, and of a sensible young woman only a few years older than herself. She had always esteemed Charlotte for her calm good sense, most particularly in the management of her husband and her bright young son, and her interest and concern over village affairs. Young Master Collins was brought each day to see his mother and baby sister by either his nurse or his father, and although he was frequently admonished by the latter not to make too much noise, and to walk quietly and sedately within the house, his natural exuberance and laughter could often be heard. He took a fancy to Anne, and when his mother was resting, or busy with the baby, he would follow Anne about, usually with one small hand firmly fastened to her gown. Sarah tutted at this, and offered to take the boy away, adding that he had probably creased beyond repair her mistress' muslin, but Anne told her quietly that if she did not mind it, then Sarah should not worry herself about it. Sarah tossed her head a little at this and said:

"You are too good, Ma'am. But what is the boy's nurse about that you should have the worry of him? I'm sure Mrs Collins never meant it sol"

"Indeed, no. But the nurse is helping with the baby and young Edward here is no trouble to me. Tell Cook if you please that I will attend her in my sitting-room in about half-an-hour. Master Collins and I are going up to the nursery. Come, Edward, there is something I want to show you that I think you will like."

So saying, Anne took the child's hand firmly and led him upstairs.

In her old nursery they found a number of Anne's playthings. Her father had been an indulgent parent and on his business trips to London he always made a point of visiting William Hamley's toy shop, 'The Noah's Ark', in Holborn. Anne, therefore, had a number of educational toys, such as a set of coloured bricks with the alphabeta engraved thereon, and a pack of Wallis' 'Educational Cards for the Amusement of Youth'. There were two elderly rag dolls elegantly dressed in silk; a small but beautifully furnished doll-house; a number of board games; Thomas Bareham's child-sized books, and a venerable rocking horse with a rolling eye and a splendid mane and tail. This had been handed down the family, and Edward galloped on it as energetically as had the de Bourgh brothers. But the most splendid toy was an ingenious device in which a marble placed at the top of a wooden slope ran down to tum a wheel, which tilted a slide and enabled the marble to run into a shallow basin which it circled twice before plopping down a hole and running out into a little gully. From here it could be retrieved and set off on its merry journey once more. Edward was enchanted with this, and would not be parted from it, so that on Anne informing him that she had to go and talk to Cook, he was put into the dilemma of wanting to play with the marvellous toy, yet not wanting to forego her company. The result was a roar of frustration, which made Sarah, coming into the nursery at that moment, exclaim:

"Good gracious Miss Anne! Whatever be the matter with the child?"

"A little conflict of interest I think. Now Edward, do be quiet and listen to me. There is no need to make such a noise. You may come with me to the sitting room, and we will take the toy with us."

Tears and roars ceased as if by magic, and Edward bestowed a smile of such sweetness upon Anne that Sarah was all amazement.

"Children," observed her mistress, "would appear to be like April weather: all storm and tears one moment and all sunshine the next. Do you but bring the toy, Sarah, Edward may need my hand upon the stairs."

"Which" Sarah said to Cook later, "left me all agog, the mistress having such away with the boy. Good as gold he is with her an' all."

In due course Charlotte's lying-in was at an end, and she removed with her family back to the parsonage. Edward was consoled in this by a promise that he could visit Rosings as often as his mother could spare him, and by being allowed to carry away with him the wonderful toy.

*

Several days passed quietly at Rosings, and at Hunsford parsonage. Mr Collins had written in his usual effusive style to Sir William and Lady Lucas on the birth of their grand-daughter: a little before her time and rather small, but a neat, healthy baby, notwithstanding. If he dwelt rather more on the fact of her having been born at Rosings Park, and on the goodness and graciousness of Miss de Bourgh: 'so like her dear mother, the Lady Catherine of blessed memory,' than on his dear Charlotte's health, this came as no surprise to the Lucases. A rather longer letter, on a single sheet but closely crossed on both sides, came from Charlotte herself, who also now found time to write and congratulate her friend Elizabeth, and inform her that Charlotte Catherine Collins had come into the world but a few weeks after Charles Edward Bennet Darcy.

'*But do not be thinking, dear Elizabeth*' wrote Mrs Collins in her neat hand, '*that we should formulate a union between Charles and Charlotte while they are still in their cradles. Such a wish, as you well know, may be doomed to failure by the interference of others who may later have the greater claim of both love and inclination.*'

Elizabeth, receiving this, could not but laugh, and in her reply to her friend said she hoped the children might have the opportunity to become acquainted, but with no other end in view but to continue the friendship their mothers had always enjoyed.

The summer was now approaching. May blew hot and cold, but the gardens of the park and the village grew bright with blooms. Mr Collins began to be busy with his bees, and Miss de Bourgh busy with the affairs of the estate and farms. She frequently rode out with her bailiff, a sensible man in his early fifties who had served Sir Lewis well, and borne with equanimity Lady Catherine's management, or rather lack of it. Thanks to the kindness and knowledge of her cousin James, Colonel Fitzwilliam, Anne was now the possessor of a pretty roan mare, soft in the mouth and easy under the hand. Anne called her Firefly and was enchanted with her. She lost no time in having a riding habit made for herself; black of course as befitted her mourning status, but of elegant cut and the newest style with epaulettes and handsome frogging. . To wear with it she had a neat hat with a grey feather curling over the brim.

When she first appeared in this, and was heard to order her mare saddled to be ready to ride out with Mr Castleton, Mrs Jenkinson uttered a scream of protest. Of this Anne took no notice at all, and indeed continued to turn a deaf ear to the usual pleas of "your poor dear mother—always so very careful—your delicate state of health"—etc. But when Mrs Jenkinson, whose anxiety on her own behalf had rendered sillier than usual, uttered the fateful words: "Remember what happened to your poor dear father," Anne turned and confronted her.

"I am not likely to forget my father, Ma'am," she said with unwonted severity, "nor to forget what a splendid horseman he was. His death was due to a series of unfortunate accidents: it being midwinter and the hunt going out over frozen ground. Your fears do you credit Mrs Jenkinson, but please observe we are now near the end of May, the weather is fine and dry and I do not intend to jump Firefly over Brook Hedge. Moreover, I shall be attended by John Groom and Mr Castleton, so do not be thinking I shall be in any danger."

Mrs Jenkinson tottered back to her sitting-room, as much shocked by Miss de Bourgh's manner as her words. After a few self-pitying sniffs, she sat down to write a letter to her sister Mrs Maria Trenton, now living in Southend-on-Sea, in which such turns of phrase as *'always served the family with devotion',* and *'in Lady Catherine's memory',* and *'having had her ladyship's complete trust in the oversight of Miss Anne since before she left the schoolroom'* ...

were interspersed with anxieties about her own future status and position. But if she expected a soft and sympathetic answer from her robust elder sister, she was disappointed.

'I beg to remind you, Sister', Mrs Trenton had written on two crossed sheets of paper for which Mrs Jenkinson had to pay sixpence, *'that we have no more claim on the de Bourgh family than any other retainer, being merely distant and poor relations of Lady Catherine's family. You should consider yourself fortunate that you have been more than adequately housed, clothed and fed, and retained as companion to the young lady since the dismissal of her governess, Miss Serena Pope, under circumstances which I consider to be heartless and peremptory. Since then, as I have observed on my several visits, you have been useful to her La 'ship in the management of a young and spirited girl, whose resemblance to her father appeared to be a matter of disapproval to her mother. Such that it is my belief that Lady Catherine prevailed upon you, and indeed her household, to deprive the child of the means of health—viz: fresh air, exercise and an adequate diet. All this under the pretext of Miss Anne's delicate and sickly constitution. As you know, Sister, I visited Rosings with you before the death of Sir Lewis, and before your appointment as companion—or should I say warden - of Miss Anne, and indeed my memory is of a bright-eyed, plump, lively and rosy little girl. Since when she has been*

rendered a semi-invalid Far be it from me to suggest that Lady Catherine, enjoying rude health herself, sought deliberately to inflict the interesting condition of sickliness on to her daughter, thus denying her the opportunity to enjoy any other life than that dictated by the determined resolution of her mother.'

Mrs Jenkinson was shocked and dismayed at her sister's words and thought at once of returning a spirited answer in contradiction to these dreadful accusations. However, the next page gave her pause.

'You cannot expect,' the letter went on, *'that conditions will remain as they were since Lady Catherine's demise. She it was who appointed you, and that appointment must be considered at an end. Unless Miss Anne has expressed a decided wish to keep you, and your letter to me suggests that she has not, then you must consider your usefulness to her to be over. She will, no doubt, wish to seek a companion nearer her own age. Perhaps Mrs Collins may fulfil that role, as far as her family commitments will allow. Be that as it may, if you are to be of no more use to the de Bourgh family, consider how much use you may be to me. As you know, I was left a good deal more than a competence by my late husband, and I am thinking of setting up a genteel boarding house ...'*

More followed of the healthfulness of Southend-on-Sea; the benefits of sea bathing; the development of the resort and the desirability of offering good accommodation to well-to-do London families of complete gentility and character, seeking recreation in the pure air of the seaside. Mrs Jenkinson was made aware of the gains to be made from such a venture, which she was invitedto share.

This letter threw the lady into a variety of conflicting emotions. She was loath to acknowledge the truth of much of her sister's letter, but on the other hand, had to admit that Miss Anne, much taken up with the business of the estate, seemed to have little time or inclination for her company. Mrs Jenkinson's advice and admonishments over Miss Anne's diet, rest, apparel, etc, were met with a mere nod and a brief smile and then ignored. Their evenings at quadrille or casino more often than not gave way to Anne saying she needed to read the latest Board of Agriculture pamphlet, or a treatise on drainage, or crop rotation or somesuch by Sir John Sinclair. The Collinses were invited to dine no more than once a week and no other invitations had been sent out to well-known families in the neighbourhood. Mrs Jenkinson did not know what to think, or what to do.

Anne herself, while feeling a trifle sorry for her companion, was at the same time becoming impatient with her. Her sighs, her expressions of anxiety over Anne's health and her constant worried expression fretted at Anne's nerves. She was reminded of a little spaniel the family had once had, who had the same mournful expression and drooping ears. Not that Mrs Jenkinson's ears drooped exactly, but she shared with the dog a little frown and a propensity to sigh heavily.

Having come into her inheritance, Anne was conscious of needing a female friend and companion with whom to share aspects of her life and thoughts which she could not confide to either Mr Clements or Mr Castleton. Both these gentlemen, being of her father's generation and with all the awareness of male superiority, treated her with patronising deference, although she had surprised them both with her clear-sightedness and knowledge of both business and rural affairs. Charlotte Collins was indeed becoming a friend to Anne, who had often wished for a closer acquaintance. Before her mother's death, she had driven the road passed the parsonage in her low phaeton and had stopped whenever possible to converse with Charlotte. Elizabeth Bennet had commented on this, remarking to Charlotte's sister Maria that she thought Miss de Bourgh very rude to keep Charlotte out in the cold wind, and why did she not come in? Had she known it, Anne would have dearly loved to go in, but had been expressly forbidden by her mother to 'so lower herself.' Of course, she always had Mrs Jenkinson with her to see such commands were carried out. Now of course she could visit Mrs Collins as much as she wished, but was conscious that as a mother and the parson's wife, Charlotte's prior concerns must be for her family and parish matters. Anne needed someone who could enter into her thoughts and feelings; someone a little nearer to her in age, with whom she could exchange books, compare the latest fashions, go for walks and discuss village affairs. And of necessity, to act as chaperone. She wanted her former governess and friend, Serena Pope.

But how to achieve an exchange of Mrs Jenkinson for Miss Pope? Anne formulated several ideas only to reject them. She could of course simply dismiss Mrs Jenkinson, but was loath to do so. Her mother, while being extravagant in some areas of life, particularly those pertaining to her own comfort, was parsimonious in others. She had maintained Mrs Jenkinson in some elegance as to dress, in order that the lady should do her credit, but Anne would have been surprised if she paid her more than very little in the way of a wage, such that Anne had no doubt that a plain dismissal would put her companion in severe financial difficulty. Nor did Anne entertain for long the idea that Mrs Jenkinson could be found a similar position in another family. The possibility of a governess situation also occurred to her; her mother having been instrumental in placing the lady's nieces, and of course sending Miss Pope to Lady Metcalfe, but although Mrs Jenkinson had been supposed to supervise Anne's later education, she had had very little in the way of accomplishments with which to achieve this.

It was at this point in her musings that fate took a hand. Like both her parents before her, Anne continued to pay a sovereign a year for an early delivery of post, and thus one morning, she found a letter in a firm, but unknown hand waiting beside her breakfast plate. She broke the seal and perused the contents with increasing surprise, and a growing consciousness that this might the answer to her dilemma. She glanced up and found Mrs Jenkinson's rather woeful expression fixed on her.

"I do hope no bad news, Miss Anne?" said that lady.

"No indeed! But the letter is of a surprising nature, and as it concerns you, you must be apprised of it."

"Concerns me?"

"It is from a Mrs Trenton. Your elder sister, I believe?"

Mrs Jenkinson acknowledged the fact and began in a flustered way to apologise that her sister should have so troubled her dear Miss de Bourgh, Maria usually being aware of the social niceties as to never venture on presumptuousness—

"Indeed she has not presumed at all," calmly interrupted Anne. "She writes with exactly the correct tone, and puts her ideas forward with a great deal of sense. She is, I gather, like yourself, a widow, but with a good competence?"

Mrs Jenkinson assented to this, but her look of an anxious spaniel increased.

"She is desirous of setting up a respectable boarding house, and begs that if I can spare you, she would be grateful for your company and your assistance."

Anne waited for her companion to reply or comment, but Mrs Jenkinson had nothing to say.

"I understand," Anne went on, "that the air of Southend-on-Sea is very conducive to good health and can offer plenty of sea bathing. My father swore by Dr Russell's book on the use of sea-water for diseases of the glands, or somesuch, and sea-bathing has come to be seen as a cure for all ills. Both the King and the Prince of Wales are advocates of it."

She paused again, but there was still no reply.

"Do not be thinking that you would not be fitted to assist Mrs Trenton in this enterprise. I cannot imagine but that your experience of easy converse with ladies and gentlemen of quality, together with your air and address resulting from your residing with us - "

Anne broke off, with the uncomfortable thought that she was beginning to sound as condescending as her mother. Mrs Jenkinson seized the moment.

"Oh my dear Miss Anne! My sister had indeed written to me with this idea, but I put her letter aside, thinking that I could not possibly leave you without a friend or companion."

"As to that," replied Anne, "you have indeed been invaluable to our household, but this seems such an opportunity for you that I would be selfish if I kept you from it. I cannot keep you at my side for ever, and if, or in fact when I come to marry, your position would be untenable you know."

Mrs Jenkinson became even more flustered and Anne thought that if she had a tail, it would by now be drooping on the floor.

"Please consider carefully your sister's kind offer. You need not decide at once but as the summer season approaches, I feel Mrs Trenton is wise to want to begin her venture as soon as possible."

Mrs Jenkinson continued to dither, and Anne continued at intervals to urge, saying that she was determined to visit her at Southend-on-Sea to see what sea bathing would do for her health, and would need such a boarding house as her sister proposed in which to stay. But it was not until the arrival of the Lady Cecilia Gould and cousin Kit that Mrs Jenkinson was finally persuaded she could safely leave her charge in competent hands. Thus she departed with sighs and tears which not even the gift of twenty guineas in a silk embroidered stocking purse could assuage. Anne watched the carriage bowl down the drive, then sped back indoors with a sense of relief and only a twinge of conscience that she could not share such grief.

***
**
*

Chapter Four

"Nothing is to be done in education without steady and regular instruction, and nobody but a governess can give it"
Jane Austen: Pride and Prejudice (1797/1813)

Lady Gould and Kit were to stay at Rosings for a month before departing for London. Kit's come-out was set for the next Season and her mother wanted her to acquire a little town-bronze during the Little Season. They would of course limit their excursions to simple amusements such as concerts of Mr Handel's sacred oratorios or Mr Beethoven's symphonies. Lady Cecilia considered that small private parties would be unexceptional, but the theatre, dances and visits to such palaces of pleasure as Ranelagh or Vauxhall she dismissed as out of the question; they were after all still in black gloves and Kit not yet eighteen.

"Not that there will be many such festivities yet, London being thin of company over the summer and even the Little Season not getting under way until September at the earliest. Then, of course, with the opening of Parliament in December, Sir Thomas will be required to be in town, and Kit will have the opportunity to become acquainted with several eligible young gentlemen before the Season gets into full swing in March. And if I could prevail upon you, Anne, to join me the following year, I am sure you will enjoy at least some of what London has to offer. We need not be giddy you know, if your health does not permit the full round of balls and routs and other pleasures. Although my dear, I have never seen you looking so well."

Regarding her niece as her sister-in-law had done but a few months previously, Lady Cecilia noted with approval a touch of healthy colour and a brightening of the eyes in Anne's hitherto pale looks. Her figure too seemed to have rounded out and was it possible she was a little taller? Certainly she carried herself with more uprightness than a mere few months ago. If she goes on in this way, thought her aunt, she may well turn out to be a beauty. It did her ladyship credit that with a pretty daughter of her own to establish she could consider bringing Anne, with her wealth and promise of increasing good looks, to the notice of London society.

Anne, unaware that she was under scrutiny, did no more than acknowledge her aunt's offer with a word or two of gratitude. She had lost no time in writing to Serena Pope informing her of the latest turn of events, and now waited impatiently for a reply. This was not long in arriving. Miss Pope wrote that as her youngest charge would be starting at Eton in September - *'and in spite of his mother's coddling, he is as ready for the rigours of the place as my instruction, discipline and strictures can make him'-* she would be able to take up her post as companion to Anne in the middle of that month. She hoped this would be acceptable, and very much looked forward to what promised to be an enjoyable relationship. Meanwhile, she sent Anne for her birthday a green calf-bound ladies' pocket-book, with an extra pocket inside for notes. As well as blank pages—*'which I hope you will fill with such anecdotes as we can discuss or laugh at together,'*—the book contained useful printed information on important calendar dates, hackney cab prices, London theatres, fashion plate engravings and the names and addresses of various banks. At the back, there were some contemporary verses by women poets. Anne resolved to put it into use at once as a day-book, and inscribed her name, the date and various comments on the new roses just then coming into bloom, and the gardener's recommendation that they should be interspersed with lavender bushes as a precaution against the Green Fly. To this she added an extract from William Blake's *Songs of Experience*, a copy of which she had received from her uncle the Dean.

Anne then unearthed from the schoolroom cupboard her paint-brushes and colours, but finding them in poor condition due to their lack of use, sent off to Merciers of Windmill Street for a further supply of good quality paper and to William Reeves for cakes of water-colour in a wide range of colours. Meanwhile she contented herself with a few pencil sketches, and was pleased to find her hand obeyed her brain and she retained some measure of her old skill.

The thought of soon being able to enjoy Serena's company brought back to Anne many of the joys of her schoolroom days. She was aware that she was fortunate to have enjoyed instruction from a governess of exceptional ability, and also to have been possessed herself of a lively and inquiring mind. Of late, her mind had been subjected to lassitude and weariness; she could not tell why this should have been so, but she dated it from the time when, following her various illnesses, her mother judged that schooldays with Miss Pope should come to an end and dismissed the governess from her employ. Up till then lessons had ranged over a wide variety of topics imparted at times in a somewhat unorthodox manner. For natural history they had rambled round the park or the village, taking note of what grew where and when, and collecting flowers, leaves, herbs, fruits and toadstools. These Anne was required to sketch with as much accuracy as possible; label according to Mr Linnaus' system of classification and add notes as to the date, location and weather conditions under which they were found. Sometimes they came across small bird or animal bones, picked clean by scavengers, and a further note went into the nature book as to what they were and what most likely had been the cause of the poor creature's demise. They observed insects, birds, beetles and other inhabitants of the woodland, and on more than one exciting occasion, Anne was bidden to rise in the night and don a warm pelisse over her night-clothes so that they could watch for bats, or the hunting of the owls.

Serena taught Anne of the science and history of medicine; of healing herbs and herb-lore, and instructed her to copy out in a fair hand a number of recipes and simples from old books, among them a very battered copy of *The Compleat Housewife* by Eliza Smith. Such remedies included a balm for sore lips and chapped hands; cures for mad dog bites and bee stings and a recipe for coral tooth powder. They presented this to Mrs Rowlands, to the housekeeper's great delight.

As well as the required French and Italian, Serena added German to Anne's languages, together with a little Latin and Greek; mathematics were part of her studies, the use of the globes and ancient and modem history. They read poetry and plays, some of which Serena wrote herself. One of these was a very cheerful Christmas piece, which caused such merriment in the schoolroom when they read it together, that Sir Lewis had called out from below:

"What's to do?"

He, then, was invited up to see a performance of *The Rogue's Christmas Pudding* and enjoyed himself so much he declared it was better than the Drury Lane Theatre.

"Best not to tell your mama you've been play-acting," he said, after pinching his daughter's cheek and declaring her to be a naughty puss. "I doubt she would approve. As for you, Ma'am," turning to Miss Pope, "you're a very clever lady but take care not to turn my girl into too much of a blue-stocking. Although she's got a good head on her shoulders and I'll be glad to have her acquire some knowledge of estate management."

Sir Lewis had a way of bringing his dark eyebrows together, with which gesture he hoped to bestow stem looks on whomever he was addressing, but inevitably the blue eyes under them always contained an irrepressible twinkle. They twinkled now and Miss Pope failed to suppress an answering smile, although she replied demurely enough:

"That is beyond my power to impart, Sir. Such instruction must come from you. My task is to teach sketching, embroidery, French and a little Italian, together with deportment and manners."

"And the rest," Sir Lewis chuckled. He turned to Anne. "Well puss, how about conning some Shakespeare for our Christmas entertainment? Her ladyship can have no objection to that!"

So on Twelfth Night, when the lesser gentry and notable members of Hunsford society came for the usual festive dinner, Anne (who was allowed to join the adults for the occasion) together with Miss Pope entertained the company with some of the comic scenes from Shakespeare's play of that name. Sad to say,

Lady Catherine did not appear to enjoy it.

Sir Lewis was very well aware of his wife's wish to bring up their daughter with the strictest propriety, and although he acknowledged she had every right to exercise complete control over the girl, he was nonetheless occasionally troubled by the rigidity of her ladyship's regime. Miss Pope knew also that in giving reign to her own notions of educating a child with as lively and receptive a mind as Anne's, she was overstepping the mark as to what was considered the limited essentials of female education. Her own father, a man of both science and letters, had taught all his children in the same way, recognising that Serena and her elder sister Sophie had as much intelligence as their brothers. Their mother was a noted blue-stocking; she was well-read in a number of languages and enjoyed the Bas Bleu soirees of Bath society, where men and women conversed together on politics, poetry and philosophy. Small wonder that Serena had been imbued with the ideas of Maria Edgeworth, who wrote that: 'it seemed women were not allowed to observe, invent or discover,' and that men: 'with the insulting injustice of an Egyptian task-master … demand the work but deny the necessary materials.'

Like another female thinker of her generation, Mary Berry, Miss Pope felt all the inequity of a system which limited women's education to a few short years before being marketable for marriage. Thus said Miss Berry: 'When men were being sent to college, women were left to gain bread, mend clothes or live in positive idleness. They were led to the fireside at an age when men had the world opened up to them.'

Serena knew better than to express openly these radical views, but she let them guide her teaching. In Anne she found an apt pupil. Without a word being uttered, they were joined in a conspiracy of silence. The schoolrooms were at the top of the house, and Miss Pope always left the door slightly ajar so as to hear the creak of the stairs should anyone approach. The second stair from the bottom had a particularly loud creak, which enabled Serena and Anne to whisk away the unsuitable book, hide the botanical drawing under the blotter and be deep in French conversation or Hester Chapone's *Letters on the Improvement of the Mind*. Thus on the rare occasions of Lady Catherine's inspection of the schoolroom, or more commonly, the housemaid coming in with more coals for the fire, they were found to be engrossed in unexceptional study.

Sad to say, out of the schoolroom, Anne's behaviour was less than unexceptional. She loved to frequent the stables and ramble round the fields of the tenant farms as well as those of Rosings Park. Although her excursions had to include either Miss Pope, or her maid Sarah, she found it easy to cajole the latter, who was only a few years older than herself, into turning a blind eye, or indeed to join in the adventures. Sarah adored her young mistress and would do anything for her, even though she often had to untangle the results of such adventures.

The prank of wading through the ford for example, when the water was high with the spring rains meant Sarah (who dared not let the washerwoman see them) had hard work to get the mud-stains from the hems of both their walking dresses, even though she used quantities of bucking. Gathering blackberries was an autumn adventure and as these went into her apron and

Anne's handkerchief, these articles became permanently, if artistically stained with purple juice. But at least Cook was pleased with the fruit and Sarah was able to ensure that Anne did not enter the house with a stained mouth.

But Sarah could not always shield her mistress and Anne's exploits did not always go unobserved. The results were often uncomfortable. Sir Lewis may have laughed over his daughter's hoydenish behaviour, but it was not to be supposed that Lady Catherine would be lenient. She remained silently grim in her husband's presence, but lost no time in recalling to Anne the seriousness of her various misdemeanours and to contrive suitable punishment. She believed firmly that children are born sinful, and although a good loud cry at their christening may be said to banish the devil, he was never so far from them but that he must frequently be beaten out of them. And Anne had not cried at all at her christening, but smiled seraphically up at the parson, giving her mother grave anxieties over her future behaviour. Punishment had therefore to be inflicted with a firm hand to bring her into obedience and polite behaviour.

Thus it was that, on the occasion of Anne climbing like a monkey to the upper branches of the great cedar tree, tearing her dress and petticoat in the process, she was made to sit all day in the schoolroom with her ankles tied to the legs of a chair. On another occasion, she was discovered creeping down to the kitchen after she had been sent to bed, and stealing a pie to give to a gypsy family she had encountered on the common. Except it was no longer the common, but had been enclosed and they should not have been there at all. For this piece of mischief, Anne was shut in the broom cupboard for a day and a night, and given only water to drink. Serena Pope, secretly sympathising with the gypsies, who had lost what little livelihood they had when the common was enclosed, and being inclined to agree with Anne's act of charity, alleviated the child's punishment somewhat by sitting on a chair outside the broom cupboard and reading stories to her from Mr John Newbery's Gilt Books: *A Christmas Box, Tale of the Fairies* and *Goody Two-shoes*.

Anne usually accepted her punishments with stoicism, although she did feel that sometimes the punishment far outweighed the crime. Such was the case when she had been out riding with papa. Sir Lewis had bought Anne's pony for her seventh birthday and she took to the saddle, he was pleased to note, like a duck to water. John Groom led her out on a leading-rein every day, but within a few weeks she was riding competently enough for her father to take her with him on some of his rides. Lady Catherine disapproved strongly of this, but for once was over-ruled. Trotting gently on her little pony behind her father's big bay, Anne visited the farms and the woodlands of the estate, and picked up pieces of information such as how to drain the lower fields ofHome Farm; when to flood the water meadows to provide lusher pasture; which trees should be felled and when to harvest the wheat and the barley. She also acquired some unsavoury pieces of a working man's vocabulary and was heard to report that: "Joe Green is a fuddlecap and a nodcock which is not surprising as his Pa is always going on the mop."

Had her father been the only recipient of this intelligence, he would have roared with laughter and told her to keep such stable talk for the horses, but unfortunately, Anne produced this gem at the breakfast table to her mother's fury. She was sent to wash her mouth with soap and water, and was then gagged with a piece of linen for the rest of the day. Worse: she was forbidden to ride out with her father for a month, a decree over which he protested, but with which he had to comply.

Anne was devastated. She refused to speak when the gag was removed and continued to sulk even when her favourite cousin, James Fitzwilliam came to stay. Two years older than Anne and the younger son of Lady Catherine's brother the fourth Earl of Matlock, he was a cheerful lad, and having a serious older brother rather enjoyed the company of a girl cousin who viewed him in the light of a bold adventurer. On his previous visits they had got into scrapes together, but his charm and imaginative explanations usually got them out of trouble, and if punishments were to be meted out he gallantly bore the brunt of them. It was not long before he had persuaded Anne out of the sulks enough to tell him the whole story.

"Well you are a ninnyhammer yourself," he told her. "Should know better than to spout cant to the parents! I know how to patter a bit of flash meself; picked it up from the stable lads, but I wouldn't dream of using it to the mater. Know when to shut me bone-box!"

This unsympathetic retort—couched in cant terms too—added salt to the wound of Anne's misery: first her beloved Miss Pope had read her a lecture on minding her tongue, and now James agreed with the adults! It was the outside of enough!

Anne compressed her lips in an unconscious imitation of her mother, and made a secret resolve to run away.

She spent the night working out a plan of action and was resolved to put it into practice the very next day. All that day she was astonishingly mild and good, meeting with her mother's approval; James's disgust at her hen heartedness and arousing Miss Pope's suspicions. That lady determined to keep an eye on her charge, but the day passed without incident and she decided her fears were groundless.

The long summer evening stretched its light well after Anne had been put to bed. The family kept country hours and by half-past nine of the clock the house was still and quiet. Anne slipped out of bed and pulled out from under it a shirt and a pair of breeches which James should have sent to the laundry room; they smelt of hay and horses and Anne sniffed in delight. She had also stolen a pair of shoes, but decided against them as they were much too big for her. She would have either to wear her own, which did not look well with the breeches, or to go barefoot. She decided to go barefoot. She struggled with the fastenings of the breeches, not being at all sure how they should go, but finally managed it. They were too big around the waist and she had to tie them with a piece of black ribbon. She found another piece of ribbon to tie her hair back in a queue, and thought she had achieved a creditable effect. She slipped down to the kitchen where once more she raided the larder for a bit of bread and cheese which she tied up in a handkerchief.

Out of the scullery door, she took a deep breath of the cool night air and set off to the stables. The dogs were a little puzzled at the mixture of smells she exuded, but as they knew them all, and although Prince stood and stretched and rattled his chain, they did no more then sniff at her hand. She let herself out by the wicket gate behind the stable block and set off down the lane to the village. From there she planned to take the London Road—just like Dick Whittington, she thought to herself—and resolved to walk until it was too dark to see, then spend the night under a hayrick or somesuch.

The last of the daylight faded and Anne was conscious of a prickle of fear as the night noises made themselves heard. A rustle in the leaves and a scurry of a small animal, the gleam of a fox's eyes and the sudden, silent swoop of an owl all made her heart pound and weakened her resolve. She remembered old tales told around the village of the night hag who carried off evening travellers on her grey mare; she was said to steal horses, or to press them in their sleep giving them bad dreams. The stables of Rosings were hung with hag-stones to ward off her attentions. Then there were the stories of Tom Tut, the Moone-calfe and other fearsome creatures of the night. Although she kept to the grassy edge of the road, walking barefoot for any distance was an uncomfortable experience, but Anne was determined and courageous. She found herself a stout stick, ate a bit of her bread and cheese, and marched on.

The moon rose over the silent village, silvering the thatches as Anne trod quietly between the dark cottages. A dog barked once, twice, then whimpered a little—and was still. At the crossroads, she peered up at the finger-post to find the London direction and set off purposefully. The farmland -began to give way to heath and scrub; although this part of the estate had been enclosed, it had not yet been brought under the plough. Soon it would be quite dark, and Anne realised she would soon have to find her hayrick. She therefore turned off the road down a lane which led, she thought, to the last of her father's tenant farmers.

She had not gone far when she heard the clop of a horse's hooves on the road. Thoughts of the hag caused her heart to beat fast, until she remembered that her grey night mare was silent and this was undoubtedly a real horse. She was just congratulating herself on having left the highway, when to her dismay, the horse and its rider turned down the same lane she had taken. She looked around wildly for a hiding place, but there was none, and she cowered down by the roadside.

Farmer Heydock, returning late from market and slightly befuddled by the quantity of ale with which he had celebrated the successful sale of several fine heifers, was nodding in the saddle, trusting to his old mare to find her own way home, when he was jerked awake by Betsy shying at a bundle of white curled up by the side of the lane.

"Whoa there, Betsy ol' girl! What's to do?" exclaimed the farmer and heaved himself out of the saddle to investigate. The white bundle turned up a pale and frightened face.

"Please sir, I'm sorry, sir, I didn' mean to scarey your 'orse."

"Bless my soul! It's nobbut more'n a lad! What might you be doin' you young varmint?"

"On me way to Lunnon, sir," stammered Anne, who retained enough presence of mind to try and speak in the vernacular.

"Lunnon is it then? Seekin' yer fortune are yer? Well, Lunnon's not on this road. This 'ere leads to my farm this does, an' if you'd gone much further you'd 'ave'ad me dogs on yer."

Anne, who knew Farmer Heydock's dogs almost as well as she knew their own, could only bite her lip.

"I was lookin' fer a rick, sir, ter sleep under," she muttered.

"A rick was it you was lookin' for me lad? You sure you weren't after me strawb'ries or somesuch? Well, you come alonga me ..." he broke off and peered at Anne's face. It was smudged with dirt and pale with fright in the moonlight, "but even so ..."

"Well bless my soul!" exclaimed Farmer Heydock again, "if it an't Miss Anne!"

"Oh please!" cried Anne, really frightened now, "please don't tell. I was running away. It was all because, it was because ..." but her nerve finally gave way and she burst into tears.

Farmer Heydock, like many men, was helpless in the face of feminine tears. "Well I don' know I'm sure," he said gruffly, "but no need to pipe yer eye Miss Anne. You'd better come up to the farm an' we'll see what the missus 'aster say about it."

Dame Heydock was a large and comfortable body who had raised eleven children, eight of them to adulthood, with cheerful placidity. She accepted her husband's late home-coming from market with the resignation   borne of experience, and the fact that he brought with him Miss Anne de Bourgh of Rosings Park, dressed in outlandish garments and with a staybit tied up in a hankercher, did little more then ruffle the surface of her calm. She bade Anne wash her hands and face; plied her with warm milk and fresh bread and honey and listened to her incoherent story. She then washed the child's dirty and bleeding feet, coaxed her into a clean night-gown - somewhat too big - and tucked a tired and tearful little girl into bed. She puffed her way down the narrow stairs, closed the door at the bottom and prepared to discuss with her man what should be done. Or rather, to tell him what she thought ought to be done.

"Now, we'm raised a brood o' childer," she said, "an' never spared the rod when it was necessary, short an' sharp. But dark cupboards an' gaggin' I don' 'old with. Not that it's any o' my business but the bantlin's no more'n seven or eight, an' 'tis obvious she was fair shrammed out of her wits to try to go trampin' to Lunnon in a boy's mish."

"That's all very well missus, but she's a lady born, an' the quality 'ave to be brought up strict. Especially little maids. 'Tis thankful I come across 'er 'cos she's no more wit than an innocent babe newborn. And whatever's Sir Lewis and Lady Catherine goin' to do when they 'ears about it?"

"They ain't a'goin' to 'ear about it. You go up to the House come mornin' early, an' ask for that Miss Pope as is governess to the young lady. If I've read 'er aright, she can be persuaded down 'ere with some suitable clothes for the lass, an' we can make out that all it was about was a stroll in the early mornin' midsummer dew."

"Well, but—" began the farmer doubtfully, but his goodwife would hear of no doubts, and cajoled him into her way of thinking in the time-honoured manner of long-married couples.

*

"And so it all worked out," Anne recounted many years later to her cousins Elizabeth and Darcy.

"Did no one know of your adventure?" asked Elizabeth, who was completely astonished at the tale.

"Only the Heydocks, Sarah and Miss Pope. And as far as I know, none of them ever breathed a word. Serena did make me copy out the whole of Fordyce's sermon on humility, but she did not scold and she fed me honey biscuits while I was doing it. And I was not allowed to go adventuring with James till it was done. The only thing I puzzled over at the time," she went on thoughtfully, "was how to fasten those breeches. As far as I could see, the opening was in quite the wrong place!"

Both Darcy and Elizabeth broke into scandalised laughter, and later, Elizabeth was to ponder how such a spirited girl of eight years old could become the pale, sickly young woman she had first met at Rosings Park

***
**
*

Chapter Five

"Good nature is more agreeable in conversation than wit, and gives a certain
air to the countenance which is more amiable than beauty."
Joseph Addison: The Spectator 1711.

Anne's visit to Darcy and Elizabeth was in the summer of 1800. Lady Cecilia
and Kit had departed for their London house, but the Darcys were remaining at
Pemberley for the summer. Elizabeth, following the fashion of the times, was
suckling her child herself and was most reluctant to subject him to the airs of
the town. Neither she nor Darcy were at all willing to exchange the shades of
Pemberley in summer or autumn for the rigours of even the little London
Season, and Anne of course was still in mourning. Country pursuits were
therefore their preferred activities.

She set out, accompanied by Sarah, John Groom and her coachman in the
large travelling carriage with as little in the way of luggage as propriety – or
indeed her maid Sarah – would allow. Sarah had more notion of what was due
to her mistress's consequence then Miss de Bourgh herself. She carried with
her greetings from the Collins; some pots of honey from their bees: a silver
rattle for baby Charles and a silk Kashmiri shawl in soft colours for Elizabeth.
For Darcy she had a half-dozen saplings of the Nonpareil apple, their roots
carefully coated in honey and wrapped in sacking. He had expressed a wish to
see how well these would grow in Derbyshire.

If Anne was a little apprehensive of furthering her acquaintance with
Elizabeth, whose sportiveness, and her mother's resulting discomfiture Anne
had silently enjoyed, Elizabeth was full of a lively curiosity concerning the
young mistress of Rosings. Since their marriage, the Darcys had received but
the one visit from Lady Catherine and her daughter, and Anne, ashamed of her
mother's overbearing attitude which led her to be scarcely civil to the new Mrs
Darcy, had remained downcast and silent. Their previous acquaintance had
been based solely on Elizabeth's visit to Rosings, and although she had heard
from Charlotte Collins of Anne's conduct since coming into her inheritance,
she did not at all know what to expect.

She was astonished therefore when the Rosings carriage drew up and the
steps were let down, to see a fashionably dressed young lady emerge and order
the disposition of trunks and parcels with clarity and firmness. Anne had
lightened her mourning, and appeared to advantage in a simple dress of pearl-

grey muslin, with a black silk pelisse and a neat bonnet trimmed with oyster-silk ribbon and a single plume. Elizabeth's memory of a small, thin, cross and sickly-looking person, with nothing to say for herself, faded before this confident young woman, who appeared to have grown at least two inches, and to have rounded out into feminine curvaceousness. Her eyes, dark blue like her father's, had acquired a brilliance almost equal to Elizabeth's own, and when she was borne into the house and had removed her bonnet, her hair, though not as red-gold as her father's had been, nonetheless had its own beauty in the colour and gloss of a ripe chestnut.

"I own I was never more astonished," Elizabeth remarked to her husband later, when he came into her dressing room. "Anne is not at all as I remembered. She was used to be so shy and quiet!"

Darcy nodded at the maid to dismiss her.

"She has certainly improved in looks," he returned, "and would appear to have more conversation than I had suspected from my previous visits to Rosings. But then she may have been constrained by the knowledge of the engagement which had been planned for us."

"Did she wish for it?" asked Elizabeth, whose curiosity on this point had never been fully satisfied.

"As little as I did I imagine. I think we neither of us gave it a great deal of thought, and had perhaps accepted the idea as a future possibility without troubling ourselves overmuch with its probability. Certainly Anne never exerted herself to please me, but then she scarcely seemed able to exert herself at all, due presumably to her ill-health. And I confess I seldom went out of my way to pay her any more marked attention than common civility required. Indeed," he went on, assisting his wife to arrange the pretty Kashmiri shawl about her shoulders, "I probably paid few women any marked attention until I met you."

"Oh!" cried Elizabeth, "you scarcely paid any attention to me, or indeed behaved with any civility at all to begin with!"

"But that was before I knew you," he acknowledged with a smile, "and before I admitted to myself what the beauty of your fine eyes was doing to my heart."

Elizabeth coloured and laughed and then grew more serious.

"Thank you for the compliment my dear sir. But tell me what was the nature of Anne's ill-health?"

"I do not know. Certainly she suffered from lethargy and ate very little, and I seem to remember Mrs Jenkinson talking of giving her a daily dose of fifteen to twenty drops of liquid laudanum."

"But laudanum is used to cure restlessness and excessiveness nervousness! Surely she did not suffer from these disorders?"

Elizabeth was indignant at what she considered to be inappropriate physicking. Had she known that Lady Catherine's doctor had also prescribed that Anne be subjected to sweating and cupping regularly after her monthly flow, she would have been even more indignant.

Their first evening together at Pemberley passed quietly but pleasantly. When the ladies withdrew after dinner, Anne was able to give an account of Charlotte and the circumstances of her daughter's birth, as well as her own enjoyment of the company of little Edward Collins. She inquired after Elizabeth's family, and learnt that Mrs Bennet and Mary had but recently returned to Longbourn after they had been at Pemberley for Elizabeth's lying-in; that Mrs Jane Bingley was expecting a happy event in the autumn, and that Miss Kitty Bennet had prevailed upon her father to allow her to accompany her Aunt Phillips to Bath, that lady having been persuaded to try what the waters would do for her rheumatics.

"Do you think Miss Kitty will like Bath?" asked Anne with interest. "I confess I did not like it above half, but then our last visit was in the Spring of '97 and it never ceased to rain."

"I have never been there, but Georgiana was there for a few months not so long ago, visiting a school-friend. What did you think of the place, Georgiana?"

"We were there in the summer you know, and the weather was kind," said Georgiana in her soft voice. "But Bath seemed very noisy and crowded, and I was aware of the amount of dust dancing in the sunlight. To be sure, there is in Bath any number of splendid shops, a good library and buildings very regular in their design and colour, but to anyone bred to country air and country quiet it was so very full of people and bustle."

"We may not like such a place," said Elizabeth, "but Kitty has always longed for such noise and bustle as you describe, so perhaps she may be comfortable there. And my Aunt Phillips means to take her to the concerts and assemblies, so she will enjoy what Bath has to offer."

The gentlemen came in at this moment. Darcy was accompanied by the Reverend Campbell, who held several of the livings in Darcy's gift, including that of Kympton – that same which had supposedly been coveted by Mr Wickham. He was a tall, broad-shouldered man who looked as if he would be more at home in the boxing ring, or riding to hounds, than in the pulpit. He was particularly fine as to dress, having a tailcoat of blue superfine over a striped waistcoat and pale pantaloons. But he was presumably a learned gentleman, having been at Oriol College in Oxford, and later a fellow of Worcester College. Anne judged him to be about five or six and thirty.

He had brought with him his curate, a slender young man, not long ordained and newly appointed. He was severely garbed in clerical black and had the modest demeanour of one who knows his inferiority both of position and stature. He had a very slight hesitation in his speech, and an unfortunate tendency to go red about the ears whenever he was addressed. As both Elizabeth and Anne were at pains to engage him in conversation in order to make him more at his ease, his ears remained in a permanent state of pinkness.

Georgiana, shy herself, merely smiled at him, but this had the effect of causing the poor young man's ears positively to glow.

Miss Darcy was prevailed upon by the company to play for them, and nothing loath, took up her position at the piano forte. Mr Campbell drew near to listen, and on taking up an air, was found to have a very mellow baritone. At the end of the song, he was warmly applauded, but laughingly refused to sing again "... unless Mr Stevens joins with me. Come now Mr Stevens, allow the ladies to have the benefit of your silver tenor. Come, I brook no refusal."

Anne, amused, thought the curate's ears would burst into flame, but he joined his senior at the piano and delighted them all by singing in perfect harmony with Mr Campbell two folk songs, and a beautiful air from Herr Mozart's 'Magic Flute', to words of a hymn by the Reverend Charles Wesley. He seemed to lose his shyness in the music, as did Georgiana. Indeed, thought Anne, watching them, they made a picturesque trio: Mr Campbell, tall and broad with the candlelight catching at the red of his hair; Mr Stevens, slender and fair and Georgiana in blue muslin, with her dark curls and serious pale face, concentrating on her playing. Anne committed the scene to memory and later, sketched it out in pencils, resolving that one day she would do a proper portrait in crayons or pastels.

The music ended, the tea-tray was brought in. The ladies continued to talk of music with Anne asking if Elizabeth still found time to play.

"Not as much as I should," she answered, "but with Georgiana playing so excellently well, I am a little cast into the shade. You never learnt I understand, although your mother felt you would have been a great proficient."

"My mother always held that any member of the de Bourgh family would have excelled in everything, but alas, she deluded herself! My governess worked hard to get me to practise my music, but I had no talent for it whatsoever. It was necessary for mama to plead my ill-health as excuse for my lack of ability. I cannot tell what excuse she found for her own."

"From what I remember of Lady Catherine," returned Elizabeth, "she needed no excuse. She was to herself everything she felt she ought, or needed to be."

"And yet, you know," said Anne, conscious that she should not be disloyal to her mother's memory, "she had her works of benevolence and charity."

"Such as any of us having wealth and position should undertake I hope. We are united in one society, albeit different in rank and station, and if the poor have been placed under the patronage of the rich, it behoves the rich to have the care of the poor. But excuse me if you will, I am required in the nursery. Perhaps Mr Stevens can take my place as an advocate of the necessity of philanthropy."

And Elizabeth, surrendering her place beside Anne to the embarrassed curate, hurried away.

"I would not imagine," said Darcy, resuming his seat after having risen to hold the door for his wife, "that philanthropy needs an advocate."

"Indeed no sir," Mr Stevens' tone was eager, "but there are those who would debate the state of the poor and what should be done for them in the way of education and relief. Many believe that nothing can improve their lot and only hunger – even starvation – will lead them into diligence and away from the evils of drink."

"But you are not of their number," said Anne, "you would have them assisted and educated, would not you?"

Mr Stevens would have replied to this, but Mr Campbell intervened.

"Indeed it is right that every care should be taken in the education of the lower classes, but charity schools should not teach that which threatens the great law of subjugation. Agreed it is the duty of the rich to provide for the poor, but surely also it is the duty of the poor to be content with their lot."

Thus, thought Anne privately, we hear the complacency of one who, to judge by the cut of his coat, enjoys a competence of probably five hundred or so pounds a year, in answer to his curate who is worth perhaps no more than fifty pounds. The thought of her own fortune at times weighed heavily on her. Aloud she said:

"Has it not been recognised that it is the right of every individual to better his own condition?"

"Thus indeed said Mr Adam Smith in his 'Theory of Moral Statements'. But such betterment needs to be limited, otherwise society will turn itself upside down."

"Perhaps," Anne ventured, "as a social experiment, we should exchange places with others of different ranks in order to see how they contrive, as in the children's tale of 'The Prince and the Pauper'. Perhaps Mr Campbell, you would agree to change place with your curate?"

Mr Campbell laughed very heartily at this, and Mr Stevens' ears turned very red once more.

"I would agree to exchange with my maid Sarah," continued Anne, "but I fear I would make sad work of furbishing up my gowns, and she I think would find the duty of the estate burdensome. Which I concede adds weight to your own point Mr Campbell, of the limitations of betterment."

"But can it not be seen in the present age," said Darcy, "that some individuals are indeed raising themselves by their own efforts to the very peak, almost, of society? Trade and industry are creating wealth, and wealth makes gentlemen of those who work hard to achieve success in those fields of enterprise."

"You cannot term such people 'gentlemen'," cried Mr Campbell. "You cannot put them on the same level as those whose birth and breeding have destined them for the elevated position they occupy."

And he bowed to Mr Darcy.

"My mother would approve of your sentiments, Mr Campbell," Anne remarked, smiling.

"And you do not?" murmured Mr Stevens to Anne.

She assented with the tiniest inclination of her head.

"We are surely what we are born to," put in Georgiana, a little timidly.

"And thus," said her brother with a smile, "must engage to fulfil our role and occupy our position to the best of our abilities and responsibilities."

The evening now being far advanced, Mr Campbell's carriage was called for, and the reverend gentlemen took their leave, Mr Campbell taking up his curate as far as the parsonage at Lambton. Anne was assured of having the pleasure of hearing Mr Stevens preach there on Sunday and she said quietly that she would look forward to it. The curate stammered his replies, and took his pink ears away with him into the night.

*

The warmth of the summer days encouraged the ladies to walk frequently in the Pemberley woods. Elizabeth was anxious to show Anne her favourite paths which ascended from the river and gave splendid views of the valley and the further hills. Anne's enjoyment of these was evident and she was happy to walk as far as Elizabeth, who was quickly recovering her strength and energy after her lying-in. After one rather strenuous outing however, Darcy was moved to ask Elizabeth to consider both her own health and that of their cousin.

"Indeed I do consider it," she replied with spirit, "and I hope I may neither give way to the limitations of sickliness nor overtax either my own strength or Anne's. She has promised to tell me if she is in the least part fatigued, but so far she has not done so."

"She has surprised you with her improvement in health and spirits, has not she?"

"So much so that I am inclined to think the poor honey I remembered as Miss de Bourgh has been stolen away by the fairies and this remarkable young woman put in her place."

"To what do you attribute the change?" asked Darcy. "Other than an exchange by the fairies, which in this Age of Reason I cannot possibly accept."

"Well then, if you will not have fairies, it must be due to the change in her circumstances. No longer is her will dictated to by another – and that other a forceful and over-bearing mother. No longer is she 'cabin'd, cribbed, confined', and thus her spirit can now take wings and her health rise in accordance with its flight!"

"Can the flight of her soul also cause the improvement in her complexion? Or do you ascribe that to Pears soap or Hungary water?"

"I will allow no such mundane considerations!" cried Elizabeth. "London women may buy their complexions, but fresh country air, healthful exercise, good food and a cheerful mind is all that is needed to transform a sickly creature into one whose bloom may take Society by storm."

"That will indeed be astonishing. She is too quiet and unassuming to make a splash in London Society."

Elizabeth acknowledged the truth of this but added:

"Nonetheless I feel that Anne may surprise us in any number of ways. It must be remembered that her fortune, coupled with her improved looks and gentle manner, if they do not make a splash as you put it, will at least guarantee some strong ripples!"

"That I own is of some concern," said Darcy gravely.

Elizabeth was right in her assertion that Anne would cause no little surprise in a number of ways. She had already made the acquaintance of the head gardener at Pemberley, and walked with him round the flower gardens, the walled kitchen garden and the succession houses. Much of the Pemberley land was laid out according to the inclination of Nature, with just such a guiding hand as Brown's or Repton's here or there: to curb Nature's over-exuberance; to add a sweeping path; build a rustic bridge, or an informal widening of the stream to form a small lake. Here were none of Cowper's 'fallen avenues', but plenty of fine woodland, well-managed for timber. Here too, a trellis-covered walk led round the side and back of the house, where informal flower gardens had been created. These contained, as well as everyone's favourite flowers, a number of the new exotics: fuchsias, acacias, camellias and veronica to name but a few. The head gardener at Rosings had persuaded Anne to try some of these and she was eager to know how they fared in the more bracing climate of Derbyshire. She was fascinated to learn of the carefully concealed alcoves in the garden walls in which slow-burning fires could be lit to protect more delicate plants against the winter cold. This, together with deep mulching ensured their survival. In the succession houses she noted some splendid vines, melons, tomatoes and cucumbers. Anne debated with the gardener the craze for growing pineapples which was sweeping the country. That seasoned man said he was more than willing to give them a try, but Mr Darcy had so far been reluctant to

"... sport his blunt, begging your pardon Miss, spend any money on such foreign fruit. Not when the finest English strawberries can be got with no more'n ordinary care and work."

He picked a strawberry for Anne to sample, and she had to agree there was little to better the taste.

From the gardens it was but a step for Anne to ask her cousin whether she could view the estate with him.

"Of course," Darcy replied. "I can place the phaeton and ponies at your disposal."

Anne hesitated.

"That would be the very thing if cousin Elizabeth wished to accompany us. But if not, I would prefer to ride. Is it possible that you could mount me?"

Darcy could scarcely conceal his astonishment, but replied with his usual civility:

"I am sure I can contrive to find a mount that would take a little lady such as yourself. When do you hope to go?"

"At your convenience, cousin."

Elizabeth disclaimed a share in the expedition, and thus a few days later, Darcy, mounted on his favourite grey, together with his steward on a sturdy cob, led out Anne on a quiet mare belonging to the squire's lady. No longer riding much herself, she was glad to allow Anne's use of it for the duration of her visit. Elizabeth watched them go from the nursery window and although no horsewoman herself, nonetheless could see how well Anne sat and how neatly she controlled the little mare.

That evening the conversation turned on the day's events, with Darcy recounting his steward's comments on Anne's ability as a horsewoman, saying that she appeared to have a good heart for riding, which was as important as having a good seat and gentle hands.

"My father was insistent that I should ride well," Anne said with some hesitation. "I had my first pony when I was seven, and after a while was used to ride with papa round the estate. Good horsemanship was very important to him. My mother however did not think it at all the thing, and, well, later, she ordered the low phaeton for my use."

Elizabeth noticed Anne's reluctance to talk on the subject and would have refrained from inquiring further had not Darcy said:

"That, I take it, was after the loss of your father. I was home from college at the time, it being Christmas, but we knew of it only when the post finally came through many days later. It had been held up by heavy snow across most of the country. I never knew the details however."

"Do not speak of it," urged Elizabeth, "if it pains you to do so."

"The memory is painful," Anne acknowledged, "but it should be spoken of. I seldom did so with my mother. Our Christmas that year had been full of all the usual festivities: carols and card-games, and bullet pudding and dancing in the servants' hall. That night we had a hard frost, but the snow you mentioned did not reach us until the following week. It had always been tradition that the hunt should ride out on the day after Christmas, and I was allowed to take the stirrup cup to my father. He leaned down to me out of the saddle and said: 'A few more years and you will be riding with us, little lady.' Then they all clattered away and we heard the master's horn blowing up a view halloo along Brook's Meadow. There is a stream there running along by the hedge."

Darcy nodded, he knew it well, it was a pleasant spot in spring and summer and full of blackberries in the autumn.

"My father would not have thought there could be any danger," continued Anne, "his horse could easily have cleared both stream and hedge together, except that the earlier rains had caused the brook to overflow and then of course to freeze. However it was, Old Soldier, that was his horse you know, slipped as he was gathering for the jump, missed the hedge and my father was flung headlong. His neck was broke and we were told he must have died at once."

She paused. Elizabeth's eyes were full of tears, and Darcy looked grave.

"It was well for him," Anne went on, "and the right way for him to depart this life. But for us, seeing him carried home on a hurdle, it was very dreadful. As far as I know, my mother did not weep at all, but she grew very hard and stern. I was forbidden to ride; indeed forbidden to stir out of the house, which I could not have done even had I so wished, for soon after the funeral I contracted influenza, and then not long after that, the measles. I became as full as I could hold with the spots and everyone was in great fear lest it should be the smallpox. But I knew it could not be that because I had had the cowpox earlier that same year. Although my mother did not know of it; Nurse and Miss Pope telling her it could be nothing but a rash caused by gathering flowers among the stinging nettles."

Perhaps it had been Anne's intention to divert her hearers' minds away from the story of Sir Lewis' fatal accident; if so she succeeded, as both Georgiana and Elizabeth exclaimed in lively astonishment at how she could possibly have contracted the cowpox.

"Next you will be telling us you became a dairymaid, like the poor French queen wanting to be a shepherdess."

"Not quite. But I did learn to milk a cow the summer I was eleven years old. That I think must have been the cause of it."

"But had you not had the inoculation?" asked Georgiana.

"No. My mother still believed it to be an unnatural process and against the will of God."

Fortunately the tea-tray coming in at that point, and Elizabeth recalling her nursery duties soon after, prevented further explanations of a time Anne wished to preserve in silence.

***
**
*

Chapter six

"In painting, the most brilliant colours, spread at random and without design, will give far less pleasure than the simple stout line of a figure."

Aristotle: Poetics.
4th century. Translated by Thomas Twining

The night was quiet and still, and when Anne had dismissed Sarah, she leaned on the windowsill to watch a full moon sail, majestic and golden, into a sky as soft and dark as blue velvet. This was just such a summer as those of her childhood, when as soon as she was dismissed from the schoolroom she would scurry to the stables to find her pony ready saddled by John Groom. Then she and her father would set off together, sometimes just for a ride, more often to visit the farms or the woodlands.

One such afternoon in late summer, they visited the Brightwell farmstead. This comprised several acres of rich meadow on which grazed a small herd of dairy cattle, and a tract of mixed woodland. Sir Lewis wished to discuss with Farmer Robert Brightwell certain improvements to this wood; which trees to fell, which should be coppiced and what new trees should be planted. Young Robert, a few years older than Anne, was gathering and bundling sticks for kindling and Anne risked her maid's displeasure by sitting on the grass to make daisy chains with the two little girls of the family. The children chatted and laughed together without either constraint on the part of the young Brightwells, or condescension on Anne's, for none were yet of an age to concern themselves over social distinctions and Sir Lewis was bluff and easy-going and well pleased to talk with a man of such good sense and good humour as Farmer Brightwell. His wife, a comely woman, brought out both strong and small beer, with milk and honey cakes for the girls. Robert whittled a piece of pinewood into the shape of a little bird and presented it to Anne and in return she flung her daisy chain round his neck. His sisters capered and laughed and declared their brother was King of the Daisies. He told them to mind their tongues and not talk such nonsense but he was laughing too, and it was obvious he was a kindly brother to the little ones. Anne wished she had such a brother. But summer idylls never last and although the memory of them may fade with age and become dulled by experience, it takes little to recall them as fresh and happy as when they were first laid down in lavender, as it were. For Anne the smell of newly chopped wood brought back that day to her, or, as now, the mention of the cow pox.

That summer Sir Lewis seemed to have occasion to ride out to the Brightwell farm more often than usual Anne would sometimes accompany him and would watch round-eyed and curious as Dame Hannah went about her tasks in the yard and the dairy. But it was Robert who taught her to milk a cow, being able as his mother said with some pride, to turn his hand to most things about the farm. Thus, it was that Anne developed on her hands the warty pock-marks well-known to dairymaids. Dame Brightwell bathed them with a lotion of her own making, telling Anne cheerfully not to mind them; she had had them, as had Robert and neither had come to any harm. Indeed it was well-known that they were a guard against the more virulent smallpox. Anne felt that if Robert had the marks then she was glad to have them too. Martha Brightwell showed Anne where to search for the hens' eggs and how to gather and dry the herbs their mother used in her medicines. Both girls would follow their brother about if he were working around the yard, and it was obvious that they adored him, being a cheerful, sensible sort of fellow, much like his father but with his mother's dark colouring. She appeared to be of Irish descent and had the dark hair and blue eyes of many of that race. Certainly it seemed that Sir Lewis found pleasure in her company, although the reasons for his visits were to discuss at length with Farmer Brightwell the plans to canalise the river for the transport of logs to the sawmills several miles away.

But these plans never came to fruition. In the autumn of that year Farmer Brightwell was out in his woods, supervising the felling of a number of large beech trees when one, rotten at its heart, fell before the woodsman could shout his warning cry of "Timber!" Robert Brightwell was crushed beneath it and died before his anxious and sweating men could heave it clear.

It was young Robert who brought the news to ·Rosings Park, and Anne who was the first to hear it. She had just returned from a ride with John Groom having spent some time in the stables seeing to the rubbing down of the pony, and was astonished to find Robert by the kitchen door with trembling hands and ashen face. When she heard his faltering words, she could not refrain from putting her arms round him and hugging him briefly, much as his sisters were wont to do, before rushing away to find her father.

Sir Lewis had a care to this little family, providing for the boy's education with the Reverend Hibberd, Mr Collins' predecessor, and arranging for the girls to attend the charity school in the village. He appointed a steward to oversee the work of the farm and also arranged for an allowance to be paid to Dame Brightwell, which he increased when her fourth child, a boy, was born in the late summer of the following year.

But at his death, such largesse ceased abruptly. The family were moved out of their pleasant farmhouse, house and land being tenanted to another farmer, and went to a tiny cottage on the edge of the estate. Robert's lessons came to an end, although Mr Hibberd, impressed with the boy's quick mind, lent him various books and urged him to continue his reading as much as possible. Now thirteen years of age, he found work on the farms as a day labourer and the girls helped their mother as she took in washing and mending, continued to make herb remedies for the village folk and sold the eggs from their poultry. She had every right to parish relief, both she and her husband having been born in the parish, but many said she was too proud to claim it. The villagers and farmers' wives gave what help they could, although there were some who were unkind enough to lay her misfortunes at her own door and to whisper and wonder at Sir Lewis's particular concern for her and her children. Especially the youngest child, the boy with the red-gold hair.

Such gossip and tale-bearing was carried across the fields, through the village, to Rosings Home Farm, and in time to Rosings Park. No-one knew if it came to Lady Catherine's ears, or if she took any notice of it if it did, but it was not long before the tiny cottage was found to be empty, and in the records of a certain cotton mill in Northamptonshire for the year 1792 there was noted:

As receiving juvenile workers from a private individual in the county of K— one male aged 13 and two females aged ten and six years.

Anne, musing at the window at Pemberley, had no knowledge of this. In the year following her father's death, when her illnesses and subsequent weakness of body and spirit kept her confined to the house, she became but vaguely aware of the Brightwell family's loss of fortune. Later when she ventured to ask of Mrs Jenkinson what had become of them, that lady purported to know nothing of the matter, or of anyone of that name. She intimated that Anne must have dreamed of them in the fever of her illness. But Anne had never had such feverish dreams, and she still had the little wooden bird Robert had carved for her on that long summer afternoon.

*

It was time for the haymaking and with the weather remaining warm and golden the men, with Darcy often among them, were out from dawn to dusk, leading in the dray horses pulling wagons piled high with the warm sweet hay. Young Master Charles Darcy was brought out into the garden at his mother's request, but swathed in shawls and swaddlings. Elizabeth, exasperated, unwrapped him and allowed him to lie on a rug in the shade of the big cedar tree, kicking his stout little legs, waving his arms and chuckling and gurgling with delight. Nurse, who was of the old school of thought and believed that children should be bound and swaddled when babies, dosed and drilled when older and trained rigorously with cold baths and the rod, was shocked at this mild and free approach and muttered darkly about troubles to come as a result, but as Mrs Darcy was not only the lady of the house, but had helped to nurse and raise three younger sisters in health and liveliness, her methods had to be obeyed. Nurse grudgingly conceded that Master Charles was a healthy, happy baby, with his father's fine features and his mother's brilliant dark eyes.

Anne found her days to be full of occupation: sometimes walking with Elizabeth or Georgiana; sometimes exploring the gardens making notes in her daybook on a number of topics, such as the care of tender plants, the taking of cuttings, rooting and grafting, pruning and mulching. She wrinkled her nose at the pile of dead and stinking fish which the gardener's boys were forking into a new bed to be ready for the autumn planting, but was assured by them of it being:

"Reet good, missus for the roots, as does love a bit o' fish dung."

At times she rode out on her borrowed mare and watched the hay-makers at work, or talked with the steward about the use of sainfoin and clover sown between the corn -rows, and turnips and mangel-wurzels both to improve the tilth and as fodder for the cattle over winter. She approved the method, which she had also instigated on the Rosings farms, of bringing the milch cows down to the yard or shed for milking, thus saving the dairymaids from having to tramp the fields with stool and pail for the milk. In summer too, standing the pails of new-drawn milk in buckets of water taken fresh and cold from the well, helped prevent it from souring too early. The maids did not quite know what to make of this fine young lady venturing into their domain, and indeed turning her hand to the milking—

"…just to see if I can still do it."

They were inclined to be rather surly at first, but were brought round by Anne's easy open manner and finally agreed she was "… neither dicked in the nob, nor a mistress princum-prancum, but an easygoing gentry-mort,"—and they put her behaviour down to one of the quirks of the quality. Anne was aware of their comments and was amused by them, especially when she recollected that she was being far more hoydenish and hob-nobbing far more with what her mother would term the lower orders than ever she had been allowed to do. Lady Catherine must be turning in her elegant oak coffin, but Anne could hear her father's hearty laughter echoing from beyond the grave and was comforted.

She had not forgotten her paints and sketchbook. She had outlined the portrait of Georgiana at the piano forte with the two clergymen in attendance and had persuaded that young lady to allow her to sketch her as she practised her playing. She had also slightly scandalised the Darcys by secretly filling in a pencil sketch of Reverend Stevens during his sermon, which, she was pleased to note, he delivered roundly and without any hesitation. Mr Campbell however, remained a shadowy figure until he next came to dinner, when, nothing loath, he had been prevailed upon to sit for half-an-hour while she filled in his features. But when the portrait was worked up with coloured crayons, it caused much surprise and pleasure, particularly to the three subjects. Mr Stevens said but little, merely gazing on Miss Darcy's likeness, while

Georgiana herself said she thought it was very fine. Mr Campbell however, was fulsome in his praise.

"How beautifully you have caught the light on Miss Darcy's hair, Miss de Bourgh!" he cried. "And you have Mr Stevens to the very life in the act of singing a splendid 'Ah!'. But I rather fear you have softened my features into a semblance of handsomeness!"

Anne disclaimed, thinking as she did so that such a disclaimer was exactly what his vanity demanded. He wanted to have confirmed from others what he privately thought: that she had caught exactly the colouring, the breadth of shoulder and regularity of features which he prided himself he possessed. Anne, however, merely said she thought she had made a reasonably good likeness of all her subjects and was saved from having to provide further fillips for Mr Campbell's consequence by Darcy asking if she would agree to have the picture framed and hung in the gallery.

"Had I known you might have wished for such a thing, I would have finished it in water-colours, or even attempted oils, but if you feel it merits such attention, then by all means, cousin."

Mr Campbell continued to praise the picture and its creator: its colour, style and proportions, for a while longer and Anne, under cover of the general talk, appealed to Elizabeth for her opinion.

"I like it very much," was the reply, "Except that you have omitted to redden Mr Steven's ears!"

A number of further sketches followed: Elizabeth in the still-room, distilling rose-water; Darcy on his grey; the hay-makers, and several of baby Charles kicking his little bare limbs on his blanket. Elizabeth was delighted with these, and Anne obligingly worked them in water colours for her to hang in her dressing-room.

*

June melted into July. Apart from the occasional thunderstorm to provide much-needed rain, the weather continued fine, indeed turned from warm to hot. The sultry weather that presaged a storm rather had its effect on Anne: she succumbed to one of her severe headaches with, Sarah reported, jagged flashes of coloured light before her eyes. Elizabeth was alarmed, but Sarah soothed her saying:

"No need to worr'it, Ma'am. Miss de Bourgh do have these migraine attacks from time to time; has done since she was quite a young thing. Its best if she stays quiet in her bed with the shades drawn and some lavender water by. In a couple of hours she'll be needing a salt-and-water purge, Ma'am, and soon after that she'll be as right as a trivet!"

"She has no fever?" Elizabeth asked anxiously. "No quickening of the pulse? If so, should I send for Doctor Groves?"

"Bless you no, Ma'am. Nothing like that at all. These attacks seldom last more'n a day or so. Miss Anne'll sleep sweet as a baby after her purge - and that only a light one, just to help nature on its way, like. She don't hold with nothing too strong."

Elizabeth was reassured and having sent up to Anne's room a large bottle of lavender water and a nosegay of roses picked from the garden, left her cousin in her maid's capable hands.

She was surprised a little later to receive a visit from Mr Campbell. He had come to Lambton for a meeting to discuss parish affairs with his curate, which Darcy had also attended. Hearing of Miss de Bourgh's indisposition, he had hastened to inquire after the fair invalid, and begged Mrs Darcy's pardon for thus calling on her without due notice.

"But being so close to Pemberley I could not let pass an opportunity to assure myself of her state of health and to ask if there is any errand I can run on her -or indeed your—behalf, Ma'am."

"Thank you, you are too kind, but there is no need. Anne's maid Sarah, who has been with her a number of years says she occasionally suffers these migraine headaches and all that is needed is that she be kept quiet and cool. So there is not the least occasion for you to put yourself out."

"But will you tell her I called to inquire?" persisted Mr Campbell anxiously.

"And assure her of my very best and warmest wishes for her speedy recovery?"

Elizabeth said all that was necessary on this point and he finally took his leave. But he later sent, by the hand of his manservant, a beautiful bouquet of lilies, together with a note. Anne, recovering exactly as Sarah had predicted, was sitting up in bed, looking rather pale and sipping weak tea when Elizabeth scratched the door and was admitted, bearing this offering.

"It seems you have an ardent admirer, my dear. How are you feeling?"

"My head feels a little light and my insides rather empty," returned Anne, "which is always the way after one of these attacks. Otherwise I am perfectly well. But what can you mean - an admirer?"

"These are from Mr Campbell. He called this morning most particularly to inquire after you and has just sent these magnificent lilies. With a note, which probably assures you of his warmest wishes."

Anne turned a look of comical dismay on her cousin.

"Surely not! Surely you don't mean he has a tendre for me?"

"Why not?" Elizabeth was laughing at Anne's stricken face. "What could be more natural? He obviously admires your looks—maybe not when you are as pale and wan as you are now—and he certainly approves your talent in drawing. Consider how warm he was in praise of your work!"

"But that was for the picture!" cried Anne.

"And why not for the artist herself?"

"Oh, you are teasing me. You cannot mean it!"

"Indeed I do mean it. When I look back on those evenings when he dined with us, I consider he paid you most particular attention."

"No he did not!" said Anne with decision. "No more attention than he paid to Georgiana, which is most understandable as she is excessively pretty!"

"So are you, my dear Anne. Always in the first style of elegance, and the new way Sarah has of doing your hair becomes you exceptionally well. Darcy tells me you have your father's colouring and looks, and he was considered a very well-looking man. Believe me, I would not tease you over Mr Campbell if I did not think he had a partiality for you."

"A partiality for my fortune perhaps," said Anne, shrewdly.

"Oh dear! Well, but consider he may have a prudent as well as a romantic motive for matrimony. Although I own it cannot be comfortable to be regarded as a prize merely for one's fortune and not for oneself alone. That I admit is a difficulty which I am happy to say I never encountered." She paused, reflecting on her husband's initial reluctance in offering her marriage, so poor and so unsuitable had she been. She turned back to Anne with a twinkle.

"I have just had a famous notion! Could you not pretend to have lost everything on change?"

In spite of herself Anne laughed.

"Indeed I could not! I could never keep up the pretence. Oh Eliza! How can I possibly face Mr Campbell after this?"

"Well you need not this evening in any case. I will have a tray sent up to you. But I will have to convey a message; should I say you have taken him in dislike?"

"Certainly not! You are being most provoking! I do not dislike him exactly. It is just that he seems to me not to think as a clergyman ought to think, and his wearing of those excessively bright waistcoats seems not at all the thing. I'm sure you will say everything that is pretty with regard to the flowers; they are indeed beautiful, but can you put them someplace else? Do not you think their scent a little overpowering?"

Elizabeth laughed and bore the lilies away, remarking that Anne obviously thought the same about the sender. She was as good as her word, and after consultation with her excellent cook, contrived to send up a light but nourishing supper such as to tempt the appetite of one recovering from a light head and empty insides.

Having done justice to this, Anne felt well enough to take a turn about the room, but finding herself still a little dizzy was glad to return to her bed. She mused on her conversation with Elizabeth and considered her feelings in relation to Mr Campbell. On her part, she had detected nothing particular in his attention to her; she thought him amiable and pleasing and as good-looking as he knew himself to be. His vanity she had already remarked; somehow he had an air of always being conscious of the effect he hoped he was having on those around him. She thought his conversation not serious enough for a clergyman, but had to admit that the only model she had for clerical behaviour was Mr

Collins - and he could hardly be said to measure up to her ideal. Except she was not at all sure what was her ideal. She had recently read some of the sermons of the late Mr John Wesley, together with Mr Hampson's 'Memories' of that eminent man, and she had been impressed. It seemed he combined a most remarkable scholarship with an ability for organisation and a deep and abiding care for the poor. She could not agree with his notions for educating the young, however, but then neither did she agree with the criticism of enthusiasm levelled at him, although she was aware this could be applied to some of his followers, many of whom were ridiculed for their credulousness over appearances of the so-called supernatural. Mr Campbell, on the other hand, seemed to regard the poor with little compassion, and even something like contempt. Unlike the shy and serious Mr Stevens. If only he had a little more address and could be got over the matter of those red ears, he might well be all she thought a clergyman ought to be.

Sarah came in to remove the tray and to ask if her mistress needed anything.

"Only a little barley water. Who are the guests this evening?"

"The two reverends, the Squire and his lady and Doctor Groves. The good doctor has said as if you was wishful to see him he would come up. What should I say?"

"That there is no need. I shall be perfectly well in the morning. Open the curtains a little way Sarah, the evening light is so beautiful."

"As you wish, Miss Anne."

The evening light was indeed beautiful and the air was now cool. Anne could faintly hear Georgiana at the piano forte and wondered if the two reverends—as Sarah put it—would be prevailed upon to add their voices to the music. The Squire, she knew, had no ear at all for music and would be playing a rubber of whist with his lady, Darcy and the doctor. She returned to her contemplation and became convinced that her heart was untouched; she further wondered whether she had met anyone at all for whom she might have formed a liking. But then she had met so few young men! True her cousins, James and Fitzwilliam, had often been at Rosings and although she liked them both, especially James, she could only think of them as cousins. She had meekly accepted the possibility that she might become the second Mrs Anne Darcy, but had been secretly relieved when this failed of its happening.

Since her father's death when she was but eleven years old, she and her mother had lived quietly, mostly at Rosings, occasionally at the London house, once or twice in Bath. But in neither of the latter places had she been allowed to attend dances or assemblies; her mother not wishing her to meet anyone for whom she might form a partiality, thus throwing a rub in the way of Lady Catherine's plans for the marriage of Anne and Fitzwilliam Darcy. That such an event had never taken place had not lessened her ladyship's determination to keep Anne closely confined, presumably either until such time as Darcy might be free to marry again, or as a dutiful spinster daughter-companion for her old age. That plan too had been overset, and Anne found herself in the position of being free to receive the addresses of any gentleman of birth, breeding and possibly fortune as might take her fancy. Except she had no idea, and no experience at all of what she might fancy. I have no means of knowing how I should go on should I meet anyone to my liking, she thought to herself. But then there is no reason why I should marry a man of birth or fortune. Or indeed why I should marry at all. A single woman of fortune may do as she pleases, and use all her resources of income to further her usefulness and activity. Perhaps I shall travel abroad, and send back letters from France or Italy like Anna Miller or Hester Piozzi, or my favourite author Mary Wollstonecraft. Except that with Napoleon marching his armies all over Europe, and being distinctly unfriendly toward England, things had become uncomfortable for English travellers abroad. Perhaps then, Anne thought, it would be better to explore the glories of my own country; there is so much here that Ihave not seen. I am sure Serena Pope would be glad to accompany me. We might even go as far as Scotland and Ireland. On this thought she settled herself down to sleep. But as she drifted out of wakefulness, there came unbidden into her mind the picture of a boy, sitting with his sisters in a daisy field, whittling a piece of wood into the likeness of a little bird.

***
**
*

Chapter Seven

"How I am changed! Alas, how I am grown A frightful spectre—to myself unknown!"
Lady Mary Wortley Montague: Eclogue, The Small Pox.

It was not at all unusual that letters should arrive from Longbourn; both Mrs Bennet and Mary, and even occasionally Mr Bennet, writing to pass on news of their visits and amusements and to ask particularly after the health and progress of the little heir to Pemberley. One morning not long after Anne's recovery from her headache, the post brought two letters: one from Longboum for Elizabeth and one for Anne from Lucas Lodge. This was from Charlotte Collins, and as neither Anne nor Elizabeth had any notion of Charlotte's intention to visit her family so soon after the birth of her daughter, it caused no little surprise. But so it was, and when Anne had perused the letter, which contained the reason for Mrs Collins' visit, she turned very pale and let it drop from her hand. Elizabeth, busy with her own correspondence, did not at first notice her cousin's distress, and was exclaiming over the same news in her own letter: that Charlotte and the children were at Meryton, when she was startled by Anne exclaiming in a very agitated manner:

"I know it! Oh, I know it! I must go home at once!"

Elizabeth and Darcy were instantly all concern. Anne took command of herself and explained that Mr Collins had sent his wife and family away in haste because there had suddenly occurred several cases of smallpox in the village.

'No one knows from whence it came,' Anne read from Charlotte's letter. *'Most of the adults have had the inoculation'*

'… oh yes, my father arranged for everyone to receive it, but that was years ago! I was still a small child and my mother, misliking the process, saw no necessity for me to go through what she considered a difficult and dangerous procedure. She believed country air would be proof enough against the contagion. Since my father's death, nothing further was done.'

She picked up Charlotte's letter again and continued to read:

'...had the inoculation, as have I, but of course my children have not received it and in any case the baby is too young. So we have come to Meryton, but Mr Collins was determined to remain, although I am greatly afraid for him as he has never received the inoculation either. But he has every intention of doing his duty by his parishioners, as he is convinced you would want him to

do, and begs me to inform you, dear Miss de Bourgh, of the situation. He says he will not write for fear of infection being sent through the mail, and he urges that if it is convenient for Mr and Mrs Darcy, that you remain at Pemberley until all danger is passed.'

Both the Darcys cried out that of course Anne must stay, but she would not hear of it.

"I am not, nor would be in any danger. Although I have received neither inoculation nor Doctor Jenner's new vaccination, I have had the cow pox have I not? And I must make haste and go home to do what I can. Mr Collins and our good Doctor Holmes must not bear the work and the burden alone!"

Once having determined on a course of action, Anne set about carrying it out with precision and organisation. Elizabeth sent her own maid to assist Sarah with the packing and Darcy immediately went himself to the stables. Anne wrote a quick letter to Charlotte, telling her not to be afraid, and another to Mr Collins. She also wrote to the family's London doctor requesting that a batch of the cowpox vaccine be sent to Rosings Park as soon as practicable.

"If the poor sufferers have been kept isolated, we may well save others if they can be vaccinated before they take the disease in the natural way."

Things were soon well in hand, and Anne left Pemberley early on the following morning. She promised to let the Darcys know how things stood, provided she could be sure that no letter would carry any possibility of infection. She was all gratitude for her visit, and apologised for leaving them, and all her acquaintances in Derbyshire in such haste.

*

"It is a most uncomfortable thing," Elizabeth said to her husband as they strolled through the shrubbery some time after Anne's departure, "to find oneself having to revise an opinion as to a person's character which has been long held. I thought I had become wise enough to base my opinions on reasonable observations, and to change them when experience informs me things are not as I once thought. But it is astonishing how such beliefs hold firm in one's mind! So here I am, having once more to throw over such firmly held beliefs. It really is too bad!"

"Who is the person who has caused you such turmoil?"

"Why, Mr Collins! I have always thought him lacking in good sense, conceited but weak, proud with self-importance but obsequious in humility. Such a combination could produce in me little but contempt—and pity for Charlotte. In remaining in Hunsford when there is every danger of contracting smallpox, I find he has done that which is worthy of my respect! My opinion of him has risen considerably. I would not have believed him capable of such an act of selfless generosity. He is truly behaving as a good shepherd of his flock should."

"Perhaps, you need not throw out all your former opinions. People may be all you observe them to be, and indeed Mr Collins remains weak in conversation, lacking in sense and overly servile. But tragedy such as the present crisis may produce quite unexpected depths in the most unlikely of persons."

"You think then I may be allowed to continue to feel a certain amount of contempt for Mr Collins?"

"Why not? Provided you allow yourself to respect his present behaviour," replied Darcy.

"Indeed I do respect it! But I am greatly relieved. I would not like to waste my contempt, it is a rare and expensive commodity!"

Darcy laughed.

"But do not you feel you must revise your opinion of Anne? She cannot be what you once thought her."

"Indeed no, she is not. But here the change is all from within herself. She was once a poor creature, but circumstances have brought her out - as a butterfly emerges from its hard little case. Whereas Mr Collins will no doubt revert to being the worm he once was, and I can be comfortable again."

"So he remains a worm, and she becomes a butterfly?"

"If you like. But worms, as Mr Gilbert White has informed us, have their uses you know! And Mr Collins seems to have found his."

"Presumably so has Anne. But I cannot help feeling she has more good sense than a butterfly is thought to possess."

"Oh yes! She is also all good-heartedness and sensibility. I hope that she may not wear herself out in her care for her people. Although she is not as weak a creature as once I thought her, she is still not strong."

*

Anne arrived at Rosings scarce two days after she had set out from Derbyshire. She found that Mr Collins and Mr Holmes between them had organised the patients: a young man recently employed by Farmer Heydock, and three children; removing them to a remote cottage where they were being capably nursed by the village midwife and wise woman, Dame Betty Dakins. She was skilled in the old knowledge of herbs of healing, and was used to concoct cordials of violets to cure the effects of excess of alcohol—a remedy much in demand on market days—tansy for women's disorders, samile and milfoil for wounds, marigolds to cheer the spirits. Although she grew most of these in her own garden, as did many of the villagers and farmers' wives, she was also used to go to and visit Dame Hannah Brightwell whenever she needed more than her own still-room could supply. But since that lady's mysterious departure, Dame Betty, never one to bemoan what could not be helped, rounded up the estate's supply of elder-flower water, which she firmly believed to be particularly good against fever, together with angelica, borage, calamint and cowslip wine. She then set off to do battle against the speckled disease.

Dame Dakins held her faith in time-honoured remedies. Mr Holmes, who did not strictly deserve Miss de Bourgh's honorific of 'doctor', being but an apothecary, was well-read in all the latest scientific and medical theories. His shop and centre of business was in Westerham, but he rode out whenever called upon to attend the inhabitants of several of the villages round about, including Hunsford. He was in the village when Anne arrived at Rosings Park, and having assured herself that all the staff at the House and on the Home Farm were safe and well, she sent a message for Mr Holmes to attend her—as soon as may be convenient:

"I do not wish you to leave those in your care until you are assured it is expedient to do so."

He came within the hour, having first washed and changed his clothes, an outhouse at the cottage being set aside for this purpose. He wished first to assure himself that Miss de Bourgh was immune and was informed of her cowpox. Swallowing his surprise, he proceeded with his report, which was grim. He believed the young man to have been the source of the infection, having but recently arrived from London where he had regrettably jumped ship. The vessel had just returned from Barbados with a cargo of sugar, and the young man had not stayed to unload the cargo, but journeyed to Kent, the county of his birth. Farmer Heydock had employed him for the haymaking.

"He seemed a broad, strong lad enough, but after two-three days failed to appear in the fields for work. The good farmer was at first annoyed at his defection, but when his wife found the lad shivering and shaking with fever in the barn, he was a bit more compassionate. They sent for Dame Dakins, who sent for me."

"Of what nature is his disease?"

"I am afraid of the worst. I fear he has the late purples, and will probably not survive."

"What of the children?" was Anne's next anxious question "There are now four, who may be said to be diseased. Two are the Heydocks' grandchildren: a boy of 12 and a girl of 14. Both went out to the hayfield to carry beer and vittles and the boy stayed to work the rest of the day. He is very full of the confluent pox, but may come through. The girl has more discrete pocks, but alas, a high fever. Two more children, aged six and seven, have been confined with headache and sweating; it remains to be seen what form their pox will take."

Anne was pacing the room.

"My father arranged for all on the estate to be inoculated. But of late—that has not been done. Can you discover for me how many have either never received inoculation, nor have had the cowpox?"

If Mr Holmes was surprised at how well Miss de Bourgh was informed, he managed to conceal it.

"It shall be done. My assistant can find this out and I will send a report."

"As soon as possible, if you please." Anne noted the apothecary's scarred face.

"You yourself are immune I take it? What of your family and servants?"

"I contracted the disease when I was working in America. It is not an experience I would wish anyone to have to undergo. My wife, three of our children and our maids have all received inoculation at my hands. The fourth child, a boy of five years, I vaccinated with the cowpox."

"You believe it to be a safe proof?"

"Doctor Jenner's paper to the Royal Society was most specific on that point, and in the intervening two years the evidence of numbers has grown."

"You do not believe that those vaccinated will develop cow-like appetites, make mooing sounds instead of speech and go about on four legs butting people with their imaginary horns?" Anne asked with a smile.

"Boanthropy scare-stories, Ma'am, put about by medical critics jealous of the good doctor's discoveries. I cannot believe you would give them credence Miss de Bourgh!"

"There may be some who are influenced by such tales," Anne returned, "but I am not one of them. Had I done so, I would not have ordered from Doctor Sutton in London a supply of the necessary vaccine. I wish everyone to have the procedure and I was unsure whether you would be able to supply enough yourself."

Mr Holmes acknowledged the truth of this and was preparing to take his leave, when Anne stayed him with a further request. She wished to be instructed how to perform the vaccination herself. The apothecary had had little to do with the new young mistress of Rosings, but remembered all too clearly her high nosed and remote mother. His astonishment now kept him silent for nearly halfa-minute. Anne was about to repeat her question when he broke into a confused rejoinder.

"Of course, Miss de Bourgh if you—but are you indeed sure? I mean, it is not a difficult process, but—I cannot be sure, but there may be any number who require it." He broke off in total dismay.

"All the more reason for you to have another assistant," Anne reassured him. "I am perfectly serious in my intent."

Well, well, thought he as he rode away, as unlike her mother as anyone can be!

Anne was also thinking of Lady Catherine and with a mixture of quite un-filial anger and contempt. Generous though some of her ladyship's donations to charities had been—and in her own view these were only those most deserving of her notice—she had nonetheless neglected the welfare of her estate workers, tenants and villagers. She may have been a magistrate in her own parish; she may have dispensed advice, scoldings and punishments on those brought to her notice as needing the benefit of her dictates; she may have had an eye to their moral lapses, but she had not felt herself obliged to concern herself with their sicknesses, nor sought, as many a great lady had done from royalty downwards, to ensure the prevention of just such an epidemic as had now occurred in her domain. This was not only uncaring and arrogant, it was short-sighted! Dependent as she was on the tithes and revenues of the estate and its farms, which had kept her in style, elegance and luxury, she could not afford to be so neglectful. Anne was determined to follow in her father's footsteps.

The next weeks were full of anxiety and busyness. Anne's first concern was for Mr Collins. Although she could not bear his sycophantic fawning, she was, like Elizabeth, both startled and surprised at his decision to save his wife and children from infection without thought for himself. He was therefore the first to receive the vaccination at her hands and he was duly sensible, indeed highly gratified by the honour. He was however, looking less the stout young gentleman she remembered. Not wishing to spread the infection, nor to contract it, he had refrained from visiting the sick in the distant cottage, but had not spared himself from visiting their afflicted families. How many of these were harbouring the dreadful contagion he could not of course be sure, but of this he would not let himself think. He sought to cheer, comfort and pray with his fearful parishioners, and to this end he opened the church on Tuesday and Thursday mornings as well as Sundays and led prayers for deliverance. In his carefully modulated sermons, Anne was thankful to note he did not dwell long on the belief that this visitation of sickness was sent as a punishment for individual or collective sin, but he did exhort everyone to clear their consciences and accept this disease coming among them as God's challenge to their behaviour - viz. in the mutual help and comfort they must now give each other.

"This is not a time," he thundered from the pulpit, "When ye should bear illwill, neighbour against neighbour, for whatever cause, whether great or small."

He lowered his tone:

"This is a time for confession, for forgiveness."

He raised his voice to a bellow,

"This is not a time to be apportioning blame and looking for revenge."

Once more he softened his approach,

"This is a time when all should truly take into their hearts the commandment: love thy neighbour as thyself."

For, perhaps, the first time in his ministry, Mr Collins' parishioners went home a little comforted.

*

The young sailor died. So did the Heydocks' grandson. Mr Collins buried the two boys on a scorching day in August, and waived his fee for both. In spite of all their precautions, three more villagers took the pox: two young children and the Collins' own maid, Molly. They were removed with all haste to the isolated cottage and Anne sent two servant girls down from the House to the Parsonage to cleanse Molly's room and wash and air her clothes. One maid remained to take her place.

But it was too late. With respect to Mr Collins, all precautions were too late. He became aware that very evening of severe pain spreading up from his back to his head and neck. At first he thought it due to the excessive amount of riding he had recently undertaken, but when in the night he found himself alternately burning with fever and sweats and shivering with cold, he knew that he may well have taken the disease in the natural way. In his distress he called out loud to God to save his wife, his children, his people and his soul. The frightened maid, hearing his cries, brought him the comfort of cool wet cloths to his head and elder-flower water for his burning throat. At first light, she scurried away to find Dame Dakins and arrange for the poor parson to be removed to the cottage.

In a few days, his fever began to abate; he became clear-headed and asked repeatedly after the welfare of the villagers. There was no sign of a rash. The estate waited with collectively bated breath so to speak; perhaps it was not the smallpox after all. But then the spots began to appear: a small red rash spreading over his face, neck, throat and flowing down his body.

"It may be the measles," reported Mr Holmes, but he was cautious and advised that all that could be done was to wait and see.

Dame Betty kept her own counsel; she had nursed too many to whatever outcome of their disease was in store for them, and knew well the difference between a rash of measles and one of the pox.

Meanwhile, another child died, and two more were stricken. Fortunately, most of them had the discrete form of the smallpox, and several, once their fevers broke and their aching heads had abated, had to be restrained from running around and giving vent to childhood's normal high spirits. Only one boy contracted the early haemorhagic form: a shy, sickly child of eight years who in his short life had taken a number of diseases badly—measles, coughs, influenza and putrid sore throat. With a constitution so lacking in robustness, Mr Holmes could hardly express surprise that he should succumb to the most virulent form of the pox, and one which was invariably fatal. It was one of those sad fates that he should be the only child of a quiet and long-married couple.

During the few days when Mr Collins was free of fever and in discomfort rather than pain while the rash bloomed over his skin, he was anxious concerning his parochial duties. Anne, visiting him as she had done for the other sufferers several times a week, reassured him that a curate from Westerham was undertaking the funerals and the Sunday services. She did not tell him however that she herself was reading prayers in the morning-room at Rosings for any who wished to attend on Tuesday and Thursdays, nor that she was defraying the cost of the burials. Mr Collins may have been able to waive his guineas; a curate could not, and those families unable to afford funeral expenses found that without their knowledge they were beholden to the lady of Rosings.

One Thursday morning, Miss de Bourgh received from Josiah Bender, apprentice apothecary and assistant to Mr Holmes, a neatly written list of all those so far struck down with the pox. His previous report had resulted in the vaccination of some eighty-four persons, mostly under the age of five-and-twenty, including forty-six children aged between three and twelve years. Mr Holmes, Mr Bender and Anne carried out the vaccinations, which Anne found to be a simple procedure: a cleansing of the area of the upper arm; a small scratch; the insertion of just enough infected matter to coat the tip of a needle and the whole swiftly bandaged. Mrs Rowlands, Sarah, and Dame Dakins' eldest daughter Susan acted as assistants to prepare the recipients; to comfort the more tearful little girls; exhort the boys to be good soldiers of the King; soothe anxious mothers, and reassure the fearful, sometimes by displaying their own impressively large inoculation scars. The few who developed the mostly mild fevers, lasting no more than a day or so, which followed the process, were duly noted in Mr Bender's neat account. The only difficulty arising from all this activity was the demand for elder-flower water. The trees, fortunately flowering late this year due to the coolness of the early summer, were totally stripped of their blooms, to the annoyance of those goodwives who regularly made elderberry wine.

"No flowers, no berries," one such farmer's wife was heard to grumble. By her own account her wine was the best in the district and she was disgruntled to think she would not make as much profit as usual. But she was roundly silenced by many who thought this was a just price to pay.

Thursday, August 14th: Anne received Mr Bender in the morning room prior to the reading of the prayers. He watched, hat in hand, as she read through his report on all those taken with the sickness. She had requested this so that they could say prayers for the afflicted families by name each week. It did not make good reading:

Date	Name	Age	Type	Outcome
July 24	Nat Boyd, sailor	17 yrs	Late Haemorhagic	Died
July 25	Rob Heydock, fmrs boy	12 yrs	Confluent	Died
July 25	Sarah Heydock, maid	14 yrs	Discrete, high fever	
July 30	Hannah Morris child	7 yrs	Discrete, mild	
July 2	Geo. Batt, child	6yrs	Early Haemorhagic	Died
July 8	Jane Smollett, child	10yrs	Crystalline, much marked	
Aug 9	Henry Smollett, child	4yrs	Discrete, mild	
Aug 9	Molly Bond, maid	16yrs	Confluent, very full	

Anne glanced up to find Josiah Bender's sharp eyes fixed on her. She thanked him for the care he had taken in the preparation of his reports and asked that she continue to be kept informed.

"Coming as you do from Westerham, Mr Bender, these people are not perhaps as well known to you as they are to me. Perhaps that makes it easier for you to prepare these reports in such a careful way. I am grateful for all the help you have given. I understand you are keeping careful notes of the progress of the disease in all our patients?"

"That is so, Ma' am," said Mr Bender tonelessly.

Anne nodded her dismissal.

"I will see you next week then," she said, "Unless you wish to stay for prayers. You would be most welcome, but I have no doubt you have much to do at the cottage."

Thus, she provided for him an escape she felt he would be glad to take. He took it, and she was relieved. For all his care, she found him a cold man.

The following Thursday, there was only one entry on Mr Bender's neatly scribed list

August 21st, Rev. Geo Collins, parson, 36 yrs. Confluent, severe. Died.

The paper trembled in Anne's hand as she read the final word. The assistant apothecary was watching, hawk -like, for her reaction.

"I had thought," her voice came a little huskily, and she cleared her throat and began again, "I had thought Mr Collins to be improving. Indeed although I knew him to be very full, I had not thought to hear—er, to hear that—that it was likely to be fatal. When did this occur?"

"According to Dame Betty, at first light, this morning. She sent for me as being nearer than Mr Holmes. I ascertained death had occurred from the gathering of fluid in the lungs." Mr Bender's tone was dry, precise and impartial. "The apothecary came as soon as he could and confirmed my diagnosis."

Anne nodded, reflecting that this young man may well make his mark in the future as a man of science and medicine, but by the ordinary folk he sought to treat he would never be esteemed, nor loved - as Mr Holmes was esteemed by those under his care. As warm and comfortable Dame Betty Dakins was loved. As, she acknowledged to herself with no little surprise, Mr Collins had come to be esteemed in these last few weeks of his ministry among them. There would be cries of astonishment and regret at prayers this morning, probably even tears from the women and among the families he had sought to help. He had indeed lived - and died - with them.

***
**
*

Book Two
Wealth and Wisdom

Chapter One

"Any man's death diminishes me, because I am involved in mankind"
John Donne: Devotions (1624)

Some thirty-five years after the events described above, Doctor Josiah Bender, graduate of the medical school of the University of Heidelberg, was to publish his report on the outbreak of smallpox in a small village with its surrounding farmland in the county of Kent, England, in the year 1800. In precise terms he detailed the number of persons who contracted the disease, the number of deaths and the number of those who were either previously inoculated or given the cowpox vaccine at the time the disease manifested itself. He compared these figures with those recorded in a similar village in 1723, before variolation, as inoculation was known then, was widely used. On that occasion, out of a population of some one hundred and eighty men, women and children, one hundred and thirteen succumbed to the smallpox and the resultant deaths numbered ninety-seven. In Hunsford in 1800, with a similar population, fourteen people were affected in all, with the death toll finally standing at a mere five. Such reports and such figures were not new; the efficacy of the vaccination procedure having been long established. Indeed, the Bishop of Worcester had informed the governors of the London Smallpox Hospital in 1752 that of one thousand five hundred inoculated patients, only three had died. He was at the time aiming to raise philanthropic support for the institution, and his cloth notwithstanding, was considered to have been guilty of exaggeration.

But such a comparison was not the aim of Dr Bender's paper. Nor did it aim merely to describe the variations of the disease as it manifested itself in its victims, nor the different stages or progressions through which they passed. All these were indeed meticulously described, but what Josiah Bender wanted to achieve in publishing his careful account so many years after he had first taken his notes, was to give support to the new theories being proposed on the transmission of diseases. Or rather the development of old ideas into new theories. Notions of the danger of miasmas, of congregations of foul airs and bad odours as disease carriers were slowly giving way to the thought, which in itself was not so new, but which many still believed to be ridiculous, that there existed tiny 'animalculae' which invaded the body and caused the fevers, sweats, rashes and boils, pustules and pocks. Girolamo Frascatoro, in the middle of the sixteenth century, had written about 'seminaria contagiosa', or 'disease seeds', which could be carried by the wind from one infected object to another. These tiny specks of living matter were producing a large debate among doctors, particularly in Germany, where Dr Bender had carried out his studies and his research. The idea was also being put forward that the body itself carried the means to combat such beings, but of this Dr Bender was by no means convinced.

However, he did support the theory that contagion was achieved by means of the physical transference of these disease specks which can be seen only with the aid of the strongest of microscopes, such that there are:

'...thousands in a bead of sweat, a drop of blood or pus, and thus being moved from hand to hand, smeared on to clothing, utensils, hair, linen, bedding, straw, animal fur and the like, are transported between persons without they are ever being aware of it.'

He theorised that from the original source of the infection - the young sailor who brought the disease from foreign parts via London to the hayfields of the Rosings estate, contact was made through the tools, clothing, indeed the hay itself, touched by him and transferred to those who worked with him. From them to other children who were playing in the hayfield; to the adults who minded these children; to those, like the parson, who visited the homes which now carried the seeds of the disease. So he wrote in 1835.

But what Dr Bender's dry and serious paper did not take into account was the human cost of the outbreak of the smallpox in Hunsford. This could not be measured in terms of the actual numbers of those who became ill, those who died, and those who remained ever afterwards pockmarked. But it was observed in the effect it had on all the families in the village, the farms and the estate. Young Robert Heydock's death grieved not only his parents, brothers, sisters, grandparents, aunts, uncles and cousins, but also Farmer Bone, whose boy he was, and Sally, Farmer Bone's daughter, who was his sweetheart.

Pretty Molly Bond, struggling for her life, was not to know that her resulting perpetual disfigurement would cause distress not only to her parents and her aunt Rawlings, but also have an effect on George Proctor, stable-hand at Rosings Park, who had entertained thoughts of marrying her, but who now turned those thoughts elsewhere, not being wishful for a pockmarked wife.

Then there was Kitty Roper, the baker's lovely daughter, only a year married to Thomas Roper the farrier, and about to be brought to bed of their first child. Two-three weeks before her expected time she was overtaken by the tell tale shivers and sweats and such pains in her back and belly that Dame Dakins and Mr Holmes between them had much difficulty in soothing her. Her screams of agony echoed through the cottage and for the sake of the other patients she was moved to the little outhouse. As the rash broke out over her body, so she also laboured to deliver her child: a flushed and yelling infant, small but lusty—and covered with tiny pocks. Kitty cradled him in her arms for two days before her second fever broke. A week later she was dead. The progress of her disease was carefully noted by the precise Josiah Bender.

Miraculously, the child survived, and was duly christened in the cottage hospital. He had been swaddled in a length of silk provided by Miss Anne de Bourgh as being kinder to his sore little body than the usual rough cotton. A wet nurse was found for him, one Ella Barker, a kindly soul already suckling her twelfth child.

"One more babe in that household," commented Dame Betty, cheerfully, to Miss Anne on her next visit, "makes no odds. But more than nursing the child we cannot ask, Ma'am, not should we. The infant's poor dead mother's father is a widower and Farrier Roper's family come from Middleham way and don't seem to take kindly to the idea of having a pocky baby foisted on 'em. An' 'tisn't right a man should have the work of childer, e'en though Thomas Roper be willin' enough to raise his son."

"It is natural enough that a man should want to watch his son grow and perhaps teach him his own trade. But he cannot always be watching a babe, or a lively youngster when he has his work to attend to. Little Tom will be fine with Dame Barker for a while. But then perhaps we might ask Eliza Batt and her husband Joseph if they would consider having the care of him, as they have lost their own little boy"

Dame Susan nodded reflectively.

"That may be so, Miss Anne. 'Tis true a ewe having lost her own may be persuaded to take on an orphan lamb; maybe this little lost 'un can be new mothered and bring a blessing to poor grievin' Eliza. Though he'd be double fathered."

"How would that be a problem? Most children in this village run in and out of each other's houses and are as welcomed by aunts and uncles and cousins as in their own homes. Even by those who are no kin to them. Little Tom will find no lack of loving care."

But the future of baby Tom Roper was not Anne's only concern. Charlotte Collins had returned to the Parsonage with her children and her mother, Lady Lucas, who came to support her through her husband's funeral. This was conducted by Parson Bride of Westerham, with his two curates and the two footmen from Rosings acting as pall-bearers. Charlotte was surprised and touched by the number of villagers who attended, some of them so recently bereaved themselves. She would have been more surprised had she been aware that many of the villagers came because they esteemed her rather more than her husband. She had been the one to visit the cottages whenever sickness or poverty required some relief; she carried the broth and the blankets, the eggs, the honey and the port-wine, oftentimes supplied by Rosings Park it is true, but it was Charlotte's presence which brought kindness and sympathy where it was needed most.

Parson Collins had taken his duties of parish visiting more seriously than many clergymen, but his excursions into the lives of his people was more often to admonish, scold and punish their lapses into reprehensible behaviour. Tales of such misdeeds he had considered his duty to report to Lady Catherine, who then sallied forth to add her voice to the weight of disapproval being brought to bear on miscreants. Certainly Mr Collins welcomed back into the fold those who made an outward show of repentance; but to those backsliders who remained impudent he was implacable. Only in this last outbreak of serious illness had he visited his parishioners to comfort and console, and in the end to suffer with them. This final act, fatal as it had been, removed some of the feelings that had formerly been less than charitable to the parson.

But Charlotte could not remain at the Parsonage for very much longer; she would have to quit it as soon as a new incumbent could be found. This exercised Anne's mind to a considerable degree. Her first thought had been to offer the living to the curate from Westerham, but that young man, though expressing himself duly sensible of the honour, had to regretfully decline as he had already accepted the living of Brightholmstone in the county of Hampshire, in which he would have the care of some three hundred souls. He was to leave Westerham at the end of the present quarter.

Anne then invited Mr Bride, Rector of Westerham to dine at Rosings and sought his advice in respect of his second curate. Mr Bride was not encouraging.

"I cannot with a good conscience recommend him Miss de Bourgh. He has not long taken his BA degree, and seems not yet to have shaken off the bad habits of his scholar days. Several times I have found him drunk when he should have been watchful; once indeed he was dead drunk, for which I had to fine him two shillings. He mended his ways somewhat after that, but has still not been attentive enough to his duties, which all in all, are not onerous."

Anne sighed, recommended the cheesecakes to her reverend guest, and turned her thoughts back to the dual problems of her duties: to find a new clergyman and to take, if necessary, responsibility for the former rector's widow.

As the smallpox outbreak in Hunsford began to wane, letters passed more frequently to and from the village. A letter from Mrs Elizabeth Darcy was brought from the receiving office to the Parsonage. She wrote to invite Charlotte and the children to Pemberley—

'For as long as you remain in black gloves and indeed longer, should you so wish.'

Admittedly, this could not be a permanent solution, but Lady Lucas lost no time in urging her daughter to accept her friend's invitation without delay. Sir William and Lady Lucas had expressed their willingness to take their widowed daughter and the grandchildren back into their own household, and although nothing was said to disprove this, Charlotte sensibly realised that with her brothers to bring through school and college and Maria to establish creditably, three extra mouths to feed would stretch the family resources a little too far. Mr Collins, with the expectation of long living, common to those who think well of themselves, had not been provident and had left his wife with but a modest competence; enough to ensure a dress allowance for her and the children but not enough to provide more than these simple necessities of life. Charlotte had been brought up to be a prudent and thrifty wife and mother, and she had entered the married state as a practical necessity, but she could not fail to see that her future prospects were poor indeed. Lady Lucas did her best to rouse her daughter from these melancholy reflections.

"My dear Charlotte, it is but natural that you should grieve for your husband, and indeed to find yourself in lowness of spirits concerning your future. But I am sure that Mr Collins, from that better place to which we all devoutly hope he is gone, would counsel you not to be over-anxious for the morrow. You have good friends about you, as this letter proves, and the company of Elizabeth and Fitzwilliam Darcy and little Charles will do you nothing but good. And you will have peace and leisure for quiet reflection in the beautiful surrounds of Pemberley. Mrs Bennet is always in raptures over the place; indeed, she takes every opportunity to talk of little else!"

She paused, then continued a little awkwardly:

"I do not like to speak of it too openly, but here between ourselves it may be mentioned. I presume that the entail on the Bennets' estate at Longboum now devolves on to Master Edward?"

Charlotte looked up, rather startled.

"I had not thought of it Mama, but I suppose that is so. Mr Bennet, however, is in excellent health and can hardly be said to be in his dotage, so it cannot affect my present situation."

"No indeed," said Lady Lucas smoothly, "but the expectation may, at some future date, be used to advantage. Should you wish to set up your own establishment for example, the banks would no doubt look favourably on a request for an advance. And there will come the need to provide for Edward's schooling."

Her daughter shook her head.

"It is good of you to think of it Mama, but at the moment I cannot think beyond the immediate future."

"Well no my dear, but then as to that, you have to thank Mrs Elizabeth Darcy!"

This was acknowledged and Charlotte lost no time in writing her grateful acceptance to her friend. She was not much given to introspection, having always that turn of mind which put prudence before romance or passion, but her mother's urging upon her a period of quiet thought awoke an answering response. To Pemberley therefore she resolved to go, and with only the delay necessitated by the disposal of the personal furnishings of the Parsonage, the arrangement for the carriage and the change of horses at the Bell in Bromley, all was soon accomplished. All that remained was to undertake farewells around the village and at Rosings Park.

"But I shall consider this to be not a final farewell my dear Charlotte," said Anne, "but an au revoir. Rest and recover your spirits at Pemberley, but consider Hunsford the home to which you will someday return. I have a scheme in mind for which you, with your great good sense and experience would be eminently suited. But I will say no more on this head for the moment; it may amount to little more than a will-o-the-wisp. Please convey my greetings to my cousins and write whenever you can."

Mrs Collins was moved to respond warmly to this, and the two young women parted as firm friends.

The final few days of August were dismal and overcast. Lady Lucas, Mrs Collins and the children departed in a drizzle of rain which was reflected in the woeful face of little Edward Collins who had not yet learned the lesson that small boys must be proof against such expression of sorrow. He clutched his favourite rolling-ball toy to his chest, but not even the knowledge that in the little velvet bag bestowed upon him by Miss Anne rested several shiny marbles and twelve silver pennies, could rouse him to more than a very watery smile.

*

The harvest was late; the oats not being carried in until the last day of the month and the wheat not reckoned to be ready for cutting for another two weeks at the very least. Heads were shaken and among those who gathered of an evening at the alehouse, many a forecast of a bad winter to follow such an unlucky summer were made. There will always be those who enjoy prognosticating gloom and misery, and enjoy things even more when their prognostications prove correct. But September came in warm and golden as if in defiance of the prophets of doom. The smallpox epidemic had finally died out, the last three to contract the disease being finally pronounced returned to health and dismissed to their homes. The housemaids from Rosings Park were sent down to the cottage to help to fumigate the rooms with brimstone and Indian pepper. Walls were brushed down and then painted, first with red lead and then with white; floors were swept; bedsteads taken outside into the sunshine and painted with mercury to kill any remaining fleas and bugs. The tiny windows were cleaned inside and out with vinegar-and-water and the chimney swept. Dame Dakins agreed to live in the smaller of the two rooms and reserve the other for the care of any sick persons who could not, for whatever reason, be nursed at home. The accounts of Rosings Park for the last quarter of the year 1800 included forty pounds:

"...for the upkeep, maintenance and expenses of a cottage on the estate to be designated a sick hospital, and for the sum of ten pounds per annum to be paid to Dame Betty Dakins to act as nurse and midwife."

Anne riding out on Firefly noted the bringing in of the wheat harvest with relief. It would not be the best of years, but with a little careful management it should not prove an ill one. She rode down with her bailiff to where the river purled placidly through the water-meadows and thought of her father's plans, formulated so many years ago, of widening, deepening and canalising it to carry barges for the transport of logs to the sawmill. She turned to Mr Castleton to ask his opinion of the scheme.

"It would need any amount of money Miss Anne," he replied with his usual caution. "We would need a good surveyor, some engineers, and a bevy of navvies. We would also need to construct a number of locks. And having widened, straightened and deepened the river, could we ensure a sufficient depth of water to carry the barges? That I doubt me."

"We cannot know unless we have the land surveyed. Perhaps at the same time we could consider drainage of some of these lower fields? At the moment they are reasonably dry, but after a wet autumn and winter, such as last year, they are bogged too much to be of any farming use well into the spring months. Do you know of any person we can ask to provide us with such a survey? And indeed to oversee the carrying out of such work?"

"There is a Mr Smith, Ma'am, who lives near Bath. He is well-known as a canal and drainage engineer. We can call him in for an inspection tour."

"Then please do so," said Anne, "And let me have his report as soon as may be." She turned her mare who picked her way daintily back up the slope. She was aware of feeling a little tired and dispirited, and with the threat of a mild headache. But she found consolation in the thought that within a few days her good Miss Pope would be with her, and it would be Harvest Home.

***
**
*

Chapter Two

"Mrs Malaprop: Observe me, Sir Anthony, I would by no means wish a daughter of mine to be a progeny of learning; I don't think so much learning becomes a young woman..."
Richard Brinsley Sheridan: The Rivals (1775)

Serena Pope was packing her belongings, which consisted of a reasonably modest number of dresses and other garments and an unreasonably large number of books, all of which were being fitted into her rather battered trunk. She was hindered in this task by Lady Metcalfe, whose excessive silliness Serena had borne with patience over the years she had been in her employ. Lady Metcalfe sank into the only comfortable chair in the room, and fanned herself vigorously, complaining fretfully of the heat, of the absence of her young son and of Serena's leaving her in this sudden fashion.

"But you have known of my departure for some months, Ma'am," Serena said calmly. "It was agreed that I should return to Rosings Park as soon as Master Gilbert left for Eton. And as all the girls are now out of the schoolroom there is no longer any need for my services."

"I do not see why Miss de Bourgh should require you as a companion," Lady Metcalfe remarked fretfully. "She has that Mrs Jenkinson, has not she, while I have no-one now all my chicks have flown the nest."

Serena could not let such a blatant misapprehension go unchecked.

"Sukey, Fanny and Theresa are all still at home; you have Sukey's wedding in October to plan and Theresa to bring out next spring. Master Gilbert will be home for the holidays and you know Mrs Jenkinson left Rosings to go and live with her sister, leaving Miss Anne without companion or chaperone."

Lady Metcalfe's mind could not hold so many ideas all at once; she therefore seized on the only part of this speech that was of immediate concern to herself.

"Sukey's wedding! Indeed I do not know how I am going to have everything arranged in time! It is to be a public ceremony you know, and there will be upwards of two hundred guests. Then Sukey's bride-clothes are not nearly ready, the warehouse having stupidly misplaced the order. Dear Miss Pope, could you not defer your going until after the event? I declare I shall be prostrate long before the happy couple have departed on their honeymoon!"

Serena privately thought it would be the servants who would be prostrate, running hither and yon, trying to fulfil her ladyship's conflicting orders. Both

Lady Metcalfe and Miss Sukey Metcalfe were constantly changing their minds over some aspect of the arrangements and the great event was still several weeks off. But all she said was that she regretted it would not be possible, as she had pledged her word to be with Miss Anne by mid-September at the latest.

"I am sure it cannot signify if you were to go a month later." Lady Metcalfe's tone was peevish. "I'm sure Miss de Bourgh can easily spare you to me for that time."

Serena merely shook her head and observing the agitation of her ladyship's fan, gently recommended her employer to seek the coolness of the small drawing room, which, as it faced east, was at this time in the afternoon blessedly free from the heat of the sun. Miss Pope forbore to point out that her room, next the schoolroom at the top of the house was always hot in summer. In winter it could be cold, but that her employer, generous of heart in spite of her silliness, insisted on fires being lit in every room of the house likely to be used by any member of the family.

"And my dear Miss Pope," she had said frequently, "I always consider you to be quite one of the family!"

It was not to be supposed that the upper servants shared this view, but in all her teaching positions Serena Pope had known how to tread the fine line between familiarity and condescension, such that she managed, most of the time, not to ruffle the sensibilities of the housekeeper, the cook or the ladies' maids, nor to assume too easy an intercourse with the mistress of the house. Nor with the master. In the Metcalfe establishment, she was spared any such dealings as Lady Metcalfe was a widow of ample means who, unlike Lady Catherine de Bourgh, whose autocratic rule Lady Metcalfe regarded with a mix of dislike and fear, governed her house and children with an easy rein. Too easy, thought Serena, the result being that the girls were as lazy and silly as their mother and the boy spoilt, petted and cosseted beyond all bounds. They had managed to rid themselves of no fewer than five previous governesses, and it was fortunate that Serena Pope was made of sterner stuff. Within a few weeks she had represented to the girls that if they wished to marry well it behoved them to acquire at least a smattering of feminine accomplishments, and to Master Gilbert that his whining and temper tantrums cut no ice with her, and she would be better pleased if he applied himself to his studies. These she made as imaginative and interesting as possible and was rewarded by some slight increase in diligence in her pupils and by hearing herself described by Lady Metcalfe as 'a treasure'. This description had gratified Lady Catherine, who had recommended Serena to Lady Metcalfe, far more than it pleased Miss Pope.

If her pupils regarded her at first with hostility, this gave way to a reluctant liking not unmixed with awe. It was obvious from their first encounter that she was not, as they had predicted, an antidote, being elegantly if simply dressed and having a lively and pleasant countenance. They watched in amazement at the number of books she unpacked from the shabby trunk and arranged on the schoolroom shelves, these included: Doctor Johnson's Dictionary; instruction manuals, such as 'Reading Made Quite Easy'; primers for French, Italian, Latin, Greek and Mathematics; books on the writing of accounts; several more on drawing and a number of music sheets. In addition she had Newbery's story books for the younger children, the 'Collection of Old Ballads' and a number of novels: 'Don Quixote', the gothic novels of Horace Walpole, Ann Radcliffe and Clara Reeve, including her latest: 'The Champion of Virtue'. All of which made the older girls open their eyes wide.

These same books, and more, were now being resettled into the trunk which had accompanied her from her father's house in Bath through her varied and interesting teaching positions. They recalled to her certain remembrances which afforded her amusement, tinged with exasperation and annoyance. Her primer on mathematics called to her mind her very first appointment, at age eighteen, to the family of Sir John Halcombe, a crusty old gentleman who had married late and whose wife had finally presented him with a son and heir after a bevy of eight daughters. He thus found himself the father of a hopeful family at a time when he should have been dandling grandchildren on his knee. Although as to dandling, Serena always thought to herself, it was doubtful if he would ever get the way of it.

She was engaged to teach his daughters, a biddable set of girls, and to instruct the boy into the rudiments of learning until such time as Sir John would engage him a tutor. He called the new governess into the book-room where he stood in front of the fire, bewigged, powdered and in a resplendent embroidered frock-coat reminiscent of an earlier decade, and outlined his notions for the education of his son.

"I will have him taught Latin and Greek, madam, and to be put to the application of sums, to train his mind. It will not be necessary to teach the girls such things. The female mind is incapable of being so trained; I doubt me you are aware even of what the term 'sums' means!"

Serena's trained mind could not but rise to the challenge.

"Ah! Sums, Sir John!" she replied in a musing tone. "Indeed you may be right in that many women's minds may not grasp such a branch of mathematics, which I understand consists of the manipulation of numbers, by addition, subtraction, multiplication and division, and which has the purpose of serving such branches of science as astronomy, architecture, engineering and physics as well as commerce and the management of money." She looked demurely apologetic. "Do I have that right?"

Sir John had harrumphed and hawed, but then decided that perhaps Miss Pope should continue to teach his son after all, and save him the extra expense of hiring a tutor. Serena recounted this ··exchange to her mother in a letter, and received the reply that she should:

'... *call to mind the Lady Margaret Moore whose display of her knowledge of Latin before King Henry, the VIIIth of that name, displeased His Grace, as he*

86

*himself could not match it. I fully understand, '(*Mistress Pope had continued in her letter*) 'your very natural desire to refute male condescension with regard to women 's mental capacities, but it does not do, my dear Serena, to antagonise an employer.'*

Serena heeded her mother's wise words and bit her lip whenever she met with similar examples of the slights and contempts which are part of the lot of a governess.

She had left Sir John Halcombe's establishment after nearly six years; the girls having passed one by one out of the schoolroom and the scion of the house being finally removed by his father from 'petticoat government'. He may have been willing to save his guineas while the boy was in short coats, but finally decided that even Miss Pope's learning could not provide the education required by an aspiring young blade, viz. to acquire a taste for drinking, gambling, fighting and the charms of young women of the Covent Garden variety. To achieve these necessary requisites he was despatched to Westminster School and Serena dismissed.

*

She carried her excellent references to her next post with Lord and Lady Spalding, with whom she stayed but eight months. They had two young sons, although other children of Lord Spalding's begetting were believed to be liberally sprinkled across the county. Lady Spalding was a lady after Serena's own heart: she was beautiful, lively, intelligent and well-read, and her interest in the education of her sons led to an early friendship with their governess. Her lord was in no way a fit companion for her. He lacked her wit, her style, her elegance of mind. But she had been brought up to accommodate herself to him, having seen her mother so behave to her brutish father, and she bore patiently his many and flagrant infidelities and occasional physical abuse. But she refused to countenance such abusive punishment towards her sons as he seemed to think was necessary for their good behaviour; neither would she bear without complaint his flaunting of his mistresses in the family's London home.

Matters came to a head late one evening, when Lord Spalding arrived at the house in Berkeley Square in his usual state of inebriation, to find her ladyship awaiting him in the book-room. She faced him as he sprawled in a chair, shouting to his valet to come and remove his boots.

"I have made arrangements my lord," she said coolly, "to take the children to Bath."

"Bath!" exclaimed his lordship. "Why should you want to go to such a fusty place, full of tittle-tattle and old women?"

"I have a mind to try the waters, and it would be beneficial to the boys' health were they to have a change of scene."

"Well I do not give you leave to go, madam," growled her lord. "Why should you waste the ready on hiring a house in Bath? And I most certainly do not give you leave to take the children anywhere."

Her ladyship bowed her head meekly.

"Then sir, would you give me leave to visit my mother?"

"As to that, you may do as you please my lady. But the boys stay with me." And he shouted again for his valet.

Lady Spalding went to the writing desk and quietly began to draw up two documents. Her lord demanded to know what she would be about.

"These are papers which I shall ask you to sign, giving me leave to visit my mother and sister near Bath for as long as I deem it necessary to do so."

His lordship gave a shout of laughter.

"Why do you need to bother with such nonsense? Is not my word good enough? I have sworn you may go, my lady, and be damned to you!"

Lady Spalding merely folded the papers and brought them to him, with a full pen. "Sign there, and there sir."

He swore, called her every kind of fool, said he would see her in hell, but scrawled his name to the papers. She placed one copy in his writing desk, folding the other into her reticule. His Lordship then shouted at her to get out of his sight, a command with which she was only too happy to comply.

As was usual with him, Lord Spalding slept till well past noon the next day, and then took himself off for the remainder of the day at the newly-opened boxing saloon in Bond Street, called Jackson's, with his cronies. He returned with a couple of so-called friends with whom he caroused well into the night, seeking his own couch in the early hours of the morning. The next day and the next, a similar pattern was repeated: the days spent shooting at Manton's gallery, or racing his phaeton in the park and the evenings at cards, or gaming at Watier's or White's, imbibing jugs of port and punch. Sometimes in his own house, he and a party, which included not only his current mistress but a number of other ladies of dubious reputation, would indulge in charades, which frequently led to displays of nakedness, followed inevitably by a bedtime romp.

His lordship seemed to be going on what his valet frequently termed a long mop. At these times the men-servants tiptoed around him, running to anticipate his every need, trying to keep out of the way of a flying boot and maintaining a tight and discreet silence among themselves. But on this occasion there was a breath-holding quality to the silence and many a furtive look cast between themselves.

"And although I cannot blame her ladyship," muttered the butler, "there'll be the devil to pay when he discovers the truth of the matter."

This mode of living meant that Lord and Lady Spalding would sometimes spend weeks without seeing each other - a fact on which the lady had relied when she finally laid her plans to leave her husband.

The day after the conversation in the book-room, Lady Spalding summoned Miss Pope to the morning-room. She seemed as calm and quiet as she always was, but Serena noted a tightening of her ladyship's slender fingers on her handkerchief and more than a touch of colour in her normally pale cheeks.

She was not prepared however, for the agitation which accompanied Lady Spalding's first words.

"You are acquainted with Bath, are not you, Miss Pope? Your father and mother reside there?"

Serena acknowledged that this was so.

"Are you also acquainted with Lady Montague? She set up a charity school some years ago, in the village of Easton, just outside Bath, where she now resides."

"Indeed I do know of it, Ma'am. My sister Sophie is one of the teachers there. It aims for a higher form of education than that normally provided by charity schools and is in fact attended by a number of children of the lesser gentry, both boys and girls."

"What do you think of it as a place for my boys?"

Serena was so astonished at this question that she remained silent for a full halfminute. Lady Spalding hastened to reassure her.

"It is not that I am at all dissatisfied with your teaching and management of the children. Indeed they could not be in better hands."

She rose and took an agitated turn about the room.

"It is of no use. I must be plain with you, Miss Pope. I have a scheme in mind…" She broke off and listened intently. The house was quiet.

"In this household," she continued, "who is there I can trust? My maid. The coachman—both of whom came with me from my mother's house when I was married. And, perhaps, you, Miss Pope."

"It is true that Lord Spalding pays my wages," said Serena with care, "but I have seen enough of his manner toward you, my lady, to assure you that I cannot condone it. In teaching your sons I have tried in simple ways, to show them that there are many examples of gentlemanly behaviour which even at their young age they can hope to emulate."

"I had hoped, indeed believed, that to be so. But do you accept that with such an example before them they cannot do otherwise than fall into similar ways? I would do anything in my power to prevent that, and I am therefore resolved to remove them from this house. Will you help me?"

"I will help you."

"In carrying out what I plan I shall be putting myself beyond the pale of respectable society. I shall be outcast and will, in all probability, have to spend the rest of my days in exile, possibly abroad. Will you still help me?"

"Yes, I will help you," and Serena took her ladyship's outstretched hand in a warm clasp.

*

She thought back, these many years later as she packed and sorted her books and belongings, of the times when she had carried out this same task. On the occasion when she had agreed to assist Lady Spalding to flee her husband, this had to be accomplished in haste, and with the reflection that she was putting herself on the outside of the law. Her upbringing had been strict and she would not have acted on such an impulse without a twinge of conscience, indeed more than just a twinge. But she had also been brought up to think for herself; to weigh up all the possible consequences of her actions; to recognise that simply because certain things had always been done, it did not necessarily imply that they were right and should continue to be done. In this instance, she felt strongly that an abusive husband and father should not have the legal right to treat his wife and children in a cruel and brutish fashion. If the law decreed that this should be so, then she thought, the law was bad and she would flout it. So she had flouted the law and had never regretted it.

*

Two days after that quiet conversation in the morning-room, there came a discreet bustle about the courtyard very early. The horses were put to the oldest of the family's coaches, which bore no crest, and a modest amount of luggage loaded on. Lady Spalding, Serena Pope, the two boys - excited at the thought of an adventure - and her ladyship's maid climbed aboard, and the coach rolled away.

The house resumed its morning quiet. Sunlight came, moved bright fingers across the floors and left. Lord Spalding snored on. The girl who had shared his bed quietly left it, dressed herself all by guess and tiptoed along the corridor and down the back stairs, having first helped herself to his lordship's watch, chain, rings, fobs and snuffbox. These she considered sufficient payment for the lively services of the night she had been required to perform. Lord Spalding snored on.

The coach rumbled swiftly through the villages to the west of London and on to the Bath Road. It was still only mid-day when they rattled through Maidenhead Thicket, the coachman aiming for the George Inn at Reading before he reckoned they would need a change of horses. But they would not stop there; it was too well-known. Past Thatcham, he reckoned to slip off the main road and take such back streets as could be found for a coach-and-four.

"Rack up for the night at one of the small villages," he muttered to Hoby, her ladyship's grim-faced maid when they got to Reading. She sniffed, having her own opinion of the strong possibility of damp sheets and poor food in a village inn, but she acknowledged the sense of such a proposition. She therefore simply nodded and stalked off to get her mistress a cup of coffee, but John Coachman stood stroking his face in some thought. He had availed himself of Cary's 'New Itinerary' and committed to memory the distances between places along their road, and the names of inns, but thought a bit of local information would not come amiss. He strolled across to chat to an ostler.

"What's best to do?" he asked. "Take the Old Road up'n'over Shepherd's Shore, or the road through Calne and Devizes? I did 'ear as 'ow they was improvin' the road to pass Chervil Hill by."

"Arr. That new road, though 'taint not so new now, be best for fast travellin'. Goes over Studley Common an' 'tis shorter by the four or five mile than the old Bath Road."

"More folks use the new road I take it? Stage coaches an' curricles an' the like? The old road being quieter?"

The ostler regarded John Coachman with a hard stare, and appeared to understand the drift of the questions. He resumed his rubbing down of a splendid chestnut and whistling through his teeth.

"Arr. The ol' road's quiet, but still good enuff on a fine day. There be good views over the Downs an' clear air an' only a few sheep if you've a mind fer a journey wivout too much trouble from uvver vehicles."

"The Bear at Sandy Lane still good as a waterin' place?"

"Sfar as I know."

After this encouraging conversation, Coachman strolled back to where the coach stood, its poles and traces let down waiting for a new team of horses.

Serena got down with the boys and let them scamper about the yard while the horses were being put to. She had been kept busy inventing stories to keep the boys amused and playing games such as guessing how many cows in a field or who would be the first to spot the next milestone. Hoby came out of the George, followed by the tapster bearing a tray with steaming cups of coffee, lemonade for the boys and a heavy-wet for John Coachman. She exchanged a startled glance with Serena as a curricle swept into the yard, but the driver gave them no more than a cursory glance before shouting for the ostler. Lady Spalding sank back against the squabs and Serena hustled the boys back into the coach, trying not to let her anxiety show. When Hoby took the tray back into the inn she used the opportunity to get a good look at the owner of the curricle. He had cast aside his many-caped coat and curly-brimmed beaver and she was thankful to see he was unknown to her.

"All the same," she reported to Coachman, "best be going as soon as may be."

On all being in readiness to depart, the eldest boy begged to be allowed to sit up in front next to the coachman. Lady Spalding was fearful, But Serena advised that this would allay any anxiety on the child's behalf.

"It is unlikely that he will be recognised, Ma'am," she said quietly, and then more brightly to Master Spalding: "Be sure to pull your hat well down over your eyes. For if we should be stopped by highwaymen you know, they may mistake you for a postillion."

The boy's eyes grew round in wonder.

"Will we be stopped by highwaymen? What an adventure that would be!"

"Not a comfortable one I think," said Serena cheerfully. "But if it should so turn out, and they ask who you are, I shall say you are both the grandchildren of the King. And then you know, they will say: 'God bless His Majesty!' and ride away."

"But that would be telling a plumper, Ma'am! And you always say we must tell the truth at all times!"

"Hoist with your own petard," murmured Lady Spalding, amused.

"Not so!" Serena was too quick-witted to be caught out. "For is not the King the Father and Grandfather of us all?"

And with that she hoisted Master Spalding up beside the coachman and spread the plain hammer cloth over his knees.

"No wriggling about now, young master," said John Coachman. "An' if we should meet any as we don't like the looks of, why you jes' pop yourself under that there cloth. 'Specially if they takes to loosin' off their pops!"

The coach rumbled off with Master Spalding animatedly demanding to know the meaning of such cant terms as John Coachman had in his vocabulary, and Master Will snuggling between Serena and his mama saying they would be much more comfortable without Georgie who tended to kick his legs about.

John Coachman's decision to take the Old Bath Road up over Bowden and Beacon Hills was a good one. They met few vehicles other than farm wagons, and were overtaken by none. Serena and Hoby elected to get out and walk the steepest parts, to assist the horses, and all were grateful that it was not too cold nor windy over the Downs. The only mishap occurred when Hoby's hat was blown away and she had to run after it, to the boys' huge delight. The Bear Inn, though no longer catering for the quality as in the days when the Princess Caroline stayed there, nonetheless was able to provide a decent meal for them all, and to Hoby's relief, warm, dry beds.

The remainder of the journey passed without any such incidents as to cause further anxiety; and early in the afternoon of the following day they arrived at Tanglewood House, the residence of Lady Spalding's mother, Lady Montague.

**
*
*

Chapter Three

"If the mind be curbed and humbled too much in children; if their spirits be abased and broken much by too strict a hand over them, they lose all their vigour and industry."
John Locke: An essay concerning Human Understanding. 1690

The summer of 1785 fluctuated, like most summers in England, between cool with rain, and sultry with thundery tempests. Lady Spalding, fearful of discovery by her husband, remained most of the time in Tanglewood House and its immediate environs, and availed herself of her mother's excellent library, while Serena took the boys to school. Unless the weather was truly inclement, they walked the short distance across the park, through the churchyard and into the village street by the smithy. Serena would not let the children linger to watch the blacksmith when they were on their way to school, but in the evenings if he was working, they always stood for a while in awed fascination. They loved to see him as he heated a horseshoe to glowing redness, then hammered it into shape before plunging it with a hiss and flurry of steam into the water-vat. Sometimes he would be making tools or mending plough-shares, and his neat deft hammering and twisting of hot metal, with the wonderful smell of iron and coal, fire and sizzling water made young Master Will sigh in delight and declare his intention of becoming a blacksmith when he grew up. His mother and grandmother, when informed of these wishes, both laughed, but did not discourage the little fellow by declaring such an idea to be an absurdity as they might have done: for, said Lady Montague,

"better to aspire to a useful occupation than to ape the idleness and dissipation of many born to his wealth and station in life."

The school which Lady Montague, together with her friend Lady Sarah Scott - another refugee from · a violent husband - had endowed, was begun twenty years earlier as a simple charity school for poor girls. Five years later this was extended to include the sons of labourers, and later still the children of farmers and artisans. At first, the parents merely wished their children to be kept harmlessly employed until old enough to be useful about the farm or in the shop, or to take up an apprenticeship; if they learned a smattering of such accomplishments as reading, writing and ciphering, well and good. But the appointment of a certain Doctor Morris Trent, formerly a governor of the Foundling Hospital and a noted educationist, led to the school being run along liberal and progressive lines, such as those set out by the Bishop of Autun in his pamphlet on Public Education. Boys and girls, rich and poor, were taught together from the ages of five to nine. They received those basics of education considered needful even by the most curmudgeonly of people, and received in addition such extras as natural history and philosophy, botany and simple astronomy. All teaching was carried out in a lively manner and time was allowed in the school day for the children to run around in the fresh air and exercise their bodies with bats and balls, hoops and tops. After the age of nine, the sons and daughters of artisans and trades-folk were taught employments considered suitable for their future positions in life; children of the lesser gentry received instruction in languages, politics and history. It would remain to be seen, Serena thought privately, whether Master Will Spalding would try to wriggle his way into the classes intended for future blacksmiths.

Master George and Master William were registered in the school in their grandmother's name. It was Lady Spalding's intention, should she need to flee abroad as she feared she must, that neither blame nor censure be laid at Miss Pope's door. By effectively removing them from their governess's charge she hoped the boys would remain safe from their father's jurisdiction and that his wrath would not descend on Serena's head. Lady Montague, she knew, would be more than a match for an enraged son-in-law, having had plenty of practice with her own brutish husband.

*

Things did not turn out as they had all feared, Serena recalled many years later when telling the sorry tale to Anne. Although it was not to be expected that Lord Spalding would remain long in ignorance of his wife's absence, several weeks were to pass before he discovered the whole truth. He was a careless parent, who had not learnt the maxim that his rights over his sons should be accompanied by a certain duty toward them, but he believed implicitly in those rights. When therefore he discovered that they had been removed from the family home, he flew into one of the rages so feared by his menservants. Boots, buckles and bottles were flung at his footmen and butler, but it was his unfortunate valet who bore the brunt of it. Seeking perhaps to allay his master's anger, the foolish man brought to his lordship's attention the paper which Lady Spalding had placed in his writing desk, signed in his own hand, giving his consent to her departure to visit Lady Montague

'Together with their sons'.

Lord Spalding attempted to seize the document and cast it into the fire, but when it fell short, took to shouting imprecations at his valet, who tried to remonstrate further and was promptly set upon and beaten with the poker. His cries brought two footmen to his assistance; they forcibly restrained the

94

enraged earl and managed to tie him up securely before raising the general alarm and running out for a constable. Events then moved astonishingly quickly. The poor valet died of his injuries and Lord Spalding, being a peer of the realm, was confined in his own house until a coroner's court could be convened within three days. The jury found the valet had died as a result of - 'a wilful and unlawful act', and commanded his lordship to be taken before his peers who committed him to the Tower. At his trial several weeks later, he was found guilty and sentenced: "to be executed according to the law, and the body immediately conveyed to the hall of the Surgeons Company there to be dissected and anatomized."

Both the Morning Post and the Gentlemen's Magazine carried lurid accounts of his behaviour throughout:

"insolent, vengeful and unrepentant", and conveyed to an interested public:

That though he be a lord of ancient and illustrious lineage, his crime is considered so horrendous that no mitigation viz. of execution by the sword, can be considered. He is therefore to be hanged by the neck in the same manner as a common criminal."

The household in the little village of Easton near Bath knew nothing of these stirring events until Serena visited her parents' home and there read of the trial and execution in copies of the Gentlemen's Magazine. Astonished, she questioned why her father had not informed her of these happenings, knowing her connection with the Spalding House, but he flapped an impatient hand at her, remarking that he never read anything in the various periodicals regularly delivered to the house other than articles which might be of interest to a man of sense and science. Serena therefore bore the magazines away with her.

In spite of the new-found freedom of her widowhood, Lady Spalding chose to remain with her mother and avoid the inevitable discussion of the scandal among her numerous London acquaintances. This of course ranged over all possible reasons for her flight, which was held to have provoked the unfortunate events described above. It was fanned by the earl's claim, during his weeks of imprisonment, that she had given him reason for a divorce. But the paper so carelessly signed by him, while not being held to be a legal document, was taken as evidence that there had been no hint of crim. con. Indeed, commented the Morning Post, how could there be? It would be unusual in the extreme for a lady to take her sons on an elopement, or on fleeing a husband's care for the Company of Another. Neither, it was argued, would she have taken a lover to the home of her mother Lady Montague! The imprisonment and subsequent execution of Lord Spalding meant the boys would be allowed by law to remain with their mother.

They loved their school and the companionship it provided and Serena Pope enjoyed her role as teacher and her lively discussions with her sister Sophie. But she also felt her employment by Lady Spalding could not continue, as she was no longer solely responsible for her sons' education. Neither could she be considered as employed by the school. An advertisement in the Lady's Magazine from a certain Lady Catherine de Bourgh of Rosings Park, Hunsford for a governess for:

"... a girl of five years, of lively mind and amenable disposition."

caught her attention. Thus in the October of that year, she came to Rosings, and met the young Miss Anne de Bourgh.

*

Anne at just over five years old was indeed lively. She was emerging from the nursery where she had caused her old nurse no little concern by taking scant interest in her dolls, her sewing and her own ornamentation, preferring to play with the bricks, the toy drum, the lead soldiers and the rocking horse - toys which were her father's and her uncles' legacy to the nursery. At their first meeting, Anne had very correctly curtsied to her new governess, but regarded her with bright-eyed and unwavering curiosity. Later when they were alone together and Miss Pope was reading her a story, Anne begged to be allowed to see the book and to follow the words as pointed out by Serena's moving finger.

In her young charge, Serena Pope saw an ideal opportunity to put her theories of education into practice. Her only regret was that Anne was an only child and had little chance to enjoy companionship and social converse with other children of a similar age. Lady Catherine, whose attention to her daughter focussed chiefly on providing her with costly dresses, held herself above too easy an acquaintance with local families. Anne and Serena therefore formed a unit of friendship which belied the twenty or so years between them, and which they enjoyed in equal measure.

*

The death of Sir Lewis de Bourgh brought about many and far-reaching changes, and Rosings became very different in atmosphere. Anne was grief stricken—a condition which partly led, so Serena believed, to her falling prey to the influenza. The day of the baronet's funeral was bitterly cold. Ice crunched underfoot on those paths which had been swept clear. Across the park, snow was pillowed and piled by the wind into strange humps which bore no resemblance to the shape of the underlying landscape. The trees bowed and cracked under the weight of accumulated snow; the streams were silent, the sky the colour of pewter. Inside the church, the collective breath of the congregation misted the air and condensed into small cold droplets on the stone pillars and tomb carvings. The church had escaped the more serious depredations of Cromwell's soldiers during the civil war, and although deprived of much of its former colourful statuary, still retained its beautiful stone rood screen. The insertion of a towering wooden pulpit and box pews had completed its transformation to Protestantism.

But it was almost as cold inside as out. The wind inserted icy fingers through the cracks in the tall perpendicular windows and whistled under the door where generations of feet had worn a hollow in the stone step. In the de Bourgh pew, Lady Catherine and her daughter sat, stood, knelt as the service demanded; Anne having been schooled by her mother to remain dry-eyed and composed as befitted the grand-daughter of an earl. But the child shivered frequently, little gasping shivers that shook her small frame uncontrollably, earning herself several glares of disapproval from Lady Catherine.

A few days later, Anne complained of a sore throat, to which her old nurse laid a warm red flannel and prescribed a soothing drink of barley water. But when Anne tried to get up the next morning, she felt so sick and dizzy, with all her limbs aching, that she was glad to obey Nurse's instruction to lie back down and be kept warm. The family physician was summoned and took a small amount of blood to bring down the fever; he was an old-fashioned practitioner, who still referred to the influenza as the 'sweating sickness' and ticked off Anne's symptoms on his fingers:

"...sweating, shivering, fever, nausea, headache, cramps, back pain, but praise the good Lord," he added, "She does not have the rash of measles or smallpox, neither yet the delirium and stupor. She must be watched constantly and bathed hourly. The crisis will come in twenty-four hours and then we may tell if she will survive. Or then, she may not."

With these encouraging words, he nodded at Nurse and took up his bag to leave, turning at the door to promise he would send up a panegyric of his own contriving.

Nurse tut-tutted after him and set about her own ways of making the poor child more comfortable. She called upon Miss Pope for aid, knowing her for a sensible woman, unlike that Mrs Jenkinson recently come to be companion to her ladyship:

"… all mops and mows and sniffs and snivels; a proper wantwit and about as much use as a chocolate teapot," according to Nurse.

Between them, Nurse and Serena bathed Anne's head and hands with apple vinegar and persuaded her to take a few sips of lemonade or barley-water. She tossed and turned and muttered, often calling for her father and complaining fretfully that he hadn't come to see her. But when Serena tentatively suggested Lady Catherine might be persuaded to come to Anne's bedside, Nurse shook her heads decisively.

"No good thinking it Miss Pope. Her Ladyship won't come near nor nigh Miss Anne till all this be over. And 'twouldn't do the poor child any good to see her neither. Between you and me, Ma'am, she and her mama will never be comfortable with each other. Lady Catherine can't never forgive the fact that

Miss Anne was not the hoped-for son, and Miss Anne has always been a mite fearful of her mother."

"Small wonder," murmured Serena, thinking of Lady Catherine's harsh discipline and unbending manner.

Frost, snow and cold winds continued to the end of February, and although Anne recovered from the influenza, due, Doctor Tanner constantly averred, to his excellent panegyric, she remained pale, tired and listless. But one fine clear day in March, with the sun coming through the rippled glass of the schoolroom window and making watery patterns on the old oak floor, she begged to be allowed to go out for a walk

"Just a little way round the gardens, you know, and perhaps down to the stables to see my pony. He will probably think I have forgotten him. I do so hope John Groom has been exercising him."

She broke off, observing a look of dismay on her governess' face. Sarah, sitting in a comer and mending a seam in a night-gown paused in her sewing; the book she had been reading aloud shook in Serena's hand; between them and Nurse came a breath-holding stillness. Anne looked from one to the other.

"What is it? What is the matter?" she asked. "He is not sick, is he? I'm sure John Groom will know exactly what to do if so."

Nurse resumed folding up some clothes and looked stony-faced.

"Poor mite will have to know," she muttered.

"Know what?" demanded Anne with a touch of her old truculence. "What is it I will have to know?"

Serena put down her book and took hold of Anne's hands.

"I am so sorry my dear, but your mama felt it was for the best. Your pony has been sold, along with your father's hunters. But Lady Catherine has said that when you are fully well, you are to have a small phaeton to drive around in …"

It would have been better, Serena thought, if Anne had stormed into one of her rare tempers. She could not bear the slow gathering of tears, nor the one tiny sob that escaped the child. Nurse soothed and petted and promised that Sarah would bring up a hot posset and her favourite biscuits, being a great believer in both for the lifting of the spirits. Sarah, near tears herself, hurried away and poured out her grief in the kitchen.

Anne would not be comforted. The weather continued to improve; primroses spangled the banks and the blossoms of the blackthorn frothed white in the hedgerows. Serena and Anne walked slowly round the gardens and the park, and Anne tried dutifully to note where the daffodils were pushing their green noses through the dark earth, or a pair of thrushes had begun to build a nest in the hawthorn hedge. She nodded when Serena called her attention to the tiny whorls of green leaves unfolding and the gold of celandines by the brook. Cook sent up a small bottle of blackcurrant robb which she assured Nurse would help to raise the poor young miss's spirits, and the head gardener presented her with a little pot of sweet white violets which he had brought on in one of the succession houses. Anne expressed her thanks very prettily, but she remained listless and quiet.

Every afternoon Anne and Miss Pope were summoned to spend an hour or so drinking tea with Lady Catherine and her companion, Mrs Jenkinson. Anne said little on these occasions; sipped her tea, carefully mindful of the instruction on how to hold the new cups with their delicate handles; did a little embroidery after tea; answered her mother's questions with a "Yes Mama," or "No Mama," and would not be drawn on any topics concerning her lessons. Sometimes she was required to show her sketchbook, or to stumble painfully through a piece of music on the piano forte. Lady Catherine looked, listened, recommended more practise and dismissed them. Daughter and governess escaped thankfully back to the schoolroom.

March having come in like a lamb, went out in a flurry of cold winds.

April came, bringing her sunshine and her showers, sometimes both together to make a rainbow. On one such day, Anne and Serena were caught out in a heavy shower and ran to shelter in the summer house. From there, they watched a wonderful double rainbow span the park, and recalled together the Bible story of Noah and the Great Flood. Anne wanted to know if the Ark was still on top of the mountain where it came to rest, and whether anyone who did not know the story would wonder and explain to themselves how a big boat could possibly get to the top of a hill

"They would not be able to imagine there being so much water that a mountain could be drowned," she said. "And what is more, if as you explained, there needs to be both sun and rain together to make a rainbow, why then it must have been still raining when they all came out of the Ark!"

Serena laughed but protested that Noah had waited a week after the rains had stopped and the little dove came back no more before they all emerged from the safety of the Ark.

"So perhaps they saw the rainbow from the windows," she said.

Anne remained unconvinced.

"Does it say there were windows in the Ark?"

"There must have been," argued Serena, thoroughly enjoying this discussion, "It would have been so very dark inside if not. And they could not risk candles you know, with it being a wooden boat."

"They could have had oil lamps, could not they? And I do not think you could see very much of a rainbow from a window!"

Miss Pope was delighted that her pupil was in one of her argumentative moods; it seemed to her that Anne was beginning to come out of the weakness which had afflicted her for so long. But as in many of their discussions, she had to admit that there were many things that even she did not know.

"I have to confess, my dear Anne that we cannot know all the details of the story as it is given to us in the Bible. Perhaps we just need to remember that the rainbow is a sign of hope and new beginnings. And look, our rainbow is fading, so as the sun is still shining it must mean the rain has stopped. We had better make haste and go indoors."

But when they reached the schoolroom, they both came in for a scolding from Nurse because they had got their feet wet.

A few nights later, Anne tossed and turned and was feverish again. Nurse, burning pastilles once more, muttered darkly that it was all only to be expected after getting wet feet.

"And if Miss Pope succumbs to whatever this turns out to be, we shall be in the suds."

Serena Pope, however, did not succumb. She accepted meekly her share of the blame and took turns nursing her restless pupil. When a rash of small red spots broke out a few days later, Doctor Tanner was summoned, looked grave and said he could have foretold that two months after the influenza Miss de Bourgh would fall prey to the measles, of which infection there were a number of sufferers in the village. It was only to be expected, he was heard to add, that the poor young lady, being already pulled down by her earlier illness and being of a delicate disposition, should be in grave danger, and only his expert knowledge would ensure her survival. Anne was then subjected to a small blood-letting and given tincture of laudanum to bring down the hectic fever, and once the rash had subsided, the doctor prescribed strengthening pills containing rhubarb and vipers' salts.

Nurse shook her head over these measures. Serena went one step further and was moved to protest to her ladyship that surely nourishing broths and gentle exercise in the fresh air would be of more benefit to Miss Anne's recovery. She had been brought up on Dr Cheyne's *Book of Health and Long Life*, with its emphasis on a simple diet and physical exercising, and held fast to its principles. But the doctor, who was sitting with her ladyship, subjected the governess to a haughty stare and dismissed these ideas as being too new fangled. Serena refrained from tartly pointing out that such ideas had been in circulation for more than seventy years, and resigned herself to trying to persuade Nurse that fresh air entering a window was not injurious to health. In this too she was unsuccessful; Anne was confined to her room, all windows kept firmly closed, and Dr Tanner further recommended increasing the dose of tincture of laudanum. Once more Serena was moved to protest to Lady Catherine, and found herself summarily dismissed.

Lady Catherine summoned the governess to her sitting room and informed her calmly that from now on Mrs Jenkinson would be in charge of Anne's education and that she had recommended Miss Pope to Lady Metcalfe:

"… a post for which you would seem to be eminently suited, and which I informed her ladyship you would be available to take up without delay."

Serena was left without a word to say; to protest would have been to forego any recommendation which Lady Catherine had in mind to provide. She turned away from Mrs Jenkinson's smug look, and went quietly away to begin packing once more.

***
**
*

Chapter Four

*I see the country of England smiling with cultivation, the grounds exhibiting all
the perfection of agriculture, parcelled out into beautiful enclosures, cornfields,
hay, pastures, woodlands and commons.*
Tobias Smollett 1760

The country seat of Lady Metcalfe was situated but fifteen miles from Rosings
Park, and Lady Catherine, priding herself on her beneficence as an employer,
had Serena Pope conveyed thence in the plain carriage. There had been scarce
time to bid farewell to Anne, but Miss Pope left her a letter in which she tried
to put the circumstances in the best possible light, and said she hoped for a
continuous correspondence between them. She also urged her pupil to continue
to work at her studies:

    '... *especially those considered by your mama to be essential for a young
lady of your standing in society.*'

    She left this on Anne's pillow as she kissed her goodbye, but Anne merely
murmured in her sleep. Serena hurried away, mindful of the need to control her
feelings before the servants, many of whom had come to wish her well. The
maids had been buzzing with indignation over her dismissal, and even Roberts
the butler had been seen to shake his head over the affair. The only person who
remained unmoved, indeed was quietly triumphant, was Mrs Jenkinson. She
slipped away to Anne's room during the flurry of Serena's leave-taking and
removed the letter from the child's pillow. From now on, acting on instructions
from her ladyship, all correspondence between Miss de Bourgh and her former
governess would be read by Mrs Jenkinson and censored by Lady Catherine.
    Anne, scarcely aware at first that she had been bereft of the joy and
companionship she had never thought to lose, became restless and fretful as
realisation dawned. Dr Tanner declared this to be but a natural outcome of the
hectic fever following such a severe bout of the measles and further increased
the dose of laudanum to ten drops daily. Thus opium-soothed, Anne slept, half-
woke, remembered her loss and counteracted the pain in more drug-induced
sleep. Nurse protested much as Miss Pope had done, but found herself over-
ruled. It was indicated to her that it was fully time that she should retire to a
cottage in the village, her services in the household no longer being required.
Mrs Jenkinson was now firmly in charge, and there began for Anne a dreary

round of schoolroom activities which consisted of embroidery, deportment and simple readings in improving books which held little interest. These Mrs Jenkinson considered sufficient, as this was all she was able and qualified to teach.

*

It was early May when Serena Pope left Rosings Park for Metcalfe Place. The farms, fields and orchards of the countryside were bright with blossom; the 'Garden of England', as Kent was fondly known by its inhabitants, looking its best in tidiness of cultivation. The hay was already lush in the meadows and the bright sun mocked Serena's low spirits.

It was a warm and golden September when she returned eight years later, and she was reminded of Psalm 126:

"They that sow in tears shall reap in joy; though he goeth on his way weeping, bearing forth the seed, he shall come again with joy, bringing his sheaves." Indeed there were sheaves standing in some of the cornfields, while the reapers working their diagonal lines across the unmown fields, were scything the standing stalks ready for the boys and women to follow and bind up the stooks. Part of the journey led through the hop fields, and Serena observed whole families employed in picking the hops, with babies in plaited rush baskets lying placidly here and there among the plants. One little maid in a ragged blue frock had woven herself a wreath of hops and set it on her curly dark head while she crooned to the baby she was minding. For a few weeks, Serena reflected, these poor folk from London Town could breathe the air of the countryside while they earned themselves enough to keep body and soul loosely together in the winter months.

The carriage rolled on and Serena reflected on times past and speculated on times to come. The intervening years had hardly touched her features; she was still upright of bearing and elegant in attire, favouring a neat round dress with a single flounce at the hem in her usual soft grey. Her pelisse, a darker shade of grey, lay beside her on the seat with her plain bonnet. Her dark hair, worn in the simplest of styles had here and there a few silver threads, but her eyes were still bright and her complexion unlined. Lady Metcalfe's coachman, handing her up into the carriage, had privately thought her to be a fine-looking woman, and as ladylike in her simplicity as the young ladies of the House with all their silks and curls and furbelows.

Little heeding the effect her unchanged appearance might have on her former pupil, Serena wondered what she might find in Anne de Bourgh. They had met but the twice in eight years: the first occasion being an Assembly at Westerham to mark the come-out of Miss Sukey Metcalfe, and the second, two years later, being a private party for Miss Fanny Metcalfe's eighteenth birthday. Serena had attended both events, chaperoning the younger girls and had been shocked and distressed at Anne's appearance and demeanour. At the Assembly, a grand affair featuring massed flowers in all the rooms and a vast quantity to eat and drink, Anne sat between her Mama and Mrs Jenkinson and did not dance at all. She glanced briefly at Serena, a look in which the governess read a kind of longing, as though she wished she could come and talk to her. But Lady Catherine laid a restraining hand on her daughter's arm, and after that one glance Anne sat with her eyes demurely cast down. Lady Metcalfe at one point coming up to where Lady de Bourgh was sitting, asked whether Anne would not like to dance as there was a young friend of the family who had expressed a wish to take her for one of the country dances, but Lady Catherine had replied firmly that her daughter had no desire to dance. As Lady Metcalfe said later to Serena Pope:

"One feels so sorry for that poor child, but what can one do?"

At the birthday party, Miss de Bourgh could not have provided a greater contrast to the lively Miss Fanny Metcalfe. Both girls were of an age, but Fanny was tall, well-formed, with a blooming complexion and dressed in one of the very latest modes in pink silk, gathered round the bust and sleeves and down the front with tiny rosebuds. Anne's dress of pale yellow muslin was also in high fashion, but her smallness and pallor, combined with the dark circles under her eyes, put her completely in the shade. On this occasion, Lady Catherine having earlier granted permission, Anne's hand was solicited for one of the country dances by a cousin of the family and she went down the set with grace and lightness of step, but she was no match for the two older Metcalfe girls. They danced every dance; they played the harp and the piano forte and sang several songs either solo or together; one of the most popular being the new verse to the National Anthem in praise of Admiral Nelson's victory over the French fleet on the River Nile. This was said to have been sung first by the infamous Lady Emma Hamilton at the celebration held in his honour:

"First on the roll of fame Him let us sing;
Spread we his name around, Honour of British ground,
Who made Nile's shores resound—God save the king!"

Flushed and triumphant with the applause this brought, Fanny and Sukey ignored Anne who, again sitting between her mother and Mrs Jenkinson seemed to dwindle in significance. Extreme lowness of spirits, thought Serena, reduces a person to a shadow, to one who can go unnoticed in a crowded ballroom. Thus was Miss Anne de Bourgh at her friend's party. No such party was ever held for her.

*

The carriage arrived: the two women met and embraced on the steps of Rosings Park and Serena regarded her former pupil, now her companion, with a critical eye. Anne at twenty and scarce six months since her mother's death, was fast becoming the bright young lady promised by her early childhood years. Serena found herself confronting a very different person to the Anne of two years before. She was still small and slender, but she was womanly and in command of herself and her household.

This became evident almost at once. Anne apologised that she had business to attend to in the afternoon, and proposed that after a light nuncheon, perhaps Serena would like to attend the meeting with Squire Probert, county magistrate and over-seer of the poor.

"If you are not too tired by your journey my dear Serena, I would be grateful for your opinion in a matter which I apprehend is of some delicacy. The squire insisted that we must begin to discuss the matter today as he wishes to go up to London to visit Tattersall's. An important matter concerning hunters and hounds before the hunting season begins, he says."

"Perfectly understandable," commented Serena laughing.

Mr Probert was the epitome of a country squire: red-faced, hearty, plump, gruff-spoken and inclined to patronise the young lady of Rosings. But Anne, Serena observed, was having none of it. The meeting was to discuss the case of a poor young woman, a widow of some two months, though not of this parish, who was claiming relief by reason of her marriage to one Tom Cooper, journeyman cobbler to the shoemaker of Hunsford village. He had died in mysterious circumstances, and the squire was firm in his opinion that the wife should return to her parents' home in Westerham and claim relief there.

"She would have right of both residence and family in Westerham town Miss de Bourgh, and there are a number of others who have the greater claim on our parish resources," he declared. "I cannot comprehend why she would wish to avail herself of our charity, nor to remain here, where she has neither kith nor kin. She has been amongst us scarce two months, and rumour has it that indeed she …" he paused and cleared his throat noisily. "Hm, hm. I will speak not of that …" as Anne raised her brows inquiringly.

"Nor do I understand," Squire Probert continued, growing even redder in the face, "why she should have accosted you, Ma'am, and troubled you with her tale."

For indeed Anne had been confronted on one of her walks by a wild-haired young woman, claiming to be Hezziah Cooper, pouring out a story of hardship and injustice, and demanding that the Mistress of Rosings ensure she receive what she considered to be hers by right.

The squire might have been reluctant to divulge the details of the case before two unmarried ladies of quality, but Anne was neither so nice nor so delicate that she failed to take note of servants' gossip. When the squire had bowed himself out, agreeing to call again in a few days' time, Anne applied to Sarah, who knew as much of what went on in the House, the Park and the village as anyone, and who was able to provide what Squire Probert omitted. Sarah was nothing loth to impart what all the village thought it knew.

"She calls herself Hezzy Cooper Miss Anne, but some say as she was never truly married to our Tom. She met him in Westerham market one day, about two three months ago that would be, where he'd gone to buy leather and do a bit of shoe-mendin', an' she set her sights on him. He were a good-lookin' feller an' she bein' a comely girl- there's some as 'ud say too comely for her own good—I s'pose they got to a bit of flirtin' and fun, like. He always said as he never promised her anything that it were only a bit o' boy an' girl stuff such as any man or maid might indulge in on a fair day. He wasn't reckonin', he said, to get wed until he'd finished his journeyman year and could set up for himself and support a wife proper. But Hezziah claimed that after what passed between them after the fair, she had every right to up an' follow him here. An' that's just what she did! He came home from work one day not long after and found she'd settled herself into his little cottage an' was callin' herself his wife. Some who knew her parents said that the old couple were mighty glad to be rid of her, but I wouldn't know about that."

"Common law wife?" queried Anne.

"Hardly even that Miss Anne, as they'd been settled together only a few months. Well, poor Tom soon found as she had a wicked temper an' he took more an' more to goin' to the inn of an evenin', every evenin', which of course was not to Hezziah's likin' at all. She went after him one night and pulled him out an' they was heard arguin' and screamin' at each other all through the village. Well the very next mornin'', when Tom didn't turn up for work, the shoemaker sent for him at his cottage, but could get no answer there. So a hunt was set up for him, and they found him dead in a ditch with a crack in the back of his head."

"Good gracious!" exclaimed Serena.

"Hezziah claimed as he'd hit her an' she showed a great bruise on her arm to prove it, an' said that she'd pushed him off an' he'd tumbled backwards into the ditch. She'd run off home, thinkin' he could stay there 'til he'd cooled down a bit an' never dreamin', she said, as how he'd done himself an injury. An' 'tis true there was a great stone there he could have hit his head on. But there's not a few folk who think she were strong enough and furious enough to have hit him with it herself An' that's about the sum of it Miss Anne. Squire Probert heard the case of course, as magistrate, but found he couldn't say for definite on the evidence."

"So he gave it out as accidental death," remembered Anne, "And she is claiming poor relief on very shaky ground."

Serena pondered the situation,

"Why, as the good squire said, should she wish to remain here, when not only has she no relatives here, but it would seem she caused Tom Cooper's death indirectly, or indeed as some believe, directly? It cannot be a comfortable situation for her, with an accusation of murder against her in people's minds."

"As to that, Ma'am," said Sarah, "She seems not to concern herself with what people think. An' she is said to have set all the young men of our village all of a tizz. An' not only the single men either! Why even our Abel here has been known to make moon eyes at her!" Sarah looked quite disgusted, having, Anne suspected, designs on the well set-up young footman herself.

106

"Anyway," she went on, "Apparently the squire's young sprig of a son has set his heart on her, so 'tis said. It's my belief she's lookin' to get another husband out of us an' the higher the better. In the meantime o' course she's livin' comfortable in Tom's cottage."

"Dear me, what a tangle! No wonder poor Squire Probert is so anxious to be rid of her if his boy is concerned in the affair! Why he cannot be more than sixteen! But I think I can see my way through," said Anne.

"Would you have the wisdom of Solomon?" asked Serena, amused.

"No. More a little low cunning I think."

Miss Anne de Bourgh met with the squire again as arranged a few days later, and herself introduced the topic on which he was so reticent.

"I understand there is some doubt," she said, "as to the legality of the marriage between Hezziah and Tom Cooper. Before she can obtain relief, I suggest she furnish us with details as to the place, day and time of the wedding ceremony, together with the name of the officiating rector. This can of course be verified by looking at the parish records. If all is in order, then I do not think we can refuse her parish relief. But if she refuses, or if, as I suspect, her words cannot be proved true, then to rid ourselves of the nuisance she may turn out to be, I suggest we make her one single payment, in recognition of the months she lived here, but on condition she leave the village of Hunsford and seek employment, or a husband elsewhere. If she be willing to work I can provide her with a recommendation to a respectable household."

"Preferably t'other side of Westerham," exclaimed the squire, who had been nodding his approval of Anne's strategy. "I shall represent this as coming from you Miss de Bourgh. She cannot then fail to accept this as a just decision. But what would you suggest as to the amount of a single payment?"

"What is the standard weekly payment for a woman with no dependent children? I presume she has not indicated that there is a child on the way?"

The squire's eyes nearly popped out of his head at this plain speaking from a maiden lady, but he managed to indicate that indeed this was the case and that two shillings would be the appropriate payment.

"Well then," continued Anne, "I would recommend thrice that amount, plus a loaf of bread and a warm cloak in lieu of the firewood she might expect were she to continue to live here. That should be sufficient for any journey she must undertake."

"I consider that more than sufficient Ma'am; it is generous."

"We should not give her an excuse to think ill of us. There are still some among us I am sorry to say, who believe in witchcraft and might think an angry Hezziah would put the evil eye on us. Indeed I have heard whispers to that effect already. They might then take the law into their own hands and carry out rough music. That would be an unpleasant situation, and you would have even more legal tangles to unravel, Mr Probert. Hezziah would seem to be the sort of woman to twist events to suit her purposes. We must keep a clear record of all that has been done for her, as I am sure you do, squire, and be careful not to provide her with that opportunity."

The squire left, promising to carry out Anne's suggestion with all haste and to report back should any further matter arise on which her counsel might be needed. Serena regarded her companion with a considerable amount of respect.

"The wisdom of Solomon indeed my dear Anne," murmured Miss Pope.

***
**
*

Chapter Five

"Here's a health to our master, the founder of the feast,
I hope to God in heaven his soul may be at rest,
That all things may prosper whate'er he takes in hand,
For we are all his servants and all at his command
So drink, boys, drink, and see you do not spill,
For if you do you shall drink two; it is our master's will."
Traditional harvest supper toast. Date unknown.

The harvest was finally gathered, garnered and celebrated in traditional fashion. It was not as plentiful as some had hoped, but it was better than many had predicted. The grain was threshed and stored, the surplus, such as it was, being taken to the corn markets; the price of wheat remained as high as it had been for the past two-three years, and out of the reach of the poorer folk. The Morning Post busied itself with articles calling on all to take heed that War, Tumult and Famine were stalking the land, and reporting on the bread riots taking place in the Midlands of England and the North. Indeed in many households in parts of England, 1800 became known as 'the poor year.' But here in Kent, fertile and fruitful as it was, things were not so bad, although many a farmer took heed to store with care, and many a farmer's wife exercised more than usual thrift. All hoped and prayed for a mild winter.

The fruit and late vegetables were gathered and housewives busied themselves salting down beans, pickling eggs, storing apples in the lofts and preserving plums and blackberries in the summer's honey. These would be used in the Christmas feasts. The old bee-master was much in demand for he could take combs from the hives without the need for the sulphur rags used by less able bee-keepers, which killed all the bees except for the queen and a handful of workers, kept for the following year. As a child, and keeping a safe distance, Anne had watched in awe as the bee-master plunged his hand into the skep and drew it away, covered in bees, with a fistful of comb, oozing with honey. He kept up a gentle murmur to the bees, and was never stung. He could even take honey from the wild bees this way, humming gently into the hollow tree as he felt his way to the golden stores without disturbing the baby bees in their little cells or the workers in their busyness. For his own skeps, he always ensured enough honey was left for the colony to survive the winter, and even on the coldest days could be seen wandering among his hives, bending his head to listen to the faint murmur within; tucking straw and sacking round them when the frost bit sharp or snow fell thick.

Much of the apple harvest went to the making of cider, which in Kent was carried out in October, while the sweeter varieties were used to make the black apple butter, always served at Rosings at Christmas. October was also the month for brewing the best and strongest beer with the new malt from the summer's barley and flavoured with Kentish hops. Some farmwives remained true to the old ways and flavoured their home-brewed ale with wormwood, mugwort or rosemary.

The harvest feast, or wheatkin as it was known hereabouts, was held, as always, in the biggest barn of Home Farm. Sir Lewis in his lifetime had never been known to miss this feast and had taken Anne with him as soon as she was old enough not to fall asleep before the celebrations were over. As a good trencherman, he had enjoyed the salt beef in old ale, cold pork, chicken, goose or hare removed with junkets, cream, apple tarts and figgy pudding, all washed down with strong ale and vintage cider. He also went with a good will to join the hopkin, when all the hops were gathered and dried, and feasted on the traditional hot oast-cakes - as many as eight or nine at a time. After his death, Lady Catherine had held aloof from such rustic jollifications, and Anne had relied on her maid Sarah to report on the fun and bring her a piece of seedcake or ginger apple tart. This year, her first as the new Lady of Rosings Park, she was determined she and Serena would join the celebrations.

The two ladies settled into their new companionship with the ease born of similar minds, the same likings and mutual respect. Serena had been delighted with her bedroom and sitting room, Mrs Jenkinson's old apartments. Anne had had them refurbished, adding a number of bookshelves, a beautiful little Queen Anne escritoire, a daybed from her mother's room and two chairs of walnut with damask seats. A Sheraton cabinet and chest-of-drawers had also been ordered; the bed well aired and provided with new damask hangings. Serena was then left to unpack her belongings and add those personal touches which stamps an owner's personality on to a room. This she did with delight, arranging her books on the shelves, music on the piano forte and a number of sketches and pictures, some of them executed by herself and some by former pupils, including Anne. When Anne scratched on the door a while later bearing an armful of late flowers from the garden, she found the shelves already filled with familiar books and a number of new ones, and Serena esconced in one of the chairs before the fire, reading.

There were many aspects of each other's lives Anne and Serena found they needed to discover. Anne was interested in stories of Sukey, Fanny and Theresa and life under a very different regime to the one she had experienced. Serena listened with sympathy to Anne's halting accounts of the previous years; although Anne was careful not to say too much, it was plain that she had suffered greatly in body, mind and spirit since Serena had been so suddenly removed from her.

But there had been moments of relief. If Serena had wondered how Anne had come to be so knowledgeable about farming methods and land management, she learnt that it was due to the fact that Anne had on many an occasion made her way to the book-room and availed herself of such journals and pamphlets as her father had left there. At first she read these merely in order to feel closer to him, but then became interested in the subject for its own sake.

*

Anne still rode out every week with Mr Castleton, or met with him in the morning-room when the weather was too wet for riding. She also corresponded regularly with Mr Clements, her man of business, to put in hand a number of repairs to the House before winter set in. She and Serena together visited the cottages of the village; in the continuing absence of a parson, Anne took it upon herself to ensure that any who were in need should be cared for. They visited Dame Dakins at the cottage hospital; as the weather grew colder and wetter, that good woman was kept busy making rosehip syrup, sage and honey infusions and hyssop tea with which to dose a number of children with putrid sore throats, and old people with coughs. One very elderly man who lived alone, she had brought into the hospital to nurse through an inflammation of the lungs. A further visit to Anne's old nurse gave Serena more insight into the state of affairs in the schoolroom at Rosings after her departure.

"Miss Anne were proper poorly, Miss Pope," had said Nurse on one occasion when they were alone. "And that weasel-faced sawbones- if you'll pardon me, Miss did her no good at all. She were kept under more laudanum than was good for a young maid, that Mrs Jenkinson measuring it out for her each day and telling the poor child as if she didn't drink it all up her Mama would be most displeased. Well, I kept meself regular informed of the state of things, and one day went up to the House and met Miss Anne in her father's book-room. She was used to go there sayin' as how she could read improvin' books and Mrs Jenkinson couldn't very well disapprove of that, bein' as she was supposed to be in charge of the girl's education. Well, I told Miss Anne that if she were ever to feel better in her health she had better try an' take less of the laudanum, and she took note o' that and tried to leave the dregs in the bottom of the cup. Sarah was that good to her mistress, she would take the cup away and get it washed quickly so's Mrs Jenkinson never noticed. But 'tis powerful stuff, Miss Pope, an' it's taken time to get my poor girl back to good health after it."

If Serena was shocked at Nurse's tale, she could not profess to be surprised.

"I knew something was very wrong on the occasions when I saw Anne. But I had no idea it was as bad as that."

"It's my belief—and forgive me for sayin' such a wicked thing—but the best thing that could have happened for Miss Anne was the death of her mother.

111

Though poor Parson Collins would be turnin' in 'is grave to hear me utter such a terrible thing!"

The absence of a regular parson for the livings of Hunsford, and the hamlets of Upper and Lower Broughton, was still occupying Anne's mind, and although Serena sympathised, she was unable to suggest a solution. Hunsford's needs with regard to the Sunday services were being met by the obliging Parson Bride of Westerham and his careless curate, a situation which to Anne's mind was less than satisfactory.

Several days of heavy rain causing streams to overflow had prompted the bailiff to hasten his enquiries concerning the hiring of a drainage engineer for the soggy plains of Home Farm. Some flooding of the main roads had also held up the Mail Coach to Canterbury; consequently it was not until the weather cleared that a bundle of letters was brought up from the receiving office in Westerham. Anne received a belated copy of the Botanists' Review, together with a number of letters: one from Mr Clements concerning the rents from the London house, this she put to one side. Another came from her aunt Lady Cecilia Gould, with news of Kit's launch into London Society:

'... I have every hope that she will take; already we have had a number of very pleasing invitations and I am accepting all which may lead to a happy outcome.'

The letter continued with an invitation to Anne to join the Gould family in London in March, when the Season should begin to be in full swing. Anne passed this communication to Serena for her comments.

On the next letter she picked up she recognised Charlotte Collins' neat hand and broke the seal with eagerness to peruse the closely crossed sheet.

Charlotte's letter began very correctly with news of the inhabitants of Pemberley and greetings from Elizabeth and Darcy. Much followed concerning the children:

'... The babies are growing fast and it is delightful to see them together. Little Lottie's hair, like my sister Maria's, is growing curly and Master Charles seems to like nothing better than to put out a plump little finger and poke—it·into a curl. The small children spend much of their time smiling at each other, which makes us laugh. Elizabeth says we need the sketch pad of an Anne de Bourgh to record these precious moments. Edward has not forgotten you and sends you a big kiss.'

There came at this point a large X, obviously written in a child's hand.

'He is learning his letters,' Charlotte's letter resumed, 'with Mr Stevens, who has taken time from his curate's many duties to instruct him with great patience and understanding Mr Stevens has also taken pains to walk and talk with me,and I find myself in charity with many of his ideas and take pleasure in his company. Indeed he has said that he also enjoys our talks together, and although I am scarce two months widowed, it would seem that we have reached an understanding whereby, once my year of mourning is passed and Mr Stevens has secured a living ...'

Anne broke off her reading at this point and regarded Serena with such a look of astonishment that she became alarmed. Anne hastened to reassure her.

"Don't distress yourself, my dear Serena. I have been such a fool! Why on earth did I not think of this before? It would be the perfect answer."

"I presume you will at some point stop talking in riddles and explain yourself."

Serena assumed her governess tones which had the effect of causing her former pupil to laugh.

"I do beg your pardon, Miss Pope! Charlotte writes of Mr Stevens, curate under the Reverend Campbell who holds the livings in Darcy's gift. I had many talks with them both while at Pemberley and found myself, like Charlotte, much in sympathy with Mr Stevens' conversation, ideas and turn of mind. Why should I then not offer him the living here at Hunsford?"

"It would seem ideal," Serena responded with caution. "But how long has been in holy orders?"

"Some two-three years I think. He took his degree at Oxford, and was a Fellow of Christchurch before his ordination. He confided that he had always felt himself called to the care of souls, like his father before him."

"A son of the Church, then?"

"Son and grandson, I believe. But his grandfather was a Nonjuror, and resigned his living. He then opened a school for the sons of those of like mind. Mr Stevens however, seems as far as I can judge, to be loyal to the House of Hanover."

"Then offer him the living by all means. Have you heard him preach?"

"I have indeed, and I was relieved to find that in the pulpit, unlike his demeanour in company, he was not shy but delivered his words with clarity and precision. I was also glad to note that his sermon was not overfull of Regeneration and Conversion."

"Well as to that," returned Serena, "There are some who may say we need as much regeneration in the Church of England as the Methodists have achieved with their new teaching. Indeed, it would be true to say there are too few parsons amongst us to whom the care of souls is a priority. It would make a pleasant change here. Mr Collins I feel, was not of that number."

"Indeed no," returned Anne with some spirit. "His only concern, at least until the latter days, was the furthering of his own prominence by flattering - my mother's vanity!"

Serena raised her eyebrows at this undutiful remark and Anne flushed slightly.

"I beg your pardon, I should not speak so. But since coming into the inheritance of Rosings Estate I have found much in Lady Catherine's management that was remiss."

"You have no need to apologise to me," Serena said amused, "And I am sure you will not echo such sentiments abroad."

"I shall remain mute on that subject of course. Have you not often said that it is better to be silent than to say either that which you do not hold to be true, or that which will neither profit the living, nor honour the dead? But there is one more thing …" Anne resumed her reading of Charlotte's letter. "It would seem that in the fullness of time and should Mr Stevens accept the living, we might expect Mrs Collins to resume her duties here as the parson's wife. I can think of no-one in Hunsford or in Rosings Park who would not be delighted at the news!"

No time was lost in writing a formal letter to Mr Stevens and a warm letter of approbation to Charlotte. Anne then set in hand the cleaning and refurbishment of the parsonage in the hope that its new occupant could take up his duties by Christmas.

Serena Pope's bundle of letters comprised a newly published copy of the *Lyrical Ballads* by Mr Wordsworth and Mr Coleridge; a letter from her mother giving news of her father's talks to the Bath Philosophical Society:

… 'Upholding the view that there have been many Noachian Deluges over time and in a number of Places on the Earth …'

And news of Mistress Pope's publications with the Bath Literary Society:

'*… on the women who have taken a stand against dishonest market trading.*'

There was also a letter from Lady Spalding, still residing in Tanglewood House, which she had inherited on the death of her mother a few years before. Lady Spalding had taken over the management of the school; her elder son George, now the Earl, was abroad and serving in a diplomatic capacity in Naples with Sir William Hamilton, he who had recently shocked the polite world by taking to wife his former mistress, the beautiful Emma. The younger son of the Spalding house, the Honourable Will, Serena was then informed, had followed his bent and was studying engineering and surveying with one William Smith: '*A man of lowly birth,*' wrote Lady Spalding, ' *but of great mind, great technical knowledge and great curiosity regarding the formation of the Earth. Will has made a special study of Mr Smith's main focus of interest, which involves rivers and canals; he has made a number of interesting discoveries in connection with the cutting of the same.*'

Sharing this letter with Anne prompted the Mistress of Rosings to ask Mr Castleton concerning their own drainage and canal project. She learned that it was indeed a Mr William Smith who had been approached, but as he was involved in a large undertaking in Norfolk, he was sending two of his assistants, both well versed in the surveying and engineering requirements of land drainage, river straightening and lock building.

"If one of these assistants should be Mr Will Spalding, you will be able to renew acquaintance with another former pupil Serena. Why should we not invite both gentlemen to drink tea with us and Mr Castleton? I will need to discuss the finances of the scheme with my bailiff in any case."

Thus it was that a few weeks later the two ladies of Rosings Park received in the Yellow Drawing-room two young men, very correctly attired for an afternoon visit, and introduced by Mr Castleton. The taller of the two a fair young man stepped forward to shake Miss Pope warmly by the hand and ask how she did. Serena laughed and declared she would not have known Mr Will Spalding he had grown so large, and she presented him to Anne. He bowed gracefully over her hand, and Anne found herself being regarded appraisingly by a pair of intelligent grey eyes in a frank and open countenance. This then was the younger son of a rake, a libertine and a murderer! If she had not known his history she would never have believed that one so honest of face could have come from such a stock. But then his mother was a lady of integrity and this young man had had the benefit of Serena's teaching. Anne, responding correctly but warmly to his address, found herself liking what she saw and hoping that all would be well with him.

She turned next to receive Mr Castleton's introduction of the other young man, who up till now had remained a little in the background. She beheld a serious dark face, weathered by his work in the open air, who looked at her intensely as Mr Castleton said:

"Mr Robert Brightwell, Ma'am."

*

The visit was over. Anne hoped she had retained enough presence of mind to say and do all that was necessary and polite. She had enquired where the young engineers were lodging and found they had not yet found accommodation in the village. She then invited them to take up residence in the East Wing at Rosings.

"You will be within easy distance of your work, and any equipment you may have can easily be stored in what used to be the gun room, which has not been in use for some years now. We can of course provide stabling for your horses. Mr Castleton will be pleased to arrange things with Mrs Rowlands and John Groom."

Mr Castleton bowed his acceptance of the task, and Mr Spalding accepted the offer with enthusiasm. Robert Brightwell also uttered his thanks politely, if somewhat reservedly.

When they had departed, Anne excused herself and fled up to her room.

She found herself disturbed at meeting again the young man who had once been known to her in her childhood, and wondered what the years between had done for him. Had they been as difficult for him as for her? Had he known of her father's death? Where were his mother and sisters? Where did they go when they left Wakefield farm? She remembered asking Mrs Jenkinson about the family, but had received no satisfactory answer. Neither had Serena known what had become of them; she too had left Rosings in the spring of '92, the year when, for Anne, everything in her life had been turned upside down. She searched in the carved Chinese box her father had bought for her one Christmas, where she kept her girlish treasures, and found the little bird Robert had carved for her. It was smooth with much handling, and Anne rubbed her fingers over the wood, allowing the soft curves to soothe her agitated feelings.

***
**
*

Chapter Six

"He that lives upon hope will die fasting"
Benjamin Franklin: The Way to Wealth (1757)

Robert Brightwell rode away from Rosings outwardly calm, but in an inner turmoil. Memories came flooding through his mind: of his early years on Wakefield farm, his father's death and all that followed. He still nursed anger and resentment against the de Bourgh family. Firstly against Sir Lewis who, in spite of his care in providing for the family's welfare, had only done so because he wished to exercise his droit de Seigneur on Robert's mother. The boy could not believe that his mother, faithful and loving wife that she had been, had accepted Sir Lewis's advances willingly; rather that, by his kindliness and generosity, he had left her little choice. At least, or so Robert hoped, he had been honourable enough not to approach Dame Hannah during her husband's lifetime. In spite of this, Robert had loved the baby brother, the child of Sir Lewis' begetting; he could not be blamed for his fathering, and he was an engaging little chap. His sisters also loved him, although Martha, the elder, was wise enough in the ways of Nature to understand the implications of his birth more than a year after their father's death. While Sir Lewis lived the family had been well looked after and it was to him that Robert owed his education with the Reverend Hibbert.

But if Robert Brightwell was honest enough with himself to recognise and appreciate Sir Lewis de Bourgh's charm and good humour, and to feel himself valued by the baronet as much for his own qualities as his being the son of his mother, for Lady Catherine de Bourgh he felt nothing but contempt. That she had been wronged as a wife he could understand, although he knew enough of the ways of the Quality to know that many a great lady had to learn to accept her lord's infidelities as a matter of course, and pretend to know nothing of them.

But she must have known of them, else why should she take so complete a revenge on the whole Brightwell family? The thought caused Robert to clench his teeth at the very memory of it.

They had been woken late one evening, a month or so after Sir Lewis' death, by a loud hammering at the door, which woke the little children and caused them to cry out in alarm. Two men pushed their way into the farmhouse and told Dame Hannah roughly that she must leave at once. She stood up to them bravely and asked on whose authority they were acting.

117

"Lady Catherine de Bourgh," came the answer.

Dame Hannah then asked where she and her family were to go.

"We neither know nor care," one of the men answered, "but you are to be gone from here. If you resist we have orders to throw you out bodily."

"That you will not," Robert spoke up stoutly, grabbing the poker and planting himself in front of his mother. "You shall not lay a finger on her!"

Hannah laid her hand gently on her son's shoulder.

"We will indeed leave this place on Lady Catherine's orders," said she, "but we will go quietly and as Christian citizens, at first light. Give us this night to pack up our belongings and we will give no trouble. I do not wish there to be violence against anyone here."

One of the men was all for insisting that they leave immediately -

"… with but the clothes you stand up in," but the other, who appeared to have the greater authority, declared they could have the night's grace and they would be back at dawn to ensure the family's removal.

When they were gone, Dame Hannah controlled her trembling with difficulty and it was some little while before she could compose herself sufficiently to rouse Martha and enlist her help with sorting and packing such household things as they might be able take with them. Robert meanwhile, gathered what he could of the tools he thought they might need and which would not be too difficult to carry away. By morning, several bundles containing clothing, linen, herbs, remedies and a few household items lay ready and tied.

But dawn did not bring the two ruffians of the night before, as they had feared. Instead came Mr Castleton himself, with apologies for the behaviour of his henchmen, who had interpreted her ladyship's orders over-enthusiastically. He brought with him a donkey-cart to transport not only their bundles, but also a few essential items of furniture, and informed them they were being provided with a small shepherd's hut on the edge of the estate. He regretted the fact that they might find it rather a mean place, but he had already arranged for it to be swept and a quantity of firewood to be provided. This kindness brought Dame Hannah more nearly to tears than the surly behaviour of the night before had done. She knew Mr Castleton to be a strict Methodist, who did not view her moral lapse with any degree of tolerance; she had not looked for compassion in him and was moved to find it.

The hut was indeed a mean dwelling. It consisted of a single small room with rough wooden steps up to a half hayloft containing a few musty bundles of hay. There was a simple hearth with a jack and a small trivet just big enough to hold a kettle or cooking pot, but in spite of the fire kindled upon it, the room remained chilly. Plaster had fallen away along one wall exposing the laths, and the roof leaked in several places. Mould grew in the corners and a goodly crop of toadstools had sprouted between the uneven flagstones of the floor. The tiny window was thick with grime. Dame Hannah and Martha did their best to clean where they could and make it more habitable; little Margaret ran out into the winter sunshine and returned with some twigs of scarlet berries which she stuck in a pot on the table. Robert constructed a serviceable earth privy against the back wall and laid flat stones around the hut to make a path.

They were not destined to stay there for long. It seemed that the Lady Catherine had not given any orders that they should be re-housed; simply that the Brightwell family be removed from their tenancy of Wakefield Farm. On June quarter-day, when Mr Castleton presented the accounts, she discovered that one Rob Brightwell was being paid for casual farm work during the hay-making season and that the family were still residing on the estate. Mr Castleton was informed he had exceeded his brief, and although he pointed out very fairly that the family had never been behindhand with the rent on what had previously been an empty dwelling, Lady Catherine was not appeased. Without her bailiff's knowledge, she arranged for them to be yet further removed and the children of working age to be bound to a cotton factory in Northamptonshire.

Robert tried to shut his memory down on the first dreadful years in Northampton. This time there had been no night's grace given for packing their belongings; no Mr Castleton to come to their aid. An open wagon conveyed them away, and although they repeatedly asked, they were not told their destination. The factory overseer, with the two assistants who had been sent to fetch them had been neither rude nor rough, but the men's refusal to answer their pleadings; their lack of any conversation with them other than the curt order that they were to be taken thence; indeed the very fact that they ignored their presence in the cart behind them were almost worse than the threats and bullyings they had experienced before. The girls huddled together and cried, but softly; Robert was tight-lipped, and all went in fear of the blunderbuss carried by one of the men. Dame Hannah appeared calm as she nursed her baby son, but she was reflecting bitterly that it had been her own sins which had brought them to this pass.

*

She hated the city. A countrywoman born and bred, she could not bear the mean streets and foul-smelling air. They were put into a small house in a row of other small houses, with one water well supplying the needs of about twenty homes. The privy was also shared by a number of families and as it seemed it was no-one's job to remove the night-soil and replace it with fresh earth, it was forever overflowing into the shallow gutter which ran along the back of the houses. Hannah reminded herself that the shepherd's hut had had but the one room, but it was surrounded on all sides by fields and woodland where they could gather firewood, and nettles, herbs and mushrooms for the pot. Here there was scarce a blade of grass to be seen.

Every morning at six they would be summoned by a loud knocking on the window as the factory caller went down the street waking all who were to be on the morning shift. Robert and the girls would make haste to join the long line of workers heading for the gates. Hannah did her best to ensure they went with clean hands and faces and with rye bread and perhaps a bit of cold bacon inside them. Every evening at eight, they would stumble home, the little girls almost dropping with tiredness and too weary even to eat much of the meal Hannah had managed to prepare.

With a baby of less than two years old and no relations in the town to help mind him, Hannah had been provided with the means of knitting stockings at home for fourpence a day, being taught the way of it by a friendly neighbour.

This neighbour was a slatternly woman, but kindly in her own bluff way, who thought Dame Brightwell a poor thing who did not know how to go on. She was also curious as to how she came there; the children had been conscripted to the mill, but she had not and could have remained in what to this poor woman sounded like a palace. She herself was housed with her man and babe in the damp basement of one of the larger houses, while her children, three boys of eleven, ten and nine and two girls of seven and six were lodged with a hundred or so other children in the big sheds by the factory gates.

"But when do you see your children?" Hannah was astonished when she heard of this arrangement.

"Of a Sunday most times. Or when I tek me work up to overseer at factory. But the boys geh ter Sunday School an' learn theirselves readin' an writin' an gets a dinnner free so I doan' see so much o' them."

"Is there not a school for the girls?"

"For gels? Nah! Why should there be?" and the woman stared at Hannah in amazement.

"Would not the girls like a school? It would be an opportunity for them to learn to knit and sew, to read a little, to write and cipher and hear the stories of the Bible."

"Nah then. An' did your gels do all that?"

"Indeed yes, at the school in the village, where we lived before."

"Well an' so." The woman was all astonishment. "Who d'ya think would do all that then?"

"I could."

"Couldst tha then? Well mebbe yer should ask. A school fer the gels." And the woman sounded wistful.

"If we could get a school going on a Sunday for the girls, would you like to come too?" Hannah asked gently.

"Nah then. What would I do with readin' and writin'? An' what my man would say ter that I dursn't think," the woman laughed scornfully.

"It probably won't come to anything, so you need not be worrying about it," said Hannah practically.

She did not let the matter rest, however. When she took her completed work up to the factory, with baby Lewis strapped to her back with her shawl as most of the women did here, she mentioned the matter to the foreman. The idea was laughed to scorn and the tale went around the factory that here was a poor crazed women offering to open a school for the mill girls. But the factory owner's daughter got to hear of it, and being a young woman of modem ideas, forthright manner and the habit of always managing to get her own way with her papa, she visited Hannah Brightwell one First Day after Meeting, for they were a Quaker family, and found her instructing her own girls in reading the Bible aloud to each other. Martha and Margaret showed their visitor the plain sewing they had done and the small books in which they had written out some verses from the Psalms. She was impressed, and the idea for a school for the girls of the factory took root. In the fullness of time, after many urgings and pleadings, Miss Patience prevailed upon her father to furbish up an old barn on the edge of the town, with a little lean-to of a building as a dwelling for the school-mistress and her family. Dame Hannah was asked if she would accept the post, so with the town at their backs and a prospect of hills and fields before them, the Brightwells found it an improvement indeed.

*

Jacob Barton, son of Isaac, was a plain Quaker from the crown of his black beaver hat to his simple white stock, grey cloth coat, black breeches and stockings and round-toed shoes with square steel buckles. He wore neither lace, diamond pin nor embroidered waistcoat, although he could have afforded all these and more, and he carried a simple polished ebony walking-stick unembellished with ivory or amber knob. He had once been tempted to marry out of the Quaker Society by the laughing dark eyes of the squire's pretty daughter; had he done so he would have been expelled from The Meeting. But he came to his senses in time and married Prudence, a distant cousin and a neat, hard working little body of a woman, who bore him eight children, raised six of them in health, kept his house, orchard and garden as precise as a pin, managed their few servants, reckoned up the household accounts, and could brew and bake, make and mend clothes and doctor the children whenever needed. Not that it was needed very often; a healthier set of youngsters than the Barton children were not to be found anywhere in the whole county.

Jacob followed the rules of the Friends scrupulously. He refused to be seduced by wealth and status, despised rank and the morals of the Quality, and made his way in the world by plain speaking, plain dealing, hard work and family solidarity. Like his father Isaac he went into the cotton industry, and rose with it, expanding into foreign exports with his finely finished products. He began in his father's mill as a factory worker, learning all the processes from sorting the bags of raw cotton imported by the thousand from the southern states of America, through carding, spinning, winding, warping, sizing, looming the web and weaving the final cloth; he had an interest too in the fulling and dying processes. He rented his first mill at the age of twenty-one, described in an advertisement as consisting of:

'Rooms for the laying up of flax or cotton, four looms, starching frames, a bookroom and counting house beside a ready supply of good water, plus a house of good size adjoining and all for sixteen pounds per annum.'

From these small beginnings the business grew until by the year 1792 he had extended the premises, employed five hundred workmen, plus women and children and had installed a carding machine, a flying shuttle and a forty-spindle jenny. The 'house of good size adjoining' was made over for his foreman, factory overseers and clerks and their families.

In the philanthropic manner of the Friends, which always had good business sense at the back of it, he provided simple terraces of cottages for his workers, and if some considered them small and mean, then they should consider the Barton's own house: larger it is true, but plain in both design and furnishings. He listened when some of the inhabitants of the cottages came to him with a complaint about the overflowing privies and promptly gave orders that each house should have its own privy; each householder being supplied with regular barrowloads of fresh earth and required to carry away their own nightsoil to the ground set aside for the communal kitchen garden. The gutter was widened and deepened, with a culvert diverted from the river to flow through it at a steady level. A Friends Meeting House, a chapel and shops were also provided and the school which the factory boys had to attend for four hours every Sunday to keep them out of mischief. One of the arguments Miss Patience brought to bear on her papa was that lasses might also get into mischief. Thus Hannah's Dame School was full of growing mill girls on a Sunday, and during the week a handful of little girls came to learn their letters and numbers. Jacob Barton, unlike some of his contemporaries, refused to employ girls in the factory under the age of seven, although from six years they might earn their fourpence by running errands, delivering outwork and sweeping the factory floor on Saturdays when the machinery would be shut down for the Sabbath- or First Day. The working mothers, having at first been scornful, wary or amused at the idea of a lasses' school, soon found it useful to get their little ones out from under their feet during the week. Dame Hannah provided but simple reading, writing and number tasks; the children learnt by rote the catechism, rhymes, stories and songs and such rules for living as:

'If you would grow and thrive, let a spider run alive',

'Dry milk on the fire, dry milk in the udder',

'Marry in Lent, you' live to repent', and

'Patience is a Virtue, Virtue is a Grace, and both put together make a pretty face'.

She also taught simple plain sewing, darning and mending, knitting, some of her country lore and the way of healing with herbs, although she wondered what use these city girls would make of it.

Like many factory owners, Jacob kept a tern eye on his employees. They had strict instructions as to their own work and duties; and notices were posted everywhere in Jacob's mill:

It is hereby given that the following practices are forbidden within the manufactory, with fines imposed thus:

Quarrelling and contention	one shilling
sleeping	Sixpence
smoaking	Sixpence
loitering	Sixpence
Consumption of spiritous liquours	two shillings

'Should contention lead to striking or otherwise abusing an overseer, the perpetrator is to lose his place'.

But honesty and industry were rewarded, and Jacob kept one eye out for malefactors and the other for exemplary workers. Thus his good eye fell one day on Robert Brightwell, who was found sweeping the cotton fluff, broken threads and dust from under the looms at the end of the working week.

"Nay lad," said Jacob, "That's women's work. Why dost thou do such a thing as sweeping?"

"I know, Sir, it is my sister Margaret's work, but she has gone home sick and could not finish today."

"What ails the lass?"

"The sweating sickness sir. As tomorrow is Sunday, my mother will keep her a-bed, so she can return to work on Monday."

"And thou hopes to take home her wages as well as thy own, then dost tha?"

Robert flushed, but looked his employer in the eye.

"No sir. She has earned her own wages this day. It was but at the end-of-day bell that she admitted to being faint and dizzy. The overseer sent her home then and I stayed to do her sweeping."

"Hm." Jacob continued to regard the boy, unsmiling. "How old art thou?"

"Nearly fifteen, sir."

"What hast thou in thy pocket?"

If Robert was surprised by the sudden sharp question, he did not show it.

"A book, Sir. I like to read in the breakfast and dinner hour," and without being asked he pulled out the little book, a copy of *De Imitatione Christi* by Thomas a Kempis; it had been a gift from his old teacher, the Reverend Hibberd.

"Dost thou read Latin?"

"A little sir. And a little Greek."

"Pah! I've no time for such polite learning. Canst thou reckon up numbers?"

"Yes, sir."

"So lad, what art thou doing in my manufactory with all thy book learning?"

But Robert—could not answer this question, it was too painful, he merely shook his head.

"Finish thy sweeping then and be off home," and Jacob Barton turned on his heel and marched out.

*

That conversation, Robert realised later, had been a turning point for him, although his next encounter with his employer was not so fortuitous. Robert had not been asked his name, nor where he lived, nor, yet, anything pertaining to his mother and sisters, but, nonetheless, these things soon became known to the sharp old man. He continued to keep an eye out for the lad, and found that he was used to wander off by himself in the half-hour dinner break and find a quiet corner to read. Sometimes his sisters would come to find him, but they too either had a little book with them, or a small piece of mending or knitting. These pursuits were however mocked and teased by some of the other factory boys, and ·one day Robert found his book knocked out of his hand, and a large lad of about sixteen years confronting him with a jeer. This had the effect of making Margaret cry out in alarm, whereupon the boy turned upon her with fists raised and a threat to:

"shut yer mouth."

Robert promptly knocked him down. For this, two things were responsible: the lad's attention had been turned away, and he had slipped on a stone as he received Robert's punch and gone down heavily. But not for long. He was immediately up on his feet and squaring up to his opponent; the other boys egged the two on, and the girls fled to the safety of a corner of the yard. Robert, though the smaller of the two, gave a good account of himself and before the overseer had come upon them and stopped the fight, had given and received a bloody nose and a number of cuts. They were both taken before Mr Barton and each fined one shilling. Although nothing was said, Robert had the impression that their employer knew much about the cause of the fight, but would give no quarter, even though his sympathies may have been engaged on Robert's behalf.

Jacob questioned his overseer as to Robert's behaviour, and also his daughter as to the running of the Dame school and found the former admitting that the lad had never been in any kind of trouble before, and that Miss Patience was impressed with the teaching and the manners of the school-mistress.

After some months, Robert found himself at the day's end, called before the overseer. He searched his conscience but could not find anything amiss, so went with his head up and stood patiently waiting for whatever would come. The overseer regarded the boy thoughtfully.

"Well, it seems yer've caught the master's eye lad," he said with a faint sneer. "Yer're to be transferred to the counting house and learn to do the accounts. Seems the master has a yen to mek a clerk of you. What d'yer say ter that then?"

Robert said he thought he would like it well enough.

"Well, then seems I'm to lose yer, and yer're a good worker on the looms. Work out this week and on Monday, report ter the chief clerk good and early".

Robert stammered his thanks and scurried away home with the news. Thus, with the setting up of the school and Robert's transfer to the counting house, it seemed the Brightwell family's fortunes were improving.

It did not last. Their second winter in Northampton was long, hard and bitter. Fever, influenza, consumption and measles swept through the town and Dame Hannah was kept busy making infusions and poultices, mixtures and decoctions to help the afflicted. Both Martha and Margaret, working amid the dust and cotton waste that pervaded the factory, succumbed to coughs and colds.

Margaret in particular, although a gallant little soul, was not strong in her body nor happy in her mind since they had left Hunsford and the countryside of Kent.

It was true that Kent suffered harsh winters, with plenty of ice and snow, but the air was clear and clean and the farmhouse of Wakefield had always been warm in winter with good fires in the kitchen hearth, plenty of logs cut and piled by their woodsman father, and good food on the table. Here, and Hannah was bitterly aware of this, it was difficult to provide decent country fare for the family and a warm house at all times. The little lean-to of a house behind the schoolhouse barn was thin-walled and damp, and although the family tried to keep a good fire going in the tiny hearth, it was difficult to keep out the cold and the chill. Margaret developed a putrid sore throat, then an inflammation of the lungs. She struggled to breathe at times and coughed deep painful sobbing coughs that left her weak and gasping. Her mother did the best she could, but her best was not good enough. At Candlemas, 1795, when the first snowdrops began to show their white heads, Margaret died. For all his life, Robert swore to himself, he would put her death at the door of Lady

***
**
*

125

Chapter Seven

"I discoursed with a man about their wages in the cotton mills, who said that men could earn two shillings per diem, women one shilling and children sixpence."
John Byng: Rides round Britain. Tour to the North. (1792)

Jacob Barton would never have become as rich as he was without being shrewd in his affairs. True, his business thrived on the fact that there had been an increase in the demand for cotton in the colonial and continental markets, which followed an improvement in the quality of the finished product by the use of modem machinery. Whereas formerly, ladies in great houses and housewives of the merchant class had preferred linen for their sheets, napery and household goods, now fine cotton was in demand, not only for these items but also for clothing. Dresses and petticoats were being made of cotton muslin in a variety of patterns; men's neck-cloths and small-clothes were fashioned of cotton poplin and handkerchiefs of the finest lawn. Mr Barton and others engaged in the business could make material delicate enough to rival the daintiest Indian cottons, and fabric sturdy enough to serve well in hangings and furnishings. Thus it was that from royalty downwards drapes and bedlinens were made of cotton, and some of the highest-born gentlemen in the land were demanding that their shirts be made of English cotton. Thousands of factory workers earned their two shillings a day, while the mill owners grew fabulously wealthy in the days when cotton was king.

Speculation was not in Jacob Barton's nature; nonetheless, when he was approached by a group of Nottinghamshire landowners and businessmen with proposal to set up an incorporated company to buy and sell shares for the financing of a short-haul canal linking a number of mills with the navigation systems of Nottingham and Leicester, he gave it serious consideration. The great Mr William Jessop, he was informed, would be approached to be the consultant engineer and the cost of the project would be defrayed over time by the reduction in haulage expenses. It was pointed out that a six ton wagon needed a team of eight strong horses, whereas one Clydesdale work-horse could tow a long barge carrying 25tons. Coal could, therefore, be brought down at little expense for the setting up of a rotatory steam engine, which had long been one of Jacob's dreams. Water wheels were durable and cheap, and swift-flowing water served the mill well, but was subject to fluctuations which could not always be controlled, as in times of drought, flood, or ice. In addition to the carrying of coal to the mill to power a steam engine, cotton bales could be transported away through the network of waterways to the warehouses and linen drapers' shops of Liverpool, London, Bristol—and beyond. But first the canal must be built.

Robert Brightwell, in his new capacity as clerk in the counting house, was involved in the costing of this, and was astonished to discover that according to figures produced by the Duke of Bridgewater - the noble pioneer of canal development - to cut a canal could cost ten thousand guineas per mile. Using an existing waterway would of course reduce that by a considerable amount. Memories of his father's investigation into canals as a means of transport came to Robert's mind. He was fascinated by the whole concept: the cutting of the canal; puddling the bed and sides with clay to make them watertight; the construction of bridges, locks, reservoirs, towpaths and junctions, all these aroused his interest. He began to read eagerly all that came his way about what was involved in the whole process.

The observant Jacob Barton noted his interest. He had acknowledged little Margaret's death with the briefest of condolences:

"I am sorry for thy loss, lad," but he believed in the ordering of human lives according to God's providence. "The Lord giveth and the Lord taketh away, and blessed be the Name of the Lord!" he would often be heard to say. Thus gains were to be accepted without pride and loss without undue mourning. He had bowed his head upon the deaths of two of his own children without complaint and expected others to bear up under similar bereavement. He was a hard man, but not an unkind one, and he sought now to further young Robert Brightwell's career. He therefore proposed that the lad take up an apprenticeship in engineering with a view to his involvement in the Barton Mill Canal scheme. Thus he hoped his sponsorship would ensure a willing worker on the project, whose honesty could be relied upon, and whose loyalty would serve the mill's interest in the construction of the canal.

Mr William Jessop was approached, accepted the task for a considerable remuneration, and promptly delegated nearly all of the work to his assistant, William Smith, who was himself a qualified surveyor and engineer. Mr Smith accepted a mere fraction of the sum offered to the great canal man himself, but as he was unaware of the terms upon which Mr Jessop agreed to undertake the project, he was not unduly perturbed. William Smith in turn allowed his journeyman and apprentices to do the actual surveying with pantograph, theodolite, dividers and steel chain, and the planning, drawing out and designing of the route of the canal. They were paid less than half between them the sum granted to Mr Smith. They then supervised the army of navvies, working with trenching tools, with pick and shovel, barrow and clay, wood props and iron girders, and their wages were but three shillings a day. On the days when it might have been supposed to be too cold, too hot, too wet or too icy to work, they received nothing at all. Thus they laboured to feed their families through all kinds of weather.

It was to Mr Smith that Robert Brightwell was bound as apprentice and from him he learned his knowledge and expertise. The work on the Barton Mill Canal took three and a half years to complete, and at the end of it, Robert, whose apprenticeship had another two and a half years to run, was required to travel the country, working on various waterways: enlarging, mending, raising bridges, constructing tunnels, joining short-haul canals to the great rivers and canals which were revolutionising transport in the heady days of the late eighteenth century.

He had not wanted to come back to Kent. Everything within him revolted at the idea of returning to the county of his birth, and most of all to the estate which had seen the happiest and also the worst of his times. But he was required to go where he was bid, to work as his master demanded. William Smith was a good master in many respects: he did not beat his apprentices any more than they needed or deserved; he shared his knowledge and enthusiasm with them and gave them as much responsibility as he felt they could hold. He held forth over dinners on the wonder and beauty of the fossils found by the workmen as they cut down through the layers of chalk, limestone, marls, sandstone or mudstone.

"The grand folk collect these," he said on one occasion, holding up particularly fine specimens of ammonites and trilobites. "They marvel at them and place them in their Chinese cabinets and show them to their friends with the same delight as a child will show a new toy. But they have no idea of the order and regularity with which Nature has disposed of these pretty things, nor of the significance—of the fact that certain groups of specimens are only found in certain layers and types of rocks. The implication of such a discovery is beyond them."

"And what is the implication, sir?" demanded William Spalding.

He and Robert were dining with Mr Smith ostensibly to pick up their instructions for the Kent project, but the master had gone off on one of his high horses, and the young men knew it would be a while before they got anything practical out of him.

"Why the implication, my dear young sir s that these are not simply figured stones, or 'lapides sui generis'—stones unto themselves—which the good God has 'planted' into rocks for our interest and amusement. They are not stones mimicking shells, insects, bones and leaves, but the actual remains of such creatures that once lived and died on this earth. They fell to the ground and were buried as you and I one day will be put into the ground and buried, and the earth hardened into rock and the rock held their shape, the same shape as you see before you now. The layers of the rocks hold the key: the lowest layers carry the earliest living creatures; the upper layers those that died more recently. But 'recently' may in fact mean many, many thousands of years ago."

"But, Sir," Robert objected, "Some of these creatures are sea animals, yet we find them in places where there is no sea, nor has there been sea in these regions within living memory."

"Aha!" and Mr Smith got up and paced about. "So, what do you deduce from this?"

"That—there was once sea, or something like it in that place, and that somehow, for some reason, there is now dry land."

"Even so," nodded William. "'And it came to pass, the waters were dried up from off the earth, and behold, the face of the ground was dried. Leaving behind dead animals of all kinds which became fossils."

"Are you saying the Great Deluge was here?" Will Spalding was amused.

"I am saying nothing of the kind. Merely, that there was a flood, or a sea over parts of this land which is now land. I do not presume to know anything of the Great Deluge, or Noah's Flood, although would not be at all surprised if Almighty God changed his mind about not wiping mankind off the face of the earth again, and has sent us any number of deluges, great and small, to try and teach us a lesson. But I am only a humble engineer and I leave all that to the theologians and philosophers. All I know is what I see, and what I can deduce from what I see. And what I see at the moment is my bed, and what I deduce is that it is time to retire to it. It is late, my good fellows, and you have a journey into Kent tomorrow. Good night." And he ambled off to the stairs, taking the only candle with him.

For all his self-taught knowledge, William Smith was not a man of business. He spent money as fast as he earned it; indeed at times he found himself seriously in debt. Thus, he took on more work than he could fairly manage, and had to rely on his underlings to carry out tasks he should have done himself. He was fortunate, as were those who employed him, that he had competent engineers and surveyors in both his journeyman, William Spalding, and senior apprentice, Robert Brightwell. Both could be relied upon to draw up the plans for the drainage, river straightening, lock and reservoir construction required for the Rosings Park river project. Mr Castleton's uncertainty over the continuing supply of sufficient water to carry barge boats for logging were not unfounded; as he learned in conversation with the two young engineers, water supply was always the most important element in the running and survival of any canal. The river could be relied upon to supply this to some extent, but the fact that the water meadows were frequently flooded and bogged in winter and the river ran sluggishly in summer meant that the flow was unpredictable, and that other measures must be put in place to ensure a good depth of water at all times. Locks need a constant supply of water and at least three would be required on the stretch of river designated to become a navigable waterway.

*

Following the tea with the Lady of Rosings and her companion, Mr Castleton and the two young men left the House by the door in the East Wing the bailiff having showed them where they would be residing—and walked round to the stable block. The wall bordering the path and separating a formal garden from the park, appeared to be of ancient stone, with a strange carving of a head, much weathered, on the end of it. Robert stopped and ran his fingers over the worn face.

"That's said to be a medieval stone carving from the chapel. Dates from when Rosings was an abbey—or so they say." Mr Castleton had noted Robert's interest. "There's another bit of carving, more like a little devil or somesuch on the wall that runs on the other side of the garden."

Robert nodded; he remembered hearing something of the history of the place from the Reverend Hibberd in their brief lessons together.

"Not much else left of the abbey stones now though. All pulled down long ago and used to build the pigsties and bits of the stables. And not a few cottages I shouldn't wonder. There's also a few humps and bumps in the park said to have Abbey foundation stones under 'em. But I wouldn't know for sure. There's a muniment room in the top of the East Wing if you're interested. Oh and a short history in a guide book: 'Seats of the Nobility and Gentry' with engravings by a Mr Angus."

The three men collected their mounts and rode through the gates into the lane. Will Spalding conversed cheerfully on the work ahead; the fineness of the trees in their late autumn glory, and the grace and kindliness of the young Miss de Bourgh.

"She may not be your usual style of beauty; the fashion being, so m'mother tells me, for small, plump, dark women. But I shouldn't wonder at it if chestnut hair and dark blue eyes don't become all the rage when Miss de Bourgh takes the London scene."

"Along with her fortune," commented Robert.

"Ah yes! One should never forget the fortune!" laughed Will. "A single woman possessed of a good fortune can have - how does Mr Sheridan put it?— 'a hump on each shoulder, be as crooked as the Crescent, her one eye shall roll like the bull in Cox's museum, she can have the skin of a mummy and the beard of a Jew' ... and still the polite world will fall over itself for her and 'write sonnets to her beauty!'"

In spite of himself Robert laughed.

"But in this instance, add to the fortune," Will continued, unabashed, "a sweet face, eyes as blue as a summer sky, a slender waist and my word, what wouldn't any man give for that? Don't consider she'd look at a younger son though, do you? No? Thought not. Daughter of a baronet and grand-daughter of an earl! She can aim as high as she likes. More likely set on becoming a duchess, or a countess at the very least!"

Mr Castleton, riding up to them at this point, adjured them strictly to keep their minds on the work in hand, at which Will bowed his head, saying in tones of mock repentance:

"I am rebuked. I promise that from henceforth I shall talk no more of the lady, but offer her my mute obedience, like a true knight. And if she bestows on me no more than the favour of her smile, I shall consider myself justly rewarded."

"Such knight errantry does you credit," said Mr Castleton in his driest tone, "But won't put food on your table. Now bustle about young sirs; talking of food, you are dining with me tonight and my wife will no doubt have a good plain dinner to set before you."

Over the good plain dinner, which in fact consisted of several courses, the bailiff tried to draw out Robert Brightwell and to gain from him a little more of his history than had been vouchsafed so far. He had recognised him at once as the quiet but hard-working lad, eldest child of Farmer Brightwell, whose death Mr Castleton recalled only too well. He had been witness to the family's early misfortunes, but since the summer of '92 had had neither sight not sound of them. It was as though they had vanished into the night. Lady Catherine had remained tight-lipped when he had ventured to ask, and he had been too concerned over his position as her bailiff to risk her further displeasure. She had already raked him down when he had dared to request the purchase of a Tullian drill for the Home Farm, and to import fertilisers such as seaweed and marl; she could never be brought to believe that such expenditure was an investment which would bring an increase in revenue. The only schemes to which her ladyship gave unqualified approval were those pertaining to the improving of Rosings Park: the construction of a shell grotto; planting flowering shrubs or extending the rose garden. To all other matters, including those of her tenant farmers— unless they fell under her magisterial displeasure—she turned a deaf ear. Useless to ask then after the Brightwell family, Mr Castleton had confided to his wife. Yet, here was the son of the family returned like the prodigal six years later, although, unlike the prodigal, grown into a good-looking young man with the end of a decent apprenticeship within his grasp. But he had an air of bitterness about him

"- as though he had suffered much from diskindness," Mrs Castleton had remarked.

But Robert would not be drawn. He mentioned briefly that his family had removed to Nottinghamshire and that he had worked for Mr Joseph Barton, mill owner, who had sponsored his apprenticeship with Mr William Smith. To enquiries concerning his mother, sisters and young brother, he said simply that they were well, but that his sister Margaret had died of consumption in the early spring of '95.

Mrs Castleton was a kindly, bustling little body and as shrewd as she could hold together. Generous of heart, she filled their good-sized, stone-built house with visiting grand-children and indigent relations and liked nothing better than to gather as many as eight or ten persons round her well-filled board. As well as providing good plain suppers, she also had a care to the general welfare of her guests and any in distress of body, mind or soul found her an ever-present help in their trouble. She was well aware of Dame Hannah's history, and had no doubt at all that Lady Catherine de Bourgh had brought about the bitterness she detected in Robert Brightwell, and to find out more—for largeness of heart must needs go with curiosity of mind—she sought out Miss Pope.

Serena however, could not enlighten her. She too had suspected that the sudden disappearance of the family was instigated by Lady Catherine, but she had been preoccupied at the time with Anne's illnesses, and later, her own dismissal. Discreet enquiries among the servants brought forth much conjecture, but few known facts.

"I am sorry I know so little, Mrs Castleton," said Serena, "And neither does Miss de Bourgh. I do know she was acquainted with the family when a child, but since her father's death and her subsequent ill health she has had little to do with the tenants. Only now is she taking pains to re-acquaint herself with matters of the estate."

"I know that, Miss Pope. Indeed the young mistress has already endeared herself to her folk, especially since the smallpox affliction which so lately came upon us. And 'tis obvious she would know nothing of the affair we speak of; why she was no more than—what—twelve years old! But what I believe is that the family were sent away; why should they have left of their own accord? Where would they have gone? They had no family elsewhere that we do know."

She lowered her voice a little, "'Tis a well-known fact, Miss Pope, that children of the poor were bound over to the great manufactories. Sent by the wagon-load by the parishes and as lost to their families as if shipped off to the West Indies. Now maybe there are some poor parents as would welcome there being fewer mouths to feed, and 'tis also obvious there'd be less call for parish relief. But for others, it was a terrible thing to have lost their young people. Mind—I'm not saying as that's how it was with the Brightwell children, but if they were so sent to this Mr Barton's cotton mill, then it would be like Hannah Brightwell to go with them."

Serena could only shake her head at this and debate with herself how much of Mrs Castleton's conjecture she should impart to Anne.

*

By the beginning of December, and in spite of much rain and not a little wind, several drainage channels had been cut down the length of Lower Field, and a lake of some considerable size, so it appeared to Anne, was being dug out and lined with clay. This, it was hoped, would serve to keep the water levels high enough to feed into the locks, and the field dry enough for pasture or crop planting. Because the cut would be supplied with flowing river water, it would prevent it becoming dark and polluted, as in some stretches of the Midland Counties where, between locks, the canal water turned black and pestiferous, a condition which had been likened to the River Styx.

In spite of the weather, Anne rode out as often as she could to view the work, but if she had secretly hoped to become better acquainted with one she had once considered a childhood friend, she was disappointed. Robert remained politely aloof, especially on those occasions when he came with Will and the bailiff in response to a formal invitation, to take tea at Rosings, or even to partake of dinner. Indeed, Serena noted that at these times, Anne responded more to Will Spalding's cheerful conversation and mild gallantries, and it was obvious she found pleasure in the conversation of that young man. But her glance strayed frequently to Robert, as Serena noted with some alarm. Miss de Bourgh's behaviour was always perfectly correct, but there was a warmth in her regard which was not lost on her companion, even though Mr Brightwell himself appeared not to notice it. There were occasions however when he seemed discomforted in Anne's presence, and that he maintained his politeness with some effort.

A week or so before Christmas, Mr and Mrs Castleton and the two engineers came to dine at Rosings. Anne had also invited Squire Probert and his lady, with their son and young daughter, she being newly and shyly emerging into polite society.

The dining-room, which had been sombre with dark red hangings in Lady Catherine's time, had been lightened with the straw-coloured drapes which had formerly embellished the morning-room; these had previously been laid aside with lavender sprinkled between the folds. Anne had had them re-made; the dark wood panelling painted in a lighter shade and extra candlesticks, designed by Mr Chippendale with sturdy and elegant pedestals, installed in the corners. The whole room now presented a cheerful appearance, and with the excellent dinner, the evening proceeded along convivial lines.

When the gentlemen joined the ladies in the drawing-room, Serena noted, without appearing to do so, that it was Will Spalding who made his way to Anne. Miss Probert was persuaded to play and sing for the company, which she did prettily but with only a modicum of talent, and Robert Brightwell went to sit near and turn the pages for her. Not once did he so much as glance in Anne's direction, and she gave her attention equally to Will and the squire's son; encouraging the one to tell of his visits around the country in connection with his work and the other to regale them with tales of his prowess in the hunting field and the purchase of two new horses, described enthusiastically as sweet goers.

The party broke up not long after the tea had been brought in and drunk; Mrs Probert being anxious about travelling even the short distance home in the frosty December night. Anne ordered the carriage to take up the Castletons and in the flurry of farewells, with Serena assisting Mrs Castleton with her cloak and Mr Castleton giving Will instructions for the morrow, Anne drew near to Robert and said:

"I hope, Mr Brightwell, that you will be able to join us for some of the Christmas festivities."

Robert responded with but a polite bow.

"Our new parson, Mr Stevens, will be arriving to take his first service with us on the twenty-first of this month, and I hope to welcome him to dinner on that day. Would you, and Mr Spalding of course, be able to join us?"

Robert's expression became frozen.

"I cannot answer for my colleague, Miss de Bourgh. For myself, I thank you for your hospitality, but although I am constrained to work for you, I would rather not be beholden to you, or indeed to receive anything other from your family than can be considered recompense for my work here. In this I hope to give satisfaction. I bid you goodnight, Madam."

With these brusque words he bowed again, not touching her outstretched hand, and strode away.

***
**
*

Book Three
High Life and Low

Chapter One

"Who has not wak'd to list the busy sounds
Of summer's morning in the sultry smoke
Of noisy London? On the pavement hot
The sooty chimney-boy, with dingy face
And tatter'd covering, shrilly bawls his trade,
Rousing the sleepy housemaid. At the door
The milk-pail rattles, and the tinkling bell
Proclaims the dustman 's office, while the street
Is lost in clouds impervious. Now begins
The din of hackney-coaches, wagons, carts,
While tinmen 's shops, and noisy trunk makers
Knife-grinders, coopers, squeaking cork-cutters,
Fruit-barrows, and the hunger-giving cries
Of vegetable vendors fill the air."
London's Summer Morning: Mary Robinson (1800)

"Would you consider it advisable, my dear Serena, for me to take up my Aunt Cecilia's invitation to spend at least a part of the London Season with her?" The two ladies were at breakfast; Anne had just received a number of letters, and was perusing one with an unmistakable London frank. Serena poured herself a cup of coffee.

"Why only a part of the Season? But to answer your question fully: indeed I not only consider it advisable but of the greatest necessity. No young woman of your standing in society should forego the pleasure of at least one London Season."

Anne regarded her former governess with some astonishment, until she perceived that slight quiver of Serena's mouth which betrayed her amusement. Anne in her tum, suppressed her responding smile and said with mock seriousness :

"I am amazed, Miss Pope, that a lady of your education and understanding should be advocating a time spent in giddiness and pleasure!"

"Now did I say that?" protested Serena, openly smiling now. "You asked my advice and I gave it. For I believe you know, that a girl's education must be well rounded, and should, if at all possible, include the experience of such pleasures as alfresco breakfasts, assemblies, balls, routs, theatre parties, and so on that mark the Season. I am in fact delighted that you should be considering such a plunge into London's heady society."

Indeed, Serena was pleased. Christmas had come—and gone, bearing with it the memories of the mummers, the carol singers, the feasting and the ceremony of the Yule Log in Rosings Park's great entrance hall. The Reverend Stevens had delivered his first sermon in Hunsford on St. Thomas' Day and his Christmas sermon on the next Thursday, and, no doubt admirably coached by Charlotte beforehand, followed both with distributions of new sixpences to the women who 'came a-Thomasing' and shillings, beef and beer to those poor who came to the parsonage on St. Stephen's Day. So far at least, his parishioners had been cautiously pleased with him, although as many an old man was heard to say over his ale at the inn:

"It be early days for 'un yet."

The New Year too had been welcomed in with the ringing of the church bells and wassailing in the orchards, and the first day of the year 1801 was observed at Rosings by welcoming all who came to call, and marred only by one of the new housemaids attempting to carry out the ashes. She had to be forcibly restrained from doing so by the other servants, as it was considered most unlucky that any remains of fire should be removed from the House on this day.

There were many older folk in the village who refused to acknowledge the new calendar and continued to observe 'Old Christmas Day'—a fact noted by Mr Stevens, who earned himself further approval by holding a special service on that day, it being a Tuesday. He rather lost commendation however when he also caused a large gilded star to be suspended from the rafters of the church to celebrate and call to their minds the visit of the—Magi some parishioners designating this as 'Popish'. But no-one objected to the distribution by Miss Anne de Bourgh of the traditional Twelfth Cakes, decorated with sugar stars, to the children, and the special spiced ale with cooked sweet apples known as 'Lamb's Wool' to their elders. Indeed throughout the festivities, the Lady of Rosings had carried out her duties with every appearance of enjoyment; only Serena, closely watching her, noted a return to her former pallor, and Sarah observed with distress traces of tears left from those moments when her mistress had thought she was alone.

Now it was Candlemas; all the pieces of the Christmas greenery had been at last removed and were ceremonially burnt, the ashes scattered over the garden beds where the spring bulbs had been planted. Mrs Rowlands breathed her annual sigh of relief; much as she loved the holly and the ivy, the laurel and the mistletoe, her housewifely eye had had to remain vigilant for falling berries, scarlet and white, squashed under the big feet of the footmen, Abel and Charles. She had also needed to keep that eye trained on some of the housemaids, who had been giggly and skittish as they manoeuvred themselves under the mistletoe boughs whenever a manservant hove in sight.

Serena had been out earlier in the day to find the first snowdrops, said by country folk to come into flower on this day in honour of the Virgin Mary. Some years the cold of winter kept the little flowers firmly buttoned up inside their green hoods, and she had thought this year would be no exception, but there had been a few under the shelter of the box hedge on the south side of the garden which had already drooped their white heads. These were now residing in a little glass vase and were opening their petals in the warmth of the breakfast room. She touched one of the flowers now as she turned back to Anne and resumed their earlier conversation.

"A London Season does not have to be completely full of idle pursuits," she said. "Think of the availability of the circulating libraries and the bookshops; Hatchard's of Piccadilly is, I believe, particularly fine. The Tombs in Westminster Abbey apparently just have to be viewed, as do the lions in the Tower, and the Mint where one can watch the stamping of the coins. Then there are the museums: Cox's has many interesting and beautiful artefacts, and I believe that if a party of five or more can be got up, tickets could be obtained for the British Museum. Astley's Amphitheatre is said to be well worth a visit, as are the pictures in Ackermann's Repository of Arts ..."

"Serena, do stop!" cried Anne. "How would we find time for all that? Aunt Cecilia writes that their days are full as it is with breakfasts, picnics, rides in the park and visits to the pleasure gardens, as well as so-called impromptu dances and grand Balls!"

"Well, I suppose, one is allowed to pick and choose what events to attend. But you said 'we', my dear Anne. Do you wish me to accompany you? After all, you will have your aunt and your cousin Kit, not to mention any other members of your family who will no doubt be in Town for the Season."

"If you will not mind it, I should very much like you with me. I cannot imagine my aunt wishing to visit the Tower, or the museums and so forth. But I can imagine you wanting to spend as much time as possible in the libraries and bookshops! Have you in fact done a London Season, Serena?"

"No. My father refused to countenance what he called such hummery-flummery, and I think my mother rather breathed a sigh of relief. She would have launched us into Society had it been considered necessary, but she was glad when father decreed otherwise. Neither Sophie nor I were presented, nor have we felt the lack of opportunity."

"Well then," Anne replied rather mischievously, "If you consider my education needs to be rounded out—as you put it—by the experience of London's pleasures, then does not your own also require the same benefit?"

"A hit, a palpable hit!" acknowledged Serena, and as both women shared their laughter, she silently blessed Lady Cecilia Gould for her renewed invitation to her niece to visit them in London.

It was not to be supposed that they could depart from Kent immediately.

Anne proposed to send a reply to Lady Cecilia, expressing her thanks prettily and suggesting that if all remained convenient, she and Miss Pope might begin their visit just after Easter. As her ladyship had expressed the hope that they might be in London from the beginning of March, when the fashionable world promises to be gay with dissipation, Serena could only wonder what Anne hoped by these extra weeks of delay. It was not that her presence was required at Rosings by reason of the ongoing work of the estate, nor to ensure the establishment of the new parson: Mr Castleton assured her that all was well in hand, and Mr Stevens was establishing himself in his round of duties. He seemed as keen as Mr Collins had been to take charge of the Parsonage garden, and to learn bee-craft from the old master. At dinner at Rosings on the first Sunday of February, he had spoken with some enthusiasm—albeit, with his habitual slight hesitancy and reddening of the ears, of the warmth of the previous few days, thus encouraging the briskness of his bees and the emergence of snowdrops and crocuses in his garden.

"In Derbyshire, Miss de Bourgh, we would not expect to look for these signs of spring for another month at least."

Anne herself did not know what prompted her to wish to remain at Rosings. Having made up her mind that a visit to her aunt and cousin would not only be pleasurable but expedient, she could only hope that to delay her departure might grant her the opportunity of another meeting with Mr Robert Brightwell. Perhaps then she might discover some reason for his strange outburst at their last encounter. She had, indeed, as her maid Sarah had observed, wept at the memory of it; her feelings had been wounded. She remembered Robert as the friend of her girlhood's bright summers, and wondered what had befallen him to bring to his countenance that sad and bitter expression noted by the Castletons. In her memory, he was the laughing 'King of the Daisies'; the boy who had guided her hands on the udders of the family's milch cow; the lad who bundled firewood for his father and dug the herb patch for his beautiful mother; the friend whose brown fingers had whittled a piece of pinewood into the shape of a little bird and presented it to her with a warm smile. But now he was the man who had spurned her hospitality with harsh words, and had turned away from her with a look of- she might almost say - hatred. What had she done, she wondered, to deserve that?

Anne realised she could confide in no one. Not in Serena, nor in Sarah. They may have shared her history and her memories, but to neither of those closest to her could she admit what she could scarcely admit to herself: that the boy Robert had so engraved himself on her heart that she wondered if any other shape could ever erase the outline of him. She had loved her father most dearly, and had lost him; now it seemed as though she had held on to the dream of another love, a childhood love, and had lost that before it could come to any semblance of adult reality.

She had welcomed the busyness of the festive season, and had entered into the round of engagements it brought as a relief from her thoughts. But now it was February, bringing, as Mr Stevens had reminded them, a promise of spring. The lengthening and brightening of the days; the increasing mildness of the air and the hope of Nature's increasing beauty all seemed to mock her lowness of spirits. She resolved to wait upon events no longer, and something of the pride of the de Bourghs reared itself in her. She would face the London world and polite society with her head held high, and find pleasure in dancing, picnics, shops, museums, libraries and all. She re-drafted her letter to her aunt Cecilia, saying she very much hoped to be with them in London at the beginning of March.

*

Lady Cecilia Gould was not normally given to self-congratulation, but she did feel that at this moment *Life was Going Well*. She had offered to launch her niece into Society in a spirit of kind-heartedness, having always deplored her autocratic sister's treatment of the girl. A few prim Assemblies at Westerham indeed, thought Cecilia, and closely chaperoned private parties in Bath—what could the poor child hope for in that? True, she had been a thin, pale, sorry looking chit; Harriet, Lady Claydon, had spoken out with her usual bluntness - fortunately not in Anne's hearing—at her appearance on one such occasion, saying that in spite of the modishness and obvious expense of her gown, the girl had nothing to recommend her. But that had been more than two years ago; the aunts, one on each side of the family, had noted her sudden blossoming and agreed between them that Anne should now be granted the opportunity to '...*have something made of her,*' as Harriet had written to Cecilia.

'*Or, it might be said, that Society should be granted the opportunity of receiving a new and well-looking Lady of Fortune.*'

The only question debated by the sisters-in-law was who should be the one to do it, and it fell to Cecilia's lot, as Harriet explained:

'It would seem that yours is to be the delightful duty, my dear sister, as my daughter Harry is expecting to be confined with her fourth child in late March and I feel I must be on hand to support her. But I shall look to be at London by the beginning of May at the earliest, and hope to have a good account of the presentation. Have you secured vouchers for Almack's? I feel sure you have everything well in hand. Anne will no doubt do you credit; when last I saw her she was in a fair way to be blossoming into beauty. However you need have no fears she will outshine Kit; her dark prettiness will serve as a charming contrast to Anne's auburn colouring. Add to which, I have been - reliably informed that if a certain young baronet can be brought up to scratch, we can expect good news concerning Kit's future status as Lady M—But no more on that head ...'

Lady Cecilia Gould was a little annoyed that Kit's possible success in the marriage stakes was already being talked of in the press—for how else would Harriet, immured in the depths of the country, have got to know of it? She wondered if bets were already being laid at White's she would not be surprised at that, but she could hardly ask Sir Thomas, busy about his parliamentary duties, to take a look in that famous betting book She could only hope that the promising young baronet, quite a matrimonial catch indeed, on whom she had set her sights and Kit her heart, could indeed be brought up to the mark. *"Up to scratch, indeed!"* she thought exasperatedly. Really, the Countess Harriet could be almost vulgar at times!

Such thoughts could not be indulged for long; Cecilia had much to do. She would begin quietly, she decided, with invitations to a private party issued to a select few of her acquaintances. But she must also arrange affairs at St. James' enlist the aid of the patronesses of Almack's—on a day when they were disposed to be charitable, she thought. Neither birth, breeding nor fortune could guarantee vouchers; indeed more than the merest hint of Anne's fortune would not win approval, but if Harriet were to be believed, an account of Anne's beauty and quiet manners might open those exclusive doors. Then she must pass under review all the eligible bachelors known to her, and consider the question of Anne's presentation gown. Not a great deal could be achieved until she was available in person to be assessed and measured, but it would be as well to alert Madame Rose Bertin, former couturier to the poor dead French queen, and who was now residing in London, having fled France when the Troubles began. It was rumoured her escape had been ignominious, but having placed her elegantly-shod foot on English soil, she had set about establishing herself with French arrogance and flair. To do her credit, her grande toilette designs were exquisite; Cecilia sighed over the memory of Kit's presentation gown.

Thus, the Gould family awaited their visitors in anticipation, and Anne, having made her resolve to at least appear to enjoy every moment of her London visit, set out from Rosings Park with the determination that no lingering regret should hinder that resolve.

***
**
*

Chapter Two

"A private ball this was called, so I expected to see four or five couple, but Lord! My dear Sir, I believe I saw half the world! Two very large rooms were full of company; in one were cards for the elderly ladies, in the other were the dancers."
Evelina: Fanny Burney (1778)

The first few days of their stay in London almost made Anne regret her resolve and flee back to the country quiet of Kent. It was not only that she disliked the incessant noise of horses, carts and carriages clattering over the cobbles and the shrill cries of the street vendors, but also that she found the smells: rich, mixed and varied, distinctly unpleasant. Whenever a wind blew from the south, the sulphurous fumes of brown coal and the smells of the manufactories on the Surrey side of the river: the tanning, soap boiling, beer brewing and dyeing works, all came drifting together over the water. At Rosings, the homely Kentish mud, the drift of woodsmoke, the smell of the stables, even the pigsties on Home Farm, she thought were positively pleasant by comparison. Grosvenor Square, where the Gould's Town House was situated, was well-paved and well-lit at night with flambeaux at the entrances to those houses that were occupied, but still the gutters ran with filth of a nature into which Anne did not dare to inquire. The urchins who earned a few pennies by sweeping the crossings were plastered from ankle to knee with greasy black mud, which they appeared to cheerfully ignore. Then too the constant press of people in the streets, the shops and warehouses was disturbing, as was the smoke and dust that seemed to linger in the air. The noise kept the country ladies awake at night, until Serena had the happy thought of plugging their ears with small pieces of cotton cloth. In time, they became as inured to the constant bustle and clatter as any other Londoner.

But nothing could have been warmer than their welcome by the Goulds. Sir Thomas was prepared to be pleased by the addition of two pretty faces to his dinner table; when he found that both his niece and her companion were well informed and well-read, the duty of being pleased became a pleasure indeed. It did not take him long to discover that Serena was a daughter of Mr Edwin Pope, man of science and letters, whose treatises on such diverse matters as: the Importance of Plants in the Production of Dephlogisticated Air; the Pattern of Earthquakes around Europe in Recent Years; the Unlikelihood of there being Life on the Moon, and the Height of the Great Pyramid Mathematically

Calculated by the Ancients, had all been taken up by the Gentleman's Magazine, and even the Ladies' Pocket Book. Sir Thomas had read a number of such works and held the writer in great esteem; it ·followed therefore that Miss Pope might be entitled to have more notice taken of her than his normal courtesy and civility would have allowed. Lady Cecilia Gould was all kindliness and amiability and Kit, feeling herself almost secure in the affections of her baronet, was happy to welcome a cousin who had obtained her inheritance and of whom she stood in some awe.

If Lady Cecilia had thought to launch Anne quietly into Society, she greatly under-estimated the gossip that carried the news of Miss de Bourgh's fortune around the clubs and gaming houses. She also forgot the fact that rumours are as ripples in a pond, such that Anne's wealth increased by the thousand at every repetition. Impoverished peers pricked up their ears on learning that a rich, young, single lady was coming on to the scene, and the mothers of extravagant sons vied with each other to claim hitherto unsuspected friendship with Lady Cecilia. Her ladyship knew to a nicety who were the wellknown rakes and fortune hunters liable to lay siege to Anne, and was prepared to put her niece on her guard, but even so, she was astonished at receiving morning calls and invitations to select parties from the likes of the Countess of Elsburg, whose estates were known to be mortgaged to the hilt; Lady Hamborough, whose husband had, on their wedding eve, lost all her substantial dowry in one night at White's club; Lady Cardington, as avid a gambler as her lord and three sons, and Lady Marston, whose eldest son was one of the Prince of Wales' set, and as extravagant and debt-ridden as his royal friend. The scions of all these noble houses, and more, were -anxious to bestow their titles or positions on Anne in return for unlimited access to her wealth, which they were prepared to squander as liberally as they had squandered their own. No doubt the Prince of Wales himself, in spite of his two wives—the second of whom he had only accepted as a means to free himself of his financial embarrassments - would have invited Miss de Bourgh to become his third wife, if he thought he could get away with it. Parliament may have towed him out of the River Tick, as the saying went, as soon as he unwillingly thrust his ring on to Princess Caroline's stubby finger, but here he was, scarce five years later, separated from his wife and floundering as deep in the murky waters as ever. A rich young wife would answer a good number of his problems, if rumour was to be believed, especially if she be a good Protestant.

It would not have mattered, as the Honourable Will Spalding had surmised, if Anne had been squat and fubsy-faced, but when she put in her first appearance at Almack's Assembly Rooms in a gown of cerulean blue gauze over an underskirt of ivory silk, with her only ornaments a delicate necklace and bracelet of sapphires and pearls, her looks drew the admiration of every man present. Those who had aspirations to write poetry rushed away to find rhymes for 'eyes of sapphire blue' and 'cheeks of pale roses and cream' and sought to lay these offerings at her feet. She also attracted the envy of a number of other debutantes, who lost no time in whispering to each other that although she might be considered well enough, her rich auburn hair was decidedly out of the fashionable mode and she was too slender and pale to be thought a real beauty. Anne was aware of both the admiration and the envy and noted both with inner amusement, but she preserved an outward appearance of quiet calm, which earned the approval of Almack's patronesses, who allowed her to be pretty behaved.

To many of the Ton, used as they were to the best of entertainments, Almack's was considered 'devilish flat'. The strict rules of decorum, the indifferent food and the insipidity of the minuets and country dances which were all that were allowed, led many a young blade, having put in a dutiful appearance and handed his voucher to the great Mr Willis, to seek livelier pleasures elsewhere. But it was the place to see and be seen, and to Anne, brought up in country seclusion, it was delightful enough. Her hand was sought for every dance; compliments were showered on her, and a number of young gallants strove with each other to take her in to supper. She chose however, to disappoint them all by electing to go down on the arm of her uncle Sir Thomas Gould. This piece of diplomacy was applauded by Lady Castlereagh, who remarked to Lady Cecilia that if there wasn't a duel fought over the fair young Lady of Rosings before the Season was out, she would be very much surprised. Cecilia was shocked and said she hoped it would be no such thing, but Lady Castlereagh only laughed, patted her on the shoulder and said in her gruff voice:

"I compliment you, Ceccy. In giving us your niece you have provided us with more than enough food for gossip and entertainment!"

Lady Cecilia could find nothing to say in answer to this, and spent the rest of the evening in thoughtful mood.

The first few weeks of their stay in London were not wholly taken up with the social round of balls, assemblies, and visits to the theatre. It did not take more than a few days for Serena to discover the joys of Hatchard's book-shop and Hookham's circulating library, and she came home from both with armfuls of books, including: Maria Edgeworth's recently published *Castle Rackrent*, poems by Mr Robert Southey and Mr William Blake and a new edition of the works of Mr William Cowper, whose death the previous year the English literary scene had duly mourned. So, while Anne felt herself compelled to be arrayed in yet another gown of twilled French silk for yet another party, Serena had the joy of curling up before a generous fire in the book-room and reading to her heart's content. She professed not to envy Anne's excursions into the pleasures of the Season, although she found herself being teased over her failure to take advantage of the opportunity to "round out" her education.

"Indeed, you need not envy me, Serena," said Anne one afternoon, when they were sitting together in the small drawing-room, "For I must confess that to be forever meeting the same faces at all the different parties, to receive the same compliments and listen to the same empty talk and gossip is beginning to pall. Aunt Cecilia assures me that London is still thin of company and that by May we shall have so many invitations we shall not know which way to tum. I can scarce bear the thought of it."

"Do you dislike it so much?"

"No indeed, I would be an ungrateful wretch if I admitted to disliking it at all! It has been a new and exciting experience to be courted and feted and have the polite world at my feet, as Aunt says. I think even she is a little surprised, but I cannot help thinking that were it known I was possessed of but a modest competence, the attention now being paid to me would be equally modest. Perhaps, I should do as Elizabeth once suggested, and give it out that I have lost all my fortune on Change."

"Do you not feel that any of your suitors place a higher value on Anne de Bourgh than on Anne de Bourgh's wealth and possessions?"

"How can I tell? Is it likely that any one of them would admit to being a fortune hunter? Oh, with the exception of Lord Hamborough. He had the honesty to tell me to my face that I would be glad to know he found me 'easy on the eye' although it would not make a ha'porth of difference to the suit he intended to make. Oh yes, and he said he thought I looked to be an amenable sort of woman who would not object to him taking his pleasures as he always had."

"Well upon my word!" exclaimed Serena, "Was that the nature of his proposal to you? What did he think he was offering you in exchange for your hand and your fortune but an absent, careless husband? I consider that a shocking want of manners!"

"Wasn't it? But I found it diverting, which was more than can be said for some of the other proposals I have received."

"Other proposals? My dear Anne, how many have there been?"

"Four—no—five I think. Young Mr Elston stammered so much I could not be sure if he ever managed to get the words out. Viscount Marston read me a poem of his own devising in which he said we were twin souls and should never be apart. Who else was there? Oh yes, the Honourable Mr Emborough, but he used so many flowery phrases and classical allusions that I quite lost the thread- of his discourse and upset him very much by asking -him to repeat it. Lord Atterbury at least very correctly asked if he might approach my uncle to be allowed to pay his addresses to me. Which was strange when you think he has the worst reputation of all. He is not known as Rake Atterbury for nothing, you know."

"I think," said Serena, "that I am quite shocked! We have been here scarce a month!"

"I know. And between shopping expeditions and dress fittings, I have seen little of London but Bond Street and the Royal Opera Arcade. I was so looking forward to those visits you promised —to the Abbey, the Tower and the British Museum!"

"We will begin tomorrow," declared Serena.

True to her word, Serena armed herself with the latest edition of the 'Guide to the Curiosities, Amusements, Exhibitions, etc. etc. in and around London' and with the weather overcast but dry, the two ladies set out in the Goulds' town carriage. Lady Cecilia threw up her hands and said they would be considered a couple of bluestockings if they were not careful:

"And if this becomes known, Anne, I declare I shall wash my hands of you!" said her ladyship.

But Anne only laughed and told her aunt not to worry her head about it.

They first visited Westminster Abbey and both agreed that what with the parties of people and the guides loudly proclaiming what should be seen, the atmosphere was not at all that of a church, while the effigies in Henry the Seventh's chapel were positively ghoulish.

"They charge sixpence to view, each head," marvelled Anne, "Which I consider monstrously unfair as Henry the Fifth did not even have his head! According to the guide it had been removed to be cleaned and was then lost!"

A drive out to the City of London followed. The clouds were beginning to break under the influence of a chilly wind and Anne was distressed to see that the further East they went, the more there seemed to be of small children, barefoot and poorly clad, huddling in doorways to be out of the wind, but racing out to beg for alms whenever a smart carriage clattered by. Anne flung a generous handful of coins out of the window and watched in some dismay as they scrabbled and fought, kicked and cursed for them in the mud.

"What can be done for such poor creatures? Are there no charity schools available for them?"

"Indeed there are," replied Serena, "And for both boys and girls. I know of a school in Blackfriars for boys; two in Covent Garden which girls can also attend, and several in Southwark, run by a friend of my mother's: Mistress Dorothy Applebee, who offers free schooling in English and mathematics. These are to name but a few."

"It does not seem to be enough," said Anne thoughtfully.

"The children cannot be compelled to attend school, and many poor parents prefer their children to earn their keep by begging on the streets. Don't distress yourself, my dear Anne. Plenty is being done for these unfortunates, although I would agree plenty more needs to be done. But think of the work of the Foundling Hospital, the Sunday Schools, the Apprentices' Schools! The tip of the iceberg it may be, but at least there are philanthropists willing and able to do more."

"And plenty more of the Upper Ten Thousand who neither know nor care," Anne thought to herself.

They arrived at the Tower and crossed the moat, which was now little more than a muddy ditch, joining a number of other visitors to this most famous of London's monuments. Here were plenty of sights to be seen: Traitor's Gate, the Bloody Tower and the famous green where once stood the scaffold on which so many notable figures of history lost their heads. They went to view the Crown

149

Jewels although Serena said she was prepared to be disappointed: she had read that, according to Mr William Thornton, these were displayed individually through a small, dark, grated window with but a glimmer of candlelight to show the glories of the jewels. This was exactly what they found and were indeed disappointed, but at least, Serena commented, she could write to her mother that she had viewed for herself the emblems of the monarchy.

They could not possibly omit from their visit the famous Royal Menagerie. It now cost one shilling each to enter the yard of the Lion Tower, where a number of animals were confined in cages. Anne privately thought she had never seen such sad-looking creatures: several tigers, leopards, a black panther, a shaggy grey wolf and a number of lions whose manes had become thin and tangled. These all regarded the curious folk who came to view them with their tawny eyes full of a supreme indifference, and their smell reminded country-bred Anne of a dozen tom-cats. Other cages contained a hyena and several racoons. The keeper, with an air of having saved the best of his show to the last, then led them to view an ostrich.

"This is the second of these we 'ave 'ad 'ere," he announced proudly. "There was one a few years back, but the pore bird died, 'cos those 'as should 'ave known better would keep feedin' it wiv bits of metal, jus' fer the joy of seein' it swaller, an' the lumps go down its long neck!"

Serena was fascinated by this creature and asked more questions of the keeper than he could fairly answer. Fortunately she was overheard by a gentleman, whose complexion indicated some time spent in warmer climes than England's. He was dressed neatly, but in a manner that betokened practicality and comfort rather than the fashions aped by the Dandies, the Corinthians and the Pinks of the Ton.

"If you will permit me, Ma'am," he addressed Serena deferentially, "I could not help but hear that you wished for information on this creature's habits. My name is Thomas Vauney, and I have travelled much in Africa - which is the home of these strange and wonderful birds. Perhaps you would allow me to be your informant?"

"Tha's right, Ma'am," broke in the keeper, "Mr Vauney 'ere 'elped bring this bird to us, and knows more'n anyone all abaht it. You couldn' do better'n to ask 'im, Ma'am."

Nothing loath, Mr Vauney expounded on the habits of the ostrich: how it could not fly, being too large and heavy in the body, but that it could run faster than a hunting leopard. This was a female bird, he informed them, but the male of the species may stand seven or eight feet tall.

"In the wilds of Africa, several birds may live together, and do so in harmony, seeming to have a liking for each others' company. I have a friend who has a farm where he keeps a flock of ostriches. Their eggs are good to eat, and the shells, being firm but malleable, are used by the natives to carry water. Then of course, the feathers make wonderful adornments for ladies' bonnets, although formerly it was the African men who wore them for ceremonial occasions."

He smiled at the ladies' surprise.

"Does the bird object to having its feathers taken?" asked Anne.

"Well, the poor creatures used to be hunted and killed for them, but it has recently been discovered that they will give up their plumage readily, and without hurt, and grow more in consequence. If you will permit me …?" and to the ladies' wonder, he calmly opened the door of the cage and stepped inside. The ostrich seemed to have no fear of him; indeed she seemed to welcome his intrusion by nibbling at his coat collar. Mr Vauney reached his hand gently into the wing feathers and delicately detached two beautiful pale plumes, which he presented to Serena and Anne.

"With the compliments of the ostrich, Ma'am."

They thanked him, and the bird, with very real pleasure and the creature stretched out her neck toward them.

"They are of a curious nature," said Mr Vauney, coming out of the cage and quietly closing the door. "You saw how this lady made an attempt to eat my coat? They normally eat only vegetable matter, but often will nibble at anything as though to see how it tastes, as did the poor bird who swallowed nails and coins, and thus brought about its own death."

The afternoon light was beginning to fade, and the gentleman asked if he could accompany the ladies to their home. Anne hastened to reassure him.

"We have a carriage, sir. Perhaps we may take you up and convey you to wherever you wish to go?"

But Mr Vauney declined this offer, with regret it seemed to Anne, as he declared he lived but a short distance from the Tower. As they began to walk away, Serena glanced back toward the ostrich, which she fancied, was regarding their departure disconsolately. She said as much and Mr Vauney laughed.

"Indeed you are right, Ma'am. I think the bird is a little lonely, but I am negotiating with my friend to bring over from Africa a companion for her. Possibly even a husband."

"I am sure she would be delighted at the prospect," said Serena gravely, and Mr Vauney laughed again.

"Indeed I hope she may. The male ostrich makes a very good husband, and takes his duties of looking after the eggs and the babies very seriously!"

He accompanied them to the carriage, and as he handed first Anne, then Serena up into it, he asked a little diffidently:

"Do you by any chance visit the Royal Institution, Ma'am, to hear the lectures? There is a young Cornishman, a Mr Humphrey Davy who has just been appointed lecturer in chemistry. He is a colleague of mine and is giving a series of lectures on the nature and uses of electricity. He is very entertaining, and I understand a number of ladies enjoy his talks."

"I have heard of him," said Serena, "and I would very much like to attend." She glanced at Anne. "Would you like it, my dear?"

"Why not?" Anne returned, smiling. "Will we have the pleasure of seeing you there, Mr Vauney?"

"I very much hope so," and Mr Vauney stepped away from the carriage, bowed gracefully and strode away with a spring in his step.

The carriage pulled away and headed back towards the West End. Serena was wrapped in her thoughts and it was left to Anne to maintain any conversation.

"Ostrich feathers!" she marvelled, drawing the plume through her fmgers. "Do you know, Serena, these cost two pounds a-piece in Grafton House Emporium; more if they are dyed and worked up by a plummassier into a hat trimming. The head-dress for my presentation, which I admit also had an edging of seed-pearls, cost nearly twenty-five pounds. And here we have a beautiful feather each, free, courtesy of a live bird! Oh and a charming gentleman of course. What do you think his work may be? Obviously something to do with natural history, and it is obvious from his complexion that he has travelled much. Indeed did he not say so? Serena? My dear, are you even listening?"

Serena gave a little start.

"Mm? Of course. Two pounds a head-dress you said? Yes, it was quite an interesting experience." Anne laughed.

"Oh Serena, I do declare you were not listening at all! I can only hope that you pay more attention to Mr Humphrey Davy's lectures on electricity at the Royal Institution!"

***
**
*

Chapter Three

"Some things I have not yet thought fit so plainly to reveal, not out of any envious design of having them buried with me, but that I may barter with those secretists, that will not part with one secret but in exchange for another"
Boyle: quoted in Dr Johnson's Dictionary (1755)

Sarah, Miss Anne's maid, had not expected to enjoy London. She had heard too many tales of haughty housekeepers, elegant ladies' maids, toplofty London butlers and ogling footmen who considered personable servant girls their legitimate prey. She had been warned by Mrs Rowlings that London was full of men of all stations in society who had nothing better to do than to have designs on a respectable girl's virtue. At Rosings, Sarah's place in the servants' hall was established and respected; she had grown up in Miss de Bourgh's service, having been taught her craft by her mother, who herself had been a lady's maid. At the age of ten, Sarah had been presented to Lady Catherine as a suitable candidate for the post of maid to her daughter, and although considerably frightened of such a formidable personage, was able to prove she knew what was expected of her. But from the first moment when the seven-year old Anne had stretched out her hand to her timid new maid and said:

"They tell me your name is Smallbone, and I am supposed to call you by that name. But I have never heard anyone called so, so if you please, I will call you Sarah. For that is your Christian name, is it not?"

And Sarah, who had been intimidated by her interview with Lady Catherine, had become Anne's devoted servant, forthwith.

Here in London, Sarah had expected to find herself snubbed or ignored, and indeed, Lady Cecilia's high and mighty dresser had been scarcely civil, while the Gould's French chef had startled her out of her wits with the oaths and curses he rained on his unfortunate underlings. She had also been quite astonished by her first sight of Lady Cecilia's little black page: darker than a climbing boy, but dressed all in silks and satins, she had thought to herself. She had stared so hard at him, that behind her ladyship's back he had poked out a little pink tongue at her. It was becoming unfashionable to have a black page, what with the slavery question being hotly debated in coffee houses and indeed in Parliament, but Lady Cecilia was fond of young Martin and determined to keep him and educate him at all costs.

If Sarah thought all the upper servants in the Gould household would act in a superior manner, she found herself surprised and comforted by Morley, Sir

Thomas' butler. He was an even more dignified personage than Roberts and twice as portly, but had been in his unbending way quite avuncular and had kindly welcomed her to the servants' hall. Then too, Miss Kit's maid, Susan, with whom Sarah shared an attic room, was all friendliness, and eager to show off the sights of London Town and to exhibit her superior knowledge to the little country mouse. The two girls sometimes found they had an afternoon or evening off together, and Susan managed to prevail upon two of the good-looking footmen to accompany them to Astley's Amphitheatre or Bartholomew Fair, or to the freak shows and exhibits of monsters. During these enjoyable excursions, Sarah thought but fleetingly of Abel, the under-footman at Rosings, but she salved her conscience with the thought that she had failed to reach an understanding with him before she left Kent, and that he was probably enjoying the company of the village girls in her absence.

Between ensuring that Miss Anne was always perfectly turned out - which seemed to involve a great deal more washing due to the fact that the coal fires used throughout the house begrimed everything with a sooty dust - and taking advantage of the leaves of absence granted by her mistress' numerous excursions to parties and dances, Sarah did not forget that she had been given a commission. Before she left Kent, Roberts had called her into the butler's pantry and given her a letter -

"... to be delivered in person, if at all possible, to Mr Fortescue, Sir Lewis de Bourgh's former valet, who since he left us, has, I believe, set up a modest tailoring business in the Strand. This is to bring him greetings from all of us who remember him, and to give him news of Rosings Park. Delivery by your hand, Sarah, will save him the expense of the post."

So on one of her early trips abroad, and with the help of Susan, she had sought out 'Fortescue's Warehouse' in the Strand, which, far from being a modest tailoring business, was a flourishing establishment selling not only cloth and suitings for gentlemen's coats - made on the premises -but also bolts of fine cotton, linen, plain and figured muslins and various silks for ladies' dresses. Mr Fortescue had profited handsomely from his employment as Sir Lewis' valet; even though in his later years there had been little to be had in the way of vails, nonetheless his retirement from service after the death of his master enabled him to set up for himself and to do very well indeed. He may not have been able to offer to the Ton the kind of service provided by such high-class tailors as Schmidt or Weston, but there were plenty of well-to-do businessmen and upper servants who relied on him for a certain elegance of cut as well as comfort in their coats.

When Sarah first entered his shop, she was a little overwhelmed by the grandeur of the surroundings and the obsequious manners of the young man who came forward to offer his services, but when she explained her errand and proffered Mr Robert's letter, Mr Fortescue came himself from the back premises and welcomed her with friendliness. He introduced her to his wife, herself a dressmaker of no mean repute, he explained, and prevailed upon her to drink a dish of tea with them while he asked for news of all at Rosings. He exclaimed over the manner of Lady Catherine's death; he had of course read the notice of it in the Morning Post, but there, little detail had been given. He was pleased to hear that Miss Anne de Bourgh was at present in the Metropolis, and staying with her aunt and uncle, Sir Thomas and Lady Cecilia Gould. He asked that his respectful remembrances be conveyed to her.

"But there is another member of the de Bourgh family known to me here in London, to whom it may be of interest to know of Miss Anne's residence here. That is, if he does not know of it already, in the way of such things being known."

Sarah looked at him in no little surprise, but he said:

"I will not say anything further. It may be that Miss Anne would not want to know of him, or he of her. But when next I visit him, as I am likely to do in the next few days, I will see whether he wishes to renew acquaintance with his—er—with Miss de Bourgh."

Well! Here was a mystery indeed! But to all Sarah's questions, Mr Fortescue would return no satisfactory answer and he adjured her to say nothing as yet to her mistress. However, he did ask if she thought he might wait upon Miss de Bourgh at the Gould's house within a few days, and Sarah having said she was sure Miss Anne would be glad to welcome her father's former valet, they parted on amicable terms.

In the event, it was several weeks before Mr Fortescue was able to follow up his request in person; thus it was the afternoon following the visit to the Tower that Anne was informed that a previous acquaintance wished to see her.

Mr Fortescue had very correctly called at the tradesmen's entrance, and explained his position to one of the under-footmen, who took his message and his trade-card to the butler, Morley. His name being well-known to all upper servants in noble houses who aspired, indeed were required to dress well, he was welcomed into the butler's pantry and offered refreshment in the form of a venerable port, over which he conveyed the delicate nature of his errand.

Morley prided himself on his knowledge of the Sir Thomas' extensive family; he could recite the Gould antecedents going back five generations. He knew the names of Sir Thomas' three brothers and five sisters; their wives' and husbands' names and positions in society as well as the names of their various offspring. He was also well acquainted with Lady Cecilia's family, including of course her in-laws, the de Bourghs. But Mr Fortescue's information caused him no little astonishment.

"I confess I am completely surprised, Mr Fortescue. I had no knowledge of this, no knowledge at all. It is also quite possible that Sir Thomas and Lady Cecilia are also in ignorance of the matter. Do you think Miss de Bourgh knows of it?"

"Of that I am not at all certain, Mr Morley. But I think she does not. You can understand that I was unsure whether to bring it to her attention, but was specifically asked if I might do so. It is a matter of some delicacy, you understand."

"Quite, quite. Another glass of port, Mr Fortescue?"

This, having been accepted, and two generous glasses poured, because of course Morley would not be so ill-mannered as to allow his guest to drink alone, they sat in silence for a short while. Eventually Mr Fortescue asked:

"What is your opinion of Miss de Bourgh, Mr Morley? She has been under your roof some little time now, I believe?"

"Nearly four weeks, yes. She seems a pleasant, quiet young lady enough, very well-looking and neat but elegant in her dress. She is not at all inclined to puff off her consequence. I gather—he gave a deprecating little cough— that she was kept in some seclusion at Rosings Park?"

"As to that, I could not say. I left Rosings when my services as Sir Lewis' valet were no longer required. I remember Miss Anne as a rosy, lively child, but I gather that after her father's death she suffered indifferent health."

"You have been in correspondence with the staff at Rosings?"

"With Mr Roberts the butler, yes. He very kindly put me in the way of acquiring my present occupation through a cousin of his."

"How did you come to an acquaintance with - er - him of whom we have been speaking?"

"Ah!" and Mr Fortescue drew his chair a little closer and disclosed the matter in a low voice. Mr Morley shook his head several times during this narrative and gave it as his opinion that Miss de Bourgh, as Mistress of Rosings, should be apprised of the situation -

"… but of course in as delicate a manner as possible Mr Fortescue."

"He has written her a letter," said Mr Fortescue, diffidently, "But I think I should tell her at least some of what I have just told you before I pass it on. Do not you think so, Mr Morley?"

"Assuredly, Mr Fortescue. If you will wait but one moment and finish your glass of port in your own time, I will inform Miss Anne de Bourgh that you are here and desirous of seeing her."

So saying, Morley rose with his usual dignity and bowed his portly frame out of the door.

*

Serena Pope had gone on an errand to Hookham's library; Lady Cecilia and Miss Kit were occupied with Madame Bertin's assistant dressmaker, who was carrying out a fitting for Kit's new ball dress. Her baronet had finally 'come up to scratch', to everyone's satisfaction, so that preparations were in hand for a grand ball to be held in Gould House to celebrate her betrothal. Anne knew she would have to order her own ball-gown soon, but at the moment, the bride-to-be was engaging everyone's attention. So Anne was glad of a few hours peace and quiet reading by herself in the book-room. Here she was found by Morley, bearing Mr Fortescue's card, who delivered the message that the gentleman in question was waiting to see her. Morley then indicated that there was a perfectly adequate fire in the morning-room, should she wish to receive her visitor there. He had strict notions as to the proprieties, and in his opinion, the book-room was a male preserve. Ladies should always receive callers in the morning-room; occupy one of the two sitting-rooms in the afternoon, and retire to the drawingroom after dinner. He also privately thought that Miss de Bourgh spent more time reading than was seemly for a young lady of fashion, as did Miss Pope, although he excused the latter on the grounds of her having been a governess.

Anne was aware of these unexpressed sentiments—Morley being perfectly able to make plain his opinions without the use of words—and she meekly agreed to remove to the morning-room, where presently Mr Fortescue was ushered in. She greeted him with pleasure; the sight of him bringing back in a rush memories of her father, and for a while they shared remembrances of those former and happier times. Anne was interested to hear of the success of his business, and asked if she might be made known to his wife—a request to which Mr Fortescue replied in a manner strongly reminiscent of Mr Collins.

But he was not to be deflected by "Miss Anne's condescension" to forget the main purpose of his visit. He introduced the topic by asking her for news of her aunt, Lady Claydon, and the de Bourgh uncles. A little surprised, Anne gave him what news she could: that Lady Claydon's daughter had just produced her fourth child, another little boy; her uncle John, Dean of Belmingham Cathedral was, as far as she knew, perfectly well; while her uncle William was at present supervising the building of a new frigate at Buckler's Hard, which, under his captaincy, was to join Admiral's Nelson's fleet in the Mediterranean.

"Do you never hear of your third uncle, Miss Anne? The Honourable Percy de Bourgh?"

"I have but the faintest memory of him. Indeed, until you mentioned his name, I had all but forgotten his very existence!"

"At that I am not at all surprised. You were very young indeed when …well, when you would last have seen him. You cannot recall his features at all?"

Anne shook her head.

"There were but two pictures of him at Rosings Park. One was in a portrait of all four de Bourgh brothers, painted by Mr Thomas Lawrence, and the other an individual picture of Mr Percy by a Mr Opie, I think. Mr Percy would have been about eighteen years of age at that time. The picture of all the brothers Sir Lewis kept in his private sitting-room, but the other was removed to the attics and the portrait of yourself, Miss Anne, as a baby in your mother's arms, painted by Miss Angelika Kaufmann was hung in its place."

"I cannot recall any picture of my four uncles anywhere in the house." Anne was puzzled.

"Well, maybe that too was removed by her ladyship. I know it was there when I sorted and cleared Sir Lewis' things—er—before I left Rosings."

"But, Mr Fortescue, why are you asking me about my uncle Percy? What do you know of him?"

"I know only what he himself has told me, Miss Anne. But he is here in London, and he knows you are here and staying with Sir Thomas and Lady Cecilia."

A number of questions came crowding into Anne's mind.

"How does he know I am here? How long has he known? And why has he not called? I cannot recollect that any card with the de Bourgh name had been left when we were out. Neither have I met anyone bearing the least resemblance to what I dimly remember of him at any social gathering."

Mr Fortescue was silent for a moment.

"Indeed you would not have met with him anywhere, Miss Anne. He is - you might say - a social recluse. And he has known of your stay here since the news of your presentation at St James' was published in both the Morning Post and the London Gazette. But as he does not go into society, he would not presume to call on Lady Cecilia Gould."

"But you know of his whereabouts, Mr Fortescue?"

"I do, yes, Miss Anne. Although due to unfortunate circumstances ..."

"What circumstances?" demanded Anne.

"That I am afraid I cannot tell you without his permission, Ma'am. But they caused his removal from the family, although Sir Lewis took care to keep himself informed of Mr Percy's—er—doings. I was occasionally commissioned to carry out certain orders with reference to Mr Percy."

"Do you mean rescuing Uncle Percy from financial embarrassment?" Anne asked bluntly.

"Among other things, yes." Mr Fortescue bowed in acknowledgement of Anne's forthrightness. "Then there were duties laid upon me under the terms of Sir Lewis' will. I hope I may say I have carried out everything as my late master would have wished."

Anne smiled at the former valet.

"My father trusted you implicitly, Mr Fortescue," she said, "and so will I. What would you have me do in respect of my uncle?"

Mr Fortescue was relieved at Anne's acceptance of the story, although whether she would be so compliant when or indeed if she knew the whole, he could not bring himself to think.

"I have a letter for you, Miss Anne, which I was requested to put into your hand after you had been informed that Mr Percy was alive, though not particularly well. He does not ask that you should meet with him however, merely that you will accept this note from his hand. With your permission, I will leave it here for you ..." and Mr Fortescue withdrew from his pocket a sealed note and laid it on the table.

"Should you wish to send a reply," he continued, "Please, would you do so through me? Your maid Sarah knows where to find me."

"Yes, she told me of her visit to you. Thank you for coming to see me, Mr Fortescue, and I would very much like to visit you and your wife—perhaps in the next few days?"

The gentleman expressed his proper gratitude and bowed himself out, leaving Anne with a sealed letter, a head full of whirling thoughts and a heart full of conflicting emotions.

***
**
*

Chapter Four

"(London) 'tis a sad place. I would not live in it on any account. One has not time to do one's duty either to God or man."
Letter to Jane: Mrs Austen (1770)

Left alone in the morning-room, Anne took up the letter and examined the seal carefully. The wax had obviously been impressed with a signet ring and the design of the seal was similar to the one she herself used, which had been passed to her after her mother's death. It was quartered: the upper half bore the crest of the de Bourghs, but carried in the bottom left quarter a tiny martlet - the insignia of a younger son. The right quarter remained blank. Her own design carried a tiny rose in this section; Uncle John's seal bore a key; Uncle William's a pennant. Thus the brothers signalled their professions. So, why was the final quarter of Uncle Percy's seal empty? Had he no work, no profession? It should have borne a soldier's mark: a horseshoe for a cavalry regiment; a lance or two three bullet points. Anne shook her head over this puzzle and then resolving to lift the seal off whole, sought her bed-chamber to find the little silver knife she kept on the dressing table.

The letter, when she unfolded it, was quite short: a single sheet, uncrossed and penned in a flowing hand. The paper was of cheap quality, as was the ink to judge by the frequent changes in depth and tone. There was no direction and no date, and was as follows:

My Honourable Niece, Should this letter make its way into your hands, and should you have the goodness to be reading it, I would not have you alarmed at the prospect of what it might contain. Here you will find no request for alms, favours or indeed anything that may distress you. Nor do I make any request that you should visit me, or indeed seek to know where I may be residing in this great Metropolis. Neither yet should you fear that I will attempt to see you, on any of your excursions, your rides in the Park, or at any social gathering. It would be quite impossible for me to do so, dear Niece, for reasons I do not choose to divulge.

I cannot hope that you might remember me; you were a tiny child of little more than two years old when I last visited Rosings Park, and since that time my relationship with your father, and more particularly your mother, was severed. If you have ever heard me spoken of, it will probably have been as the

Black Sheep of the family. I do not propose to explain the reasons for my banishment from Rosings, nor do I seek to justify myself or my actions.

So what might be supposed would be my reasons for writing to you? These are but three: that whatever bad you may have heard of me, my life could have been both worse - and better; that even black sheep may turn grey with age and wisdom, and most importantly, that I wish you well in all you may do.

I remain, Madam,
Your obedient servant, Mr Peter de La Bole,
The Honourable Percival Trethallan de Bourgh.'

Anne read this through several times and found her surprise increasing rather than diminishing with each perusal. Why did he give no direction to his letter? Was he impoverished, and therefore ashamed to disclose that he lived in one of the poorer parts of the Town? But Mr Fortescue had intimated that he had been requested by Sir Lewis to relieve any such anxieties. Besides, the letter clearly stated that he was asking for nothing. Then, there was the mention of his banishment from Rosings, and the severing of his relationship, particularly with Lady Catherine. Well, whatever had been the nature of the 'bad' he had done, Anne reflected, her mother would have had no hesitation in condemning it. And he had never been spoken of - either as a black sheep, or anything else! Anne was amused by the notion of him as a sheep, turning grey with age and wisdom, but then was immediately sobered by the re-reading of the two signatures. In what way was he both Percival de Bourgh and Peter de la Bole? That name seemed vaguely familiar, but Anne could not recall where or in what connection she might have heard it.

A glance at her timepiece showed it would soon be time to dress for dinner, and she thrust the letter to the back of a drawer and rang the bell for Sarah. She resolved upon three things: she would write a reply; prevail upon Sarah to accompany her to Fortescue's Warehouse, and try to persuade that gentleman to furnish her with Uncle Percy's abode in London.

The evening was one of the rare occasions when the family dined alone at home. Anne was quiet during dinner a fact which escaped everyone except Serena Pope. Sir Thomas was full of the important news of Mr William Pitt's resignation as Prime Minister, and speculation as to who might be his successor. Mr Henry Addington was a strong contender:

"Whether he will do any better over the Irish Question remains to be seen. Mr Pitt may have carried the House with him over British and Irish Union had he not also insisted on the Catholic Rights. He must have known that many in both parties would be opposed to such a measure, as would the King himself."

Lady Cecilia agreed and soothed as she always did, understanding nothing of the political situation, and Kit was lost in a happy dream of ball-gowns and bride clothes. It was left to Serena to ask Sir Thomas what he understood to be the evils of Catholic emancipation in Ireland, and he stared at her in some surprise.

"You cannot fail to remember, Ma'am, the problems in Scotland, which led to the Gordon riots?"

"It was more than twenty years ago, sir. I was but two years into my first post in the depths of Devon County. News did not travel so far nor so fast in those days."

"Hmph. Well it was the day of your birth, Niece," continued Sir Thomas, nodding toward Anne. "Lord George Gordon presented a petition to repeal the Roman Catholic Relief Bill and marched to Parliament with a large unruly crowd made up of the more brutal and lawless elements of society."

"Poor things," murmured Anne, remembering the gypsies she had once befriended as a child, "are they not lawless because they are starving?"

"And why are they starving, Miss?" demanded her uncle. "Surely it is because they are lazy and feckless."

Anne forbore to quote Mr John Wesley, who had found in his visits to the very poorest of the poor that indeed the reverse was the case. Sir Thomas would not have accepted this, and was indeed anxious to continue with his peroration, rather as he would were he in the very House of Commons.

"The petition was thus presented, but a decision was postponed for five days. During that time violence and rioting took place and five of the miscreants were committed to prison. A further postponement of decision caused more rioting. The prisons—Newgate, the Clink, the King's Bench— were attacked and a number of prisoners set free to add to the noise and confusion. The houses and businesses of those known to be Catholic, or sympathetic to the Catholic cause were set on fire. But finally after a few days when much damage had been done, the troops were sent in and Lord George Gordon was committed to the Tower. And here is Mr Pitt proposing a Catholic Rights Bill for Ireland! Ireland! The land remember, which was the refuge of the Old Pretender! Any whiff of acceding to Popery and there may well be a resurgence of the Stuart uprisings. That, Ma'am, cannot be countenanced. Besides, the Protestant landowners in Ireland need to guard their political power in the interests of the English constitution and monarchy."

Serena was fully prepared to argue this point, but that Lady Cecilia in some haste gave the signal for the ladies to withdraw.

Over coffee, Kit and her mother discussed the relative merits of spangled gauze or Italian crepe for the overdress of the new ball-gown and whether it should have pearls or tiny diamonds for the centre of the deep pink roses which were to embellish the hem, the front and the bodice.

"Diamonds with spangles would be too much," Lady Cecilia was heard to declare, "but the pearls with crepe would be unexceptional."

Serena brought Anne a cup of coffee.

"Why so quiet my dear? Are you considering Sir Thomas' remarks over the Irish question?"

"No, I am afraid not. My mind was otherwhere. I have been presented with an interesting problem, Serena, and would be grateful for your opinion. I cannot explain now, but if you would come to my room before you retire, I will lay it before you. Meanwhile, tell me what you have discovered about the lectures at the Royal Institution. You went to discover more about them, I believe?"

Nothing loath, Serena reported on the dates and times of the lectures she had indeed discovered on a handbill at Hookham's, together with the interesting fact that a certain Mr Vauney was billed to give a talk on the wild life of Southern Africa at a not too distant date, and that she sincerely hoped Anne would be able to accompany her for that event.

Later that evening, Serena came as requested to Anne's room. She told her of the visit she had received during the afternoon; laid her uncle's letter before her, and watched her read it with the same look of perplexity she herself must have shown. Anne asked what, if anything, Serena knew.

"I am afraid I know nothing of the Honourable Percy, Anne. Indeed I did not even know your father had a third brother. How old would he be?"

"I am not at all sure. I have not looked at the family records for a very long time.

I remember my mother showing me where they were kept in the Muniments Room, and telling me I must be sure and record the names of all who came after me, including the offspring of my Aunt Harriet and my Uncles John and William. Neither of whom, in fact, are married. Which reminds me I must remember to add the name and date of birth of Cousin Harry's latest son. But I have no recollection of ever seeing Uncle Percy's certificate of baptism. Or any note of his birth." She took the letter from Serena's fingers. "Who do you think is this Peter de la Bole?"

"I have no idea at all. What do intend to do?"

"Try to discover more. Visit Mr Fortescue, Sarah knows his direction. Should I reply to my uncle's letter do you think?"

"Why not? He is a relative after all."

Thus a few days later, Mr and Mrs Fortescue welcomed Miss de Bourgh to their establishment; Mrs Fortescue resolving to have it known that the carriage standing at their door belonged to none other than the eminent Member ef Parliament, Sir Thomas Gould. Such news spread around the neighbourhood could not but be good for business. Sarah was entertained in a lively manner in the kitchen: the Fortescue's little maid-of-all-work regarding her with open mouthed worship, and Cook being determined to show she could produce cakes as fine and light as any in a grand London household.

In the drawing-room, Anne was finding that while the former valet and his wife were kindly hosts, pressing her to sample Cook's offerings of a number of sweet-cakes laid out upon the beaufet with her dish of tea, they were reluctant to answer any more questions about Percy de Bourgh. Or Peter de la Bole. But Anne had not been mistress of her own house for a year without having learnt to be firm in her dealings in order to pursue what she felt to be a right course. She explained that she had written a reply to her uncle, but that she thought it her duty to deliver it in person, and to see for herself whether he needed help or succour.

"For although he plainly states in the letter that he wants nothing from me in the way of alms of favours, yet the very fact that it is the first thing he mentions suggests that he has indeed been, and may still be in want of such things. Were he to be completely beforehand with the world, he would have no need to mention them. You yourself, Mr Fortescue, mentioned that there were 'unfortunate circumstances', although you also felt you could not explain what they were."

"I have not been given leave to explain, Miss de Bourgh."

"That I understand. But I have not given you leave to withhold information which I surely have the right of family to know. Which I am afraid places in you in an awkward situation, does it not?"

Mr Fortescue looked sorely troubled, and Anne felt sorry for the poor man, torn as he was between her demands and what he felt to be loyalty to her uncle.

"I regret that I have put you in this situation," she said, "and I would not have you distress yourself. But I cannot feel that my uncle would blame you for disclosing his direction at my insistence. Nor for the fact that I am asking you to take me to him. Believe me, I am not in the least bit afraid of even the poorest parts of London."

"You cannot know the worst of them, ma'am. And were I to comply with what you ask, it would lead you to an even worse situation than you could ever imagine."

Anne was silent for a moment, wondering what he could possibly mean. Then she said:

"Surely if my father's brother is in such a situation, then it is up to me to do what he himself would have done, is it not?"

At this point, Mrs Fortescue, who had remained quite silent throughout, intervened in a gentle way:

"I think I understand the young lady's feelings, Mr Fortescue. Were one of my family in as bad a way as I believe Mr Percy to be, I would not rest until I had done all I could to bring him help and comfort."

"You do not know the whole of it, Madam," returned her husband.

"No, maybe not, but I know a great deal and am not under the same obligation as you feel yourself to be. So if you wish it, I will furnish Miss de Bourgh with what she needs to know. Unless of course, you expressly forbid it."

Something in the lady's manner of speaking, quiet as it was, suggested to Anne that here was one well able to overcome any obstacles her husband might see fit to put in her way. What this power might be Anne could not possibly hazard a guess, but she was grateful that Mrs Fortescue had allied herself to her cause.

Mr Fortescue gave a small groan.

"There will be no need for you to put yourself out, my dear. We have plenty of orders on hand for you to be too much occupied to undertake the office of accompanying Miss de Bourgh to—to wherever she wishes to go. But I hope …" turning to Anne, "That neither you nor I, Ma'am, will regret this day's work. All I ask is that you bring a stout-hearted female to bear you company, and that you yourself try not to faint away at what I am about to disclose."

"I am not prone to fainting fits," said Anne.

"Very well then. Your uncle, Percy de Bourgh, is in Newgate Prison."

*

For a moment, Anne felt that her proud boast would be found to be false, and that she would indeed faint away. Mrs Fortescue was ready with some smelling salts, but although Anne turned very pale, she held fast to the arms of her chair and her consciousness.

"Take several deep breaths," she heard Mrs Fortescue advise. "I knew it would be a shock, but you were quite right to want to know."

Anne mastered herself sufficiently to ask several questions concerning the reasons for her uncle's incarceration, but Mr Fortescue shook his head.

"That I will leave him to tell you, Miss Anne for indeed I do not know the full story. It only remains for me to arrange matters, if you are determined on your course and still wish to visit. But I cannot emphasise strongly enough that it will be a most unpleasant experience."

But Anne remained firm in her resolve, and with the greatest reluctance Mr Fortescue agreed to convey her letter to Mr Percy and arrange for Anne to visit him:

"… if he agrees of course," he remarked heavily.

*

The visit took place in early April. Anne had said nothing to her aunt concerning her discoveries; as she had suspected, Lady Cecilia seemed to know only of Percy de Bourgh by name. Anne had brought it up in casual conversation, as it were, when talking of her visit to Mr Fortescue:

"…who had been with my father for many years and asked for news of the Reverend John and Captain William. Oh, and of Mr Percy of course."

She could not be sure but that Aunt Cecilia had jumped at the mention, but recovering quickly had said with a little laugh:

"Percy, dear me, yes, to be sure. It is many years since I heard of him. There was some scandal attached to his name and I believe, though I cannot be sure, that he was sent abroad. You cannot have any recollection of him Anne, surely?"

"No, none at all. I could give no news of him to Mr Fortescue," and Anne turned the conversation to the forthcoming ball—a topic on which Lady Cecilia was only too relieved to converse.

So it was that Serena accompanied Anne on her next visit to the Fortescue's. They had informed Lady Cecilia that Serena was to order two new gowns from Mrs Fortescue and that she was required to select the designs and the materials. This was no pretext either, Anne having described the pattern books available and Serena being more than happy to give them her custom. Anne too thought she might order a morning dress made by Mrs Fortescue's clever fingers, feeling that her custom might go some way toward alleviating any problems her determination to visit her uncle may have caused.

Their business being concluded and Serena having expressed herself satisfied that the dresses she had ordered would be ready in a sennight, the two ladies set forth with Mr Fortescue in a hired hack. He had sent the coachman back, explaining that he would undertake to deliver the ladies to Gould House in due course. Armed with pomanders supplied by Mrs Fortescue, they set out toward Newgate Street and came to the walls of the prison, set with high, small, grated windows. They passed the main door, thick and solid and set with iron bands and spikes and came to a smaller door set into what appeared to be a lodge. On this, the entry to the governor's house, Mr Fortescue knocked several times before they were admitted. They were shown into a little room in the porter's lodge to wait until the officer who had the duty of showing visitors to the prison could be found. He wore a plain black coat and knee breeches, and would have looked like a Quaker but for the great bunch of keys hanging at his belt. He required them to sign the visitors' book:

"We looks in that there book to see 'oo needs to be conducted aht, jes' in case you 'as a fancy to be stoppin' 'ere the night," he remarked in a jocular tone.

If London streets smelt bad to Anne before, the stench that arose as they were admitted through the porter's lodge into the yard was almost indescribable.

It was a warm spring day, and the sun, shining slantwise into the corner of the prison yard, seemed to draw up a smell that could almost be felt, it was so thick and rancid. Both Anne and Serena plied their pomanders in haste, but while Serena looked around at the prisoners, walking round and round the yard 'taking the air'—such as it was—and noting with concern how bedraggled and filthy they were, Anne could not bear to look at them. But she smelt their odour and heard the cries, curses and shouts for alms which accompanied the clank and rattle of the ankle chains some of them were compelled to wear.

Following the warden, they crossed the yard, and entered the building opposite through a dark doorway; the gate which barred and locked it being barred and locked again behind them. They were conducted up a flight of steep, narrow stairs and along a dim corridor. At every door, or entrance, there was a sort of ceremony of unlocking and locking, all of which added to the feeling of oppression which had assailed them as soon as they stepped through the main gate of the prison.

"These 'ere are the gen'l'men's quarters," the warden said with a sneer, "Everyfin' of the wery best provided. All requests met, when the said gen'l'men are able to provide the means of acquirin' the same. An' this 'ere is the gen'l'man as you was astin' for."

So saying, he inserted a great iron key into a formidable-looking lock, swung open the heavy door, ushered them in and clanged the door shut behind them.

The room they entered was small and low, and immediately made considerably smaller by the introduction of three more persons into it—the turnkey remaining outside. It had but the one tiny barred window high in the wall. Under it was a narrow shelf which apparently had to do duty as a bed and was covered with a rough horse blanket; in the corner a necessary article. There was a plain deal table, with writing paper and a standish, a blob of sealing wax and a tallow candle in a battered tin holder. Before the table was a wooden stool on which a man was sitting, a quill in his hand. He turned and rose at their entrance—and Anne found herself face to face with her uncle, the Honourable Percival Trethallan de Bourgh.

***
**
*

Chapter Five

*"Many die, overborne with sorrow, consumed by famine or putrified by filth.
The misery of gaols is not half their evil, they are filled with … the rage of want
and the malignity of despair."*
The Gentleman's Magazine (1759) (attributed to Dr Johnson)

Uncle and niece regarded each other steadily for a few moments, each looking for some recognition of their kinship in the other. This was at once apparent. Anne saw a younger, albeit thinner and more haggard version of her father; Percy saw a younger, more delicate version of his beloved sister Harriet. Then Anne made her curtsey and introduced Serena Pope, who also curtsied to him. The depth of the gentleman's bow in return signalled that he had not forgotten the courtesies-of-the age. The fact that he was astonished at their greeting he did not attempt to conceal, although he said nothing. It was Anne who opened the budget, as it were.

"I am very happy to meet you at last, Uncle."

Percy gave a short harsh laugh and bowed again, more deeply than before.

"Niece, you do me too much honour. Pray will you be seated?"

He indicated the stool and turned to Serena.

"Ma'am, I can only offer you—this…" and he gestured toward the bench.

Both ladies thanked him and seated themselves. Mr Fortescue remained standing by the door, and Percy leaned against the wall.

"Why did you insist on seeing me, Niece?" He was blunt in his questioning.

"Because you are my uncle and because Mr Fortescue introduced your name to me, presumably at your request and I imagine to gauge my reaction to it. Had I responded with indignation, or with fear, or indifference, there the matter would have rested. But I was both ignorant and curious, and determined to follow up the lead I was offered. So, here am I."

"Well done, Ma'am. Your reasoning is sound, as far as it goes. Now you are here, what think you of my humble abode?"

"The dwelling does not befit the man," Anne answered, "but the man ennobles the dwelling. Why are you here?"

The direct approach, thought Serena, following this exchange with interest, would seem to be a family trait. Sir Lewis had had it too, as did Lady Harriet, and William de Bourgh was known to be a bluff, straightforward sailor. Percy seemed not at all discomforted by Anne's question.

"I am here because I deserve to be. I committed crimes, was caught out in them, tried, and sentenced to be whipped, branded and imprisoned."

Anne nodded.

"I often heard my father say that though there are many points of failure in our penal system, justice is more often seen to be done than not. Did you receive justice, Uncle?"

"I did."

"And was your punishment deserved?"

"It was."

"And could not the whole course of events—the crimes, the trial, the punishment—have been prevented at an earlier time?" Anne was more hesitant now in her questioning.

"It could, perhaps, had I not been both arrogant and angry in my youth. You never knew your grandfather, the fourth baronet, did you?"

Anne shook her head.

"Nor your grandmother, the Lady Amelia Trethallan? No, probably not, although her death occurred some several years after you were born I think. But she retired to the fastness of the de Bourgh London house and refused to set foot in Rosings Park when your mother entered it. I think she recognised a kindred spirit, and resented it. Indeed she often said there could never be two Mistresses of the House, but the truth was she could not abide your mother and even the Dower House was too close for her comfort. Whenever your parents visited London, she took refuge with Harriet. Both my parents—your grandparents—were implacable in their views, and ordered the lives of their children without regard for our wishes. What had always been done in the de Bourgh family would continue to be done. It was fortunate for them that Lewis, John and William did as they were expected to do: the eldest received the inheritance, the next went to the Church and the third son to the Navy. Harriet too did not fail to marry to please her family. But when I was told I was destined for the Army, and would no doubt be sent immediately to America –I rebelled."

"Why?"

Percy paused and looked at Anne reflectively, as though wondering how much he should reveal of himself, his failures and his weaknesses. What he read in the steady look she gave in return spoke of interest and sympathy, and determined his response.

"I hated the thought of having to kill another human being of whatever kind, in the name of King and Country. I dislike even the necessary slaughter of animals; I would never go to watch the pigs being killed and wept like a child when my horse broke a leg and had to be destroyed. All of which," his tone became bitter and sarcastic, "Makes me a weakling and unfit to bear the noble name of de Bourgh, does it not?"

Anne shook her head.

"I too hate it when the pigs have to be killed- they squeal so, as if begging us to save them. And when my little spaniel was caught in a trap, I cried for days."

"Such sensibility in a woman is worthy of praise, Ma'am. But in a boy expected to make his way in His Brittanic Majesty's Army, it is totally unacceptable. But there! I was a child who could never be brought to conform to good behaviour!"

"Ah, now wait!"

He turned toward the tiny window as he spoke, holding up a finger. This side of the prison faced the west and as the sun began the journey towards its setting, it shone briefly through the aperture, throwing the shadows of the bars across the floor and part of the opposite wall. The light hung there for a few minutes, reddened, faded and was gone. Percy sighed.

"My glimpse of the sun and harbinger of heaven! On some days, and in the depths of winter, he does not visit me at all. Are the Lenten lilies in flower yet, niece?"

"Yes. The park is full of their gold."

"The sun on the daffodils, what a glorious sight! In the House, Rosings, in my childhood days, the sun was never allowed to enter. The servants were instructed to pull the blinds as soon as a finger of a sunbeam dared intrude itself across the floor! It might fade the carpets, or the yellow silk chairs! Or the red damask drapes in the dining room! But I loved the sun, and escaped as soon as lessons were done, out into the park. I rode round the estate and across the common; talked to the gypsies; went fishing and fell in the river; climbed trees and tore my breeches."

Anne exchanged a look with Serena, and both smiled, remembering Anne's own youthful escapades.

"For all of which, of course, suitable punishments were meted out. I took the beatings and continued on my merry way. But the greatest punishment of all came on the day when I was called into the book-room and my father informed me he was buying me a pair of colours—in a foot regiment! Not even inthe cavalry! It was to teach me the discipline he had obviously failed to impart, he said. Arguments were vain."

"So, you ran away?" hazarded Anne. "On a moonlit night, having raided the larder for bread and cheese?" Percy burst out laughing.

"Now how on earth could you know that?"

"It is what I would have done. So what did you do? Where did you go? To London, to seek your fortune?"

"Not quite. Not immediately. I joined the gypsies. You know they travel on every time the youngest child has a particular dream? To atone for their sin, or so they believe. But what great sin lies on their heads I never could discover. Certainly, they consider it no sin at all to steal from all who are not Romanitshel. So, I became as one of them; proving myself by stealing a stray chicken here, a few mangel-wurzels there, an odd garment or so hung out on the bushes to dry. I became adept at evading capture, and skilful, fast and silent in making my escapes. But then one day I excelled myself—or so I thought. I stole a horse. No—let's say I acquired a horse. Not merely any horse, such as the sturdy, piebald ponies the gypsies use, but a beautiful, thoroughbred mare. She came to me one moonlight night, stepping delicately over the silvered grass, and she was fully accoutred, with two saddle-bags full of gold."

The ladies exclaimed in wonder, and Mr Fortescue stirred.

"Tell what else you found."

"Ah yes! I found the rider. Dead, in a ditch with a bullet wound in his head."

There was a moment of silence, then Anne asked:

"Did you kill him, Uncle?"

"No Niece, I did not. I hate killing, you may remember, and I carried no firearms. Nor did any men of the gypsy tribe. They caught their rabbits for the pot with simple traps or sling-shots."

"Tell what manner of man he was," Mr Fortescue spoke up again.

"He was masked, and wearing a greatcoat with many pockets. All of them full of fobs, watches, rings, seals, necklaces. He had also a holster with two plain duelling pistols, but as far as I could see neither had been fired."

"He was a highwayman?"

"Just so. As I found him, so I left him, almost. I deprived him of his mask, for no reason I could think of except it might be a useful thing to have. Then I led the mare I now considered mine back to the camp. I distributed the gold, explaining how I came by it, but to my astonishment, I was met with sullen silence and dark looks."

"Did they not believe you had not killed the man?"

"Oh yes, they believed that, but this was gold from a dead man's hand and therefore could bring nothing but bad luck. So although they took it, most of it, I, as the bearer of it, was shunned. I think they also feared they would be blamed when the man was found; they had too often had experience of being made scapegoats. I was sent out of the camp to sleep, and when I woke in the morning, they had gone. The place was deserted and silent and as though they had never been there."

"What did you do?"

"Travelled by easy stages, mostly by night and came to London. I had gold in my pockets, but looked too disreputable to be thought the legal owner of it."

"Which you were not, Mr Percy," growled Mr Fortescue.

Percy bowed.

"Just so. Thus I worked at labouring or haymaking and earned pennies enough to buy some decent clothes and get myself a wash and shave. That was by day, when I kept my mare out of sight. On certain nights, I became another man altogether. I became Peter Burden, highwayman." Serena gave an exclamation.

"Peter Burden! But he became a legend! He was known as the 'gentleman highwayman', who requested but a portion of the gold or jewellery from those he held up, and who never fired a shot. What is more, he was never caught!"

"Indeed not, ma'am; he was never caught because he did not exist! So, having reached London, I found lodgings, stabling for my mare and assumed another identity - that of businessman: Peter de la Bole."

"What kind of businessman?" Anne was puzzled.

"Oh, come now, Niece! You cannot be so naive. What do you think a highwayman would do with his ill-gotten gains? I set up a shop, selling watches, fobs and jewellery. And as your knowledgeable companion has pointed out, I took but a portion of goods—nothing in fact that could be distinguished or recognized by any mark."

"Too clever by half," sighed Mr Fortescue.

"Maybe so, but as far as it went, my business was quite legal and my prices fair."

Mr Fortescue sniffed in disapproval.

"There is much that I do not understand," said Anne. "If, as Peter Burden you were never caught, what were your crimes and how came you here?"

"By greed, mischance and perhaps, ignorance. Sometimes when sorting through what I had acquired by my night's work, I came across a piece of jewellery, a ring or a fob which was distinctive and which I felt might be recognised by its owner. I passed these items quickly on to a jeweller, whose name I will not mention. He would break the piece down and remake it, or arrange to sell it abroad, and would pay for what I passed to him with a promissory note, or bond. Alas! I was neither so sharp nor as clever as I had supposed! The bonds were forged; I was found with them in my possession and held to be responsible for them. My jeweller 'friend', having somehow become aware that discovery was inevitable, vanished into the night, and I was committed to trial. A further unfortunate twist was that he had learned of my true identity, and it was as both Peter de la Bole and Percy de Bourgh that I appeared in Bow Street Court."

"Did my grandfather get to hear of this?"

"No, he had died a few years before and Lewis was now the fifth baronet. He got to hear of it; the Morning Post made much of the news, and he came in haste to London. At first, things went well. I was discharged for want of prosecution, and was borne back to Rosings in disgrace. By that time, Lewis was married to Catherine and you were a delightful child of nearly two years."

"What happened to your business?"

"Forfeit to the Crown. Lewis however did buy back my beloved mare. But if I thought my fortunes were about to change for the better, I was wrong. First, Lady Catherine refused to have me at Rosings so I removed to the Dower House. I had besmirched the long and honourable name of de Bourgh. She considered I should have been transported to the colonies .. I tried to make myself useful on the estate, as a sort of secondary bailiff to the estimable Mr

Castleton, but Lewis was having none of it. Then a few months later, my so-called friend the jeweller, whose dealings had led me to this pass, bestirred himself once more to implicate me further, possibly in an attempt to clear his own name. I was arrested again and this time received the sentence I am now serving. My only consolation is that my false friend, in seeking to convict me, also convicted himself- and was hung for it. So there you have my story, dear Niece, and you may call it the fall and fall of Percy de Bourgh."

*

There was a long silence; no-one felt inclined to comment, or question. Percy stood with head bowed, as though waiting sentence of censure or blame to be passed on him from the court of three persons here assembled. None came. Anne sat as she had throughout, her fingers tightly interlaced; Serena remained calm and Mr Fortescue held his post by the door and cleared his throat.

"Miss de Bourgh, Miss Pope, it is time I should be returning you both to Gould House."

Anne acknowledged this remark but continued to look towards her uncle.

"And you consider that you received justice, Uncle? It seems a harsh sentence for a crime you could not really be said to have committed."

"Such is our system. I should have taken more care in my dealings with the underworld. Indeed I should not have had such dealings in the first place! But so it is. You steal a handkerchief; you take a life. You rob a fellow of all he possesses; you accept a false note. What difference does it make? Prison, the pillory, the whip, transportation, or indeed the gallows. Some form of justice must be seen to be done."

There was another short silence.

"Is there anything you need from me Uncle?" Anne finally asked.

He bowed. ·

"I am not in want—except my freedom. Courtesy of my brother's will, Mr Fortescue visits and provides me with the necessities of life: newspapers, books from the circulating library, paper and ink. And the services of a barber from time to time. The days pass, have passed. I walk around the yard, read, write letters. Indeed at one point, I was able to do a favour for one of my gypsy friends, captured for a crime I knew he could not possibly have committed. I wrote letters on his behalf and a certain Mr Coke, an ardent Methodist, took up his cause. He was freed for want of prosecution and in spite of his hatred of London Town, also visits me from time to time. Mr Coke too has been busy on my behalf, but I have not as yet seen any result from his well-meaning interventions. However, it is just possible that in this year of Our Lord, 1801, I may be freed. Deo voluntas, Deo gratias."

"And then- what would you do?"

"I have no idea."

"Miss de Bourgh, please," Mr Fortescue was growing increasingly anxious. "It grows late."

Anne rose.

"Mr Fortescue, I thank you for your patience, but you are right we must be going. May I visit you again, Uncle?" and she gave Percy her hand.

"I did not dare to hope you would wish to do so, my dear Anne. Madam," turning to Serena, "I thank you that throughout my long and perhaps tedious story you did not once portray by look or word any sense of outrage or disgust."

"Because I felt none, sir. You were but a rebellious child, and had you met with less severe punishment and more understanding, things may have turned out very different for you."

Mr Fortescue now thumped upon the door to alert the warden that they wished to depart.

"By your leave, Mr Percy, I will bring your clean shirts and smalls in a few days. Do you have any further errands for me?"

"None, thank you. You have done much for me already. I know you will escort my niece and her companion safely home. Do not, I beg you Anne, remember me to your aunt and uncle. They would not appreciate the reminder."

Anne shook her head, half smiling. The great key grated in the lock and the door swung open. As it swung shut behind them and the key was heard to turn once more, Anne wondered, what were the thoughts and feelings at this moment of the man locked into that tiny room, where the sun entered but briefly towards the end of the day.

***
**
*

174

Chapter Six

"The farm is smiling amidst the frowns and gloomy aspects of politicks. After all, it is the best trade to stick to. Though one can do less good, one is liable to do less mischief. The pleasures are less owing to vanity and it gives you health."
Letter from the Duke of Richmond to Edward Burke (1770)

Mr Castleton rode out early, as was his wont, on a fine morning in early April, intent on first going the rounds of the estate, the Park and the Home Farm before turning his attention back to the canal project. This had progressed but slowly due to the variability of the weather over the past few weeks; after a warm and dry February, March had seen a return to winter, and they had been subjected to wind and storm, hail, sleet and even a few flakes of snow, with consequent difficulties in that the roads turned to mud and mire through which the great shire horses pulling the heavy wagons bearing clay, stone and wood struggled, laboured and frequently stuck. But a week of increasing warmth, sunshine and drying winds pleased not only the prudent housewives intent on completing the great spring wash, but also farmers, gardeners and the canal navvies and engineers. Today it was hoped that the second of the three locks would be completed and the third section of the river to be canalised would begin to have its banks straightened and reinforced with seasoned wood and stone blocks. The engineers Robert Brightwell and Will Spalding were working downstream on the construction of the steam pumping engine which, it was hoped, would pump water taken down the locks back up to the summit level.

The fields sown with spring wheat were greening already and Mr Castleton was pleased to note that the winter work of hedge-layering and ditchclearing had mostly been completed. The woodlands of Wakefield Farm, the Brightwells' former home, were thick with tiny wild daffodils at their edges, and the green spears of the bluebells were pushing through the leaf-fall, eager to catch the sunlight as it fell through the still bare branches.

Riding the boundary of Wakefield brought Robert Brightwell to the front of Mr Castleton's mind. Both he and his wife had taken him under their wing and he had attended several of the weekly Methodist class meetings held in their home, duly paying his penny and listening in silence to the Bible readings, exhortations, confessions and testimonies that formed the content of the meeting. Mrs Castleton had given him a copy of Mr Charles Wesley's hymns, but he had not been prevailed upon to join in the singing which was always enthusiastic if not always tuneful. Mrs Castleton would play the tunes on the pianoforte with one hand and conduct the little group with the other, but even this encouragement did not often result in them keeping perfect time either. Although the Methodists had officially separated from the Church of England some six years before, the small group of adherents in Hunsford, like a number of others in small villages across the country, not having a church building of their own, continued to attend the parish church of a Sunday morning to hear the Reverend Stevens preach. Indeed, they were found to be more assiduous in their church-going than many another villager who considered himself to be a regular member of the Church of England. Even when such regularity consisted of but once a year on Christmas Day. Robert Brightwell, the Castletons were pleased to note, also attended church every week; unlike the Honourable Will Spalding, who preferred to spend Sunday mornings taking his gun out after rabbits, or riding the lanes and byways, or fishing the river.

Class meetings were not the only occasions when Robert met with the Castletons. Both he and Will often took dinner with them; enjoying Mrs Castleton's good plain meals. They were served by Susan Heydock, a shy, quiet girl who would have been extremely pretty had it not been for the pock-marks that disfigured her face. Robert found himself looking at her with interest and this prompted Mrs Castleton to enlighten him when Susan had left the room:

"She is a good girl, and will be an excellent wife and housekeeper to some fortunate man, provided one can be found who will overlook her disfigurement."

"I imagine, Ma'am," said Will, "That there must exist the man who will love and admire her for her talents and her trim figure. Then too, she is quiet and calm, and I am sure would never fret a fellow's nerves with chatter or nagging."

"Indeed no," Mrs Castleton sighed, "but she was used to be much livelier and always laughing. Her brother's death from the smallpox, which left her marked, seemed to drain all animation and cheerfulness from her."

The two young men looked surprised at this intelligence as well they might. Mrs Castleton went on to tell of the outbreak of the disease the previous year, which had caused five deaths in the village, including those of Susan's brother Rob Heydock and Parson Collins.

"There may well have been more had not Miss Anne de Bourgh acted with sense and swiftness. She was staying with her cousins, the Darcys, when the outbreak occurred, but she came straight from Pemberley; ordered up supplies of the cowpox vaccine for all those who had not previously had the inoculation; carried out many of the vaccinations with her own hands, and indeed visited the sick daily. Which is a good deal more than her mother would have done! She had taken no steps to prevent such an outbreak occurring, having failed to ensure that her dependants received the inoculation!"

"Was Miss de Bourgh not fearful of contracting the disease herself?" asked Will.

"No, for she had somehow taken the cowpox as a small girl."

Robert gave a small start at this and an exclamation escaped him, which he turned at once into a cough.

"Not that such a thing was to be wondered at," continued Mrs Castleton, "as Miss Anne was a harum-scarum child and friends with everybody—people and animals alike—on the estate and the farms."

"Very like her father," put in her husband, "but after his death she was never the same again."

"Indeed no, the poor child was hardly seen again, her mother keeping her close confined. Almost a prisoner in her own home you might say. Lady Catherine was determined, it would seem, to turn the girl into a proper lady; by which was meant one who did nothing and was not allowed to know anything! Then too, the governess, Miss Pope, was dismissed and that Mrs Jenkinson put in charge of the girl's education. Not much good came of that, I'll be bound! But since coming into her inheritance Miss Anne has taken more trouble than ever her mother did to further the well-being of everyone under her eye. She is proving to be a good mistress and a good landlady. Even old Joe Green speaks well of her, at least some of the time!"

Mr Castleton laughed.

"That's because she told him straight out that his rheumatics would get better if only he took care to mend his cottage and not let the roof leak on to his bed. And when he complained he had not the strength to do it, she sent down an estate carpenter to carry out the repairs and promised to provide a regular supply of firing. She knows as well as the rest of us he's just too lazy to get on and do things for himself, but she will not let him have cause to complain of neglect."

The evening drew to a close shortly after this, and the two young men rode back to their lodgings in the East Wing of Rosings Park, both quiet and deeply immersed in their own thoughts.

Having completed his rounds, Mr Castleton retraced his steps along the river path to where the work was being carried out. The path was still wet and muddy from its recent flooding where the river had been partially dammed in order for the lock to be dug and the new gates fitted. The bailiff dismounted and led his horse which picked its way mincingly in the wet. The scene before him was one of intense activity. The lock gates had been lowered into place and several men were hauling on the beams to close them against the water which, released from the dam which had held it, was already walling up on the higher level. All seemed to be well; the mechanism was working smoothly, when suddenly the gate on the side of the path struck an obstruction in the river bed. It halted; the rush of water pushing against it from the higher side was too strong for the men to hold. Mr Castleton hastily tethered his horse and went to add his weight to the team of haulers, but as he did so, the gate broke free, the beam swung over, knocking the men off their feet and Mr Castleton slipped, was struck on the head by the beam and fell into the swirling river.

A great shout went up as he was swept downstream and the men working below dropped their tools and attempted to halt the poor man's progress. Will Spalding, working further upstream than Robert Brightwell, heard the commotion and realising only that a man had fallen into the river jumped in himself in an attempt to effect a rescue. Alas! Before he could reach him, he was struck by a low branch and he too went under. By this time, several of the navvies had reached the scene, as had Robert, who, alerted by the shouts, raced to find what was amiss. Together they managed to draw both men out of the water and on to the bank. Robert despatched a man to fetch the apothecary and others to take a gate from the lower field in order to carry the unconscious Mr Castleton to his home. Will was found to have injured his leg, but after coughing up a quantity of river water was otherwise unhurt; nonetheless he too was carried to the Castelton's house. Work was halted for the day until repairs could be carried out on the damaged lock gate; Robert taking it upon himself to assure the men they would receive a full day's pay, before he too followed the sad little procession across the fields.

Robert could not help but admire Mrs Castleton's demeanour when her husband's soaking and apparently lifeless body was carried into the house. She did indeed turn pale, but she neither fainted nor fell into hysterics. She examined the livid bruise on her husband's head before turning to the shivering Will Spalding and ordering that he be taken to the guest-room and that Mr Castelton's man hasten to bring him dry clothes.

"My husband is in the arms of the Lord and there is nothing we can do for him," she told the distraught valet, "But Mr Spalding is not beyond our help. Neither are the men who have carried them here."

So saying, she instructed Susan to prepare a hot posset for Will, and to draw off a quantity of ale for Robert and the workmen. Only then did she go down on her knees beside her husband. Later she would wash and lay him out herself.

Mr Holmes arrived in haste from Westerham and ascertained that the cause of Mr Castelton's death was probably the blow to his head as he fell. Thus unconscious, he fell into the near-freezing water which only served to hasten his end. Will was found to have broken his leg just below the knee, and he submitted with gritted teeth as Mr Holmes drew it straight and bound it firmly to a splint. But he grinned cheerfully when Robert came to ask how he did and to bring the hot posset which Susan had so carefully brewed.

"You are to have it all," said Robert, "the grace, the curds and the beer. It will do you as much good as the panegyric Mr Holmes is preparing for you I dare say."

The apothecary assented to this and said his medicine was to help the patient sleep.

"No doubt he will be as right as rain in a few days," was his comment. "That leg is as healthy a piece of flesh as I have seen in a long while, and should heal with no trouble at all. But I will check on your progress in a day or so Mr Will. Meanwhile, I must go and ask the good lady of the house if she needs anything and whether she can keep you here until you can get about again."

He nodded at Will and departed.

"My dancing days would seem to be over for a while," commented that gentleman, "and I will have to hobble to work on crutches no doubt. But Mr Smith will have to be informed of events, as will Miss de Bourgh, and both as soon as possible. If I write letters, would you carry the news to Miss Anne in London? It would be better than receiving such tidings by the post. Could you at the same time seek out my mother and brother, both of whom are also in London? I will furnish you with the address. From her last letter my mother informed me that George has a fancy to open up our town house since his return from Naples, and she has consented to join him there for a short while."

He winced as he inadvertently moved his leg, and Robert adjuring him to lie still, drink up his posset and not to worry his head, said he was willing to do all that was necessary.

*

Gould House was a hive of activity. The ballroom at the back of the house had been opened up and swept; the chandeliers thoroughly cleaned so that every crystal sparkled; spare plates, glasses, cutlery and napkins were washed and counted while hundreds of the best beeswax candles, flowers and bottles of top quality wines and champagnes were delivered to the house. It seemed to Kit that everybody who could be counted as anybody had accepted the invitations to her betrothal ball, and a large number of family members had promised to add their support and congratulations. Harriet, Lady Claydon had agreed to leave her daughter and latest grandson to the ministrations of the very capable nurse; Elizabeth and Darcy were also venturing up to Town, bringing Georgiana with them to attend her very first grand London ball, as was Charles, 5th Earl of Matlock and his shy little wife Mary. All these were only to be expected, but Lady Cecilia had cast her net wide.

Serena Pope, returning with Anne from the lecture by Mr Vauney at the Royal Institution was astonished to find she had received a formal invitation, as had the eminent natural scientist whose talk they had just heard. Apparently this was at Sir Thomas' insistence; if, he said, he was being required to fill his house at great expense with the Pink of the Ton—and indeed he had no objection to doing so in order to celebrate his daughter's betrothal—then he must be allowed to invite those with whom he could have some intellectual conversation over dinner. Unbeknownst to Serena and Anne, he too had been present at Mr Vauney's lecture and been much impressed with his quiet, gentlemanly behaviour, the excellence of his talk and his attention to Miss Pope and Miss de Bourgh when he had invited them to take tea with him at Gunter's after the event. Sir Thomas was not a man to concern himself with matchmaking, leaving all that kind of nonsense to his wife and sisters, but he did hold Serena Pope in high esteem and thought fleetingly that Mr Vauney might be the very man for her. None of this however, was conveyed to Lady Cecilia when he desired her to issue invitations to his niece's companion and her scientist acquaintance, preferring to give as his reasons those already outlined.

Further surprises over the guest list were in store. Among the bridegroom's friends were a number of Anne's hopeful suitors, and Lord George Spalding, whose gilt-edged acceptance card Serena had picked up with another exclamation of astonishment.

"I had no idea George Spalding was back in England, let alone London! I shall look forward to meeting him again and introducing you to him that is if I recognise him. It is after all many years since we have seen each other. My dear! Just look at all these replies! Miss Gould must be delighted. It seems as though the whole of the polite world will be at her betrothal ball. And I have just realised that I ought to prevail upon Mrs Fortescue to make me a ball-gown. Do you know I have never owned such a thing in my life?"

"I am sure you will look utterly charming in it, Serena. Only promise me it will be any colour other than grey!"

Serena laughed and promised, leaving Anne to spare some thought from her several preoccupations to bestow on her own gown for the event.

The great day dawned and the entire staff of Gould House were up betimes, polishing already gleaming furniture; cleaning already clean windows, floors, candle-sconces and lamps; setting out card tables; arranging banks of flowers up the grand staircase and in the ballroom. The kitchen was perhaps the busiest place in the house, with the Gould's French chef shouting the imprecations without which he was convinced his staff would be incapable of carrying out his orders. The ladies' maids were also anxiously looking over their mistresses' toilettes: under garments, gowns, shoes, silk stockings, gloves, jewellery, gauze scarves and flowers for the hair, all were checked and laid out in order that the ladies should do credit to the care and creativity of their maids.

Mrs Fortescue had excelled herself over Serena's gown: it was in a rich shade of blue, bordering on purple, with blond lace trimming the bust and sleeves. Anne had decided on pale apricot silk with gold lace edging down the front and gold coloured long gloves. Kit of course, having settled on the pearls with gauze trimming over her pink silk under-dress was looking her absolute best, glowing with love and pride beside her handsome baronet as she stood at the top of the stairs to receive her guests.

Anne de Bourgh soon gathered her usual court around her, and was responding to their empty compliments with her quiet charm, allowing nothing of the boredom she was feeling to show in her face and manner. In this she was observed by her aunt, Lady Harriet Claydon, who congratulated her sister-in-law:

"You have done well, Cecilia! Not only have you managed to establish Kit creditably, and by the way she is looking particularly radiant tonight, but you have brought Anne in great beauty to the notice of the polite world. Except that those buzzing around her like wasps to a honey-pot would seem to be, without exception, most unsuitable. Do I not see Hamborough? And upon my word, Rake Atterbury!"

"I know it," said Cecilia crossly, "but really Harriet, I have never put it about that Anne's fortune was anything out of the ordinary! Why such penniless coxcombs as Tom Hamborough and Charlie Elston persist in their attentions I cannot say. I would have thought they would both be hanging out for a much richer wife!"

"Well at any rate, Anne does not seem to be taking any of them at all seriously. One would almost imagine her heart to be completely untouched, or that she is setting her sights higher. As indeed, why should she not? Ah, now here is a very personable young man come to claim your attention. Do you know him?"

"Of course! He is Lord George Spalding, Earl of Rettingborough. Do not look so disapproving I beg you, Harriet! Whatever you may remember of his father, he is of the first respectability. Serena Pope was his governess you know, and he has been serving with Lord and Lady Hamilton in Naples."

Harriet raised her eyebrows at this, but Cecilia continued in some haste:

"He is reputed to always have conducted himself with the greatest propriety I do assure you, and if, as I imagine, he wishes to be presented to Anne, I shall have no hesitation in doing so."

In this, Lady Cecilia was right and she carried out the introduction without further ado. Anne received Lord George with every appearance of pleasure and lost no time in telling him that she had met his brother, and that he was engaged in engineering work at Rosings Park. George laughed and explained that Will had ever since early childhood had a fascination for all things mechanical or of a practical nature, and went on to exchange with Anne memories of Miss Pope's teaching. He in turn seemed much struck with her, and continued to converse with great animation, telling her of his experiences in Naples and of the astonishing and fearful scene of the latest eruption of Vesuvius.

"It was an amazing sight, Miss de Bourgh. I had been detailed to escort Lady Hamilton and a vast quantity of baggage twenty miles down the coast, but even from that distance, the heat could be felt, and great fires shooting high into the sky could easily be seen."

Serena joined them at this point, flushed and sparkling on the arm of Mr Vauney, saying she wished to renew her acquaintance with another former pupil. George jumped to shake her by the hand.

"By Jove, Miss Pope, you do look well! And not a day older I do declare. My brother wrote to tell me he had met you, and said it was as though it were but yesterday. You were, he said, exactly as he remembered, and indeed he was right!"

Serena laughed and protested a little and presented him to Mr Vauney. The two men were soon engaged in conversation on the wonders and delights of the natural world, and Serena took her seat beside Anne.

"So what do you think of Lord George, my dear?" she asked quietly. "He seems to have grown into a personable young man indeed."

Anne consented to this, but said:

"He does not appear to have the cheerful openness of countenance of his brother. although he is very affable, his face seems to bear a trace of, how shall I put it? Weariness? Perhaps, his experiences abroad were rather more exacting than pleasurable."

"Hm, yes. Perhaps, you are right. He appears older than his years I think."

A new set was forming, and George promptly solicited Anne's hand for the dance. Young Mr Elston, who had continued to hover nearby, started forward to protest that Anne was promised to him, but she shook her head at him, laughing:

"Indeed, I did not promise. Would you have me censured as fast? I have danced with you twice already Mr Elston, and even in this crowded ballroom, it was sure to have been noticed. But there are so many pretty girls here, who would I am sure, much appreciate standing up with a gentleman of your address."

Mollified, Mr Elston retired, and Lord George whispered as they took their places in the set:

"Very prettily done, Miss de Bourgh! It would seem you have had some practice in delicate refusals!"

*

A grand ball, especially one as successful and therefore as crowded as this one, is not the place to exchange news or impart confidences. Anne had little time for conversation with her cousins Elizabeth and Fitzwilliam, or Georgiana, but towards the end of the evening, they stood together for a while in the hall, while the Darcy's carriage was called for, and agreed that Anne should call at their town house next day:

"For you must see how little Charles has grown!" said the fond mama. Promises to meet were in fact being exchanged between a number of persons: parties, rides, concerts and plays were discussed and George Spalding elicited from Anne a half-promise to attend with Serena a party of his contriving at Vauxhall Gardens in the near future. As he had already gained Mr Vauney's promise of attendance, Serena accepted with more alacrity than her conscience ought to have dictated. Anne later teased her former governess over this and was astonished when Serena told her in all seriousness that in all her years she had never met a man who could so engage her mind and heart.

"I would never have imagined that having reached the maturity of almost forty-one years and having enjoyed being an educationist all my life, I would ever be granted the opportunity of matrimony."

"Has Mr Vauney spoken to you on this subject?" Anne was surprised into asking.

Serena nodded and continued:

"But I am aware we have known each other but a few weeks only. I have given him to understand that although I am not averse to his suit, we need more time to understand one another, and that on no account would I leave you."

Anne responded to this with assurances that Serena's future happiness was of supreme importance to her, and the two ladies retired each having much to contemplate over the events of the evening.

***
**
*

Chapter Seven

"Those marriages generally abound most with love and constancy that are preceded by a long courtship. The passion should strike root and gather strength before marriage be grafted on to it."
Joseph Addison 'The Spectator' 1711 / 12

Weariness of mind and limb is the usual condition of ladies, and indeed some gentlemen, after a ball, thus the ladies at Gould House would not be expected to leave their bedchambers before noon. Not so the servants; they must of necessity be up early and work as hard at removing all traces of the festivity as they had been at setting it up. The ladies' maids too were up betimes, restoring order to gowns and slippers which had been danced in all night, but they would not expect to take their mistresses' chocolate to them at an hour earlier than eleven of the clock. Sarah was surprised therefore to be alerted by her mistress's bell well before this hour, and to be informed that Miss Anne wished to make a number of morning calls.

The first of these was to Mr and Mrs Fortescue; first to assure the latter that the gown she had fashioned for Miss Pope had been much admired, and that her name had been whispered to several ladies of the Ton who desired to know the name of the modiste who had designed and made it. The Fortescue's were much gratified by this intelligence. Anne then asked after her uncle, and was assured that he was as well as may be expected, and indeed in daily expectation of hearing from Mr Coke that his case was to be brought again before the court and his sentence revoked.

"Was it not given at his trial that he should serve but a fixed period of years in prison?"

Mr Fortescue shook his head.

"That practice has only been adopted of late, as has the discontinuation of branding as a punishment. At the time of Mr Percy's trial, he was committed to be burned in the hand and to be imprisoned to await His Majesty's pleasure. The recent practice of stating fixed terms of incarceration is one Mr Coke hopes to invoke, retrospectively, as it were."

Anne nodded at this.

"I only hope he may. Please convey my good wishes to my uncle, Mr Fortescue, and assure him I hope to visit him again shortly. Also that I have his future as a free man very much in mind."

Anne's next call was to Elizabeth and Darcy. They welcomed her warmly to their house in Park Lane and assured her that she would soon have the joy of seeing her small cousin, who had been taken for a walk in the park by his nurse.

"I only hope she can dissuade him from escaping his leading strings and picking the flowers," said Elizabeth. "He shows a particular delight in the yellow ones, and the daffodils will be a great temptation to him."

"Perhaps because his mother always appears to advantage in yellow," said Anne laughing and advancing to shake hands with Darcy. "How do you do, cousin? I hope all is well at Pemberley?"

Darcy assented to this, and saying he would leave his wife to acquaint Anne with all the news from Derbyshire, excused himself on the grounds that he had business to attend to.

Elizabeth then invited Anne up to her sitting-room, where she said they could be comfortable. She asked first about Anne's impressions and experiences of London, and laughed heartily over her descriptions of the parties and balls she had attended and the strange offers of marriage she had received. But she shrewdly observed that Anne had no intention whatsoever of accepting any one of them, and that, as far as Elizabeth could surmise, she was not in the least attracted to any of the young men she had met so far. Yet she learned that a number of them were good-looking, most were pleasant mannered, all were elegantly dressed and highly regarded by the Ton.

"Although very few of them have anything interesting to say," Anne explained, "and I feel I must blame Serena for having given me more education than can be satisfied by the small topics of insipid conversation."

Mention of Serena brought to Anne's mind that lady's recent disclosures, but she did not feel she could talk of these. She did however, tell of their visits to Westminster Abbey, the Tower with its menagerie, and their introduction to a charming natural scientist and an equally charming ostrich (Elizabeth was much amused by this) and their attendance at the Royal Institution lectures. Anne was also hesitant to mention her uncle Percy, but feeling that Darcy may know more than he had ever disclosed, she gave Elizabeth as much of Percy's history as she felt confident could be told. Elizabeth was a good listener and beyond one small exclamation of surprise, heard Anne out in silence. She expressed concern however over Anne's visit to Newgate:

"Are you sure you took no harm from such a visit? No sickness, no fever?"

"None. Yet although the stench in the prison yard was very bad, and many of the prisoners wretched in their dirt and rags, my uncle's room, though small, was at least swept and through the good offices of Mr Fortescue, he has access to clean linen. For the rest, I am sure that whatever their crimes, those poor men—and women too—should not be condemned to live in worse conditions than my pigs at Rosings Park farm!"

"I agree, but there are many who would say they have only what they deserve."

Anne shook her head over these melancholy reflections and changed the subject by asking of news of Charlotte Collins and her family.

"They have gone to visit Sir William and Lady Lucas at Meryton. Then I believe Charlotte would like to go to Hunsford in the summer. You know I think, of the situation there, I suppose?"

"Indeed yes, and I am delighted for her. She will be welcomed back by all in the village and on the estate. Mr Stevens seems to be settling in very well at Hunsford, but the Parsonage is in need of just such a hand as Charlotte's to give it the feminine touch. I had an idea that I would like Charlotte to help run a small circulating library in the village, with perhaps Serena's help, and I am hoping she will give due consideration to the scheme. But I also hope to return home in the early summer, and if Charlotte and the children can come to me there, she shall be married from Rosings Park."

"I am so glad you feel you can offer that. I have every hope that my dear friend will achieve the felicity in her second marriage that I fear was absent from her first."

Mention of Rosings Park brought to Anne's mind the various schemes and developments that were already afoot there, and she informed Elizabeth of the canal project, her meeting with the Honourable Will Spalding, and of course his brother Lord George at Kit's ball.

"Ah yes, the attentive young lord!" Elizabeth had observed George Spalding the previous evening. "Did you like him, Anne?"

"Well enough on a first acquaintance. I shall be able to give more of an opinion after his party at Vauxhall in a few days' time."

The entrance at this point of Master Charles Bennet Darcy with his nurse, who had indeed successfully prevented him from picking the daffodils, brought any further conversation to an end, and after exclaiming over the young man's growth, his prowess in walking at just over a year old, his obvious intellect and liveliness and his likeness to his father, Anne took her leave.

*

In spite of the many excursions of pleasure Anne had attended since she came to London, she had never visited the famous gardens at Vauxhall. Apparently the best way to approach them, especially for those visiting for the first time, was by water; thus the party took boats across· the river to land at the water-gate, and from there to view the paths and groves lit by hundreds of swinging lamps. They made their way slowly and wide-eyed with wonder to the brightly-lit Rotunda, where an orchestra was playing some of Herr Mozart's livelier music. Lord George had bespoke a box in which they were to have supper, which, they were assured, had to include the thin-sliced ham and rack punch for which Vauxhall was famous. Anne had to confess that she disliked the taste of this, and was much obliged to their host for having been thoughtful enough to also provide orgeat and lemonade. During supper, George was particularly attentive to Anne, helping her to delicate pieces of chicken and green salad, persuading her to try a water ice flavoured with peaches and peeling an apple for her. She was a little perturbed by this, and although good manners forbade her to behave in any other way than with polite gratitude, she found herself somewhat unwilling to receive such close attentions. They were, she felt, just a little too practised, and lacked the earnestness of, for example, the absurdly young Mr Elston. He, no doubt, encouraged by his mother to pay his addresses to Anne for her supposed wealth, had had the misfortune to think himself truly head over heels in love with her, which led him to declare on several occasions that he wished her as poor as a church mouse, so that they might enjoy eternal felicity in a humble cottage.Anne laughing gently at him, had asked where he thought he might stable his beloved team of hunters in a cottage, at which he had stammered that he would willingly forego all such pleasures for her sake. She had then assured him she had no wish to deprive him of anything, and had turned to speak to Lord Marston, who had muttered sourly that Charlie Elston should stop making such a cake of himself.

The evening at Vauxhall passed pleasantly enough. Following the concert and supper, there was a display of fireworks, after which the little group strolled along the Broad Walk where the lights were suspended between graceful colonnades in gently swinging loops. Anne found herself walking with Mr Vauney, and ventured to ask him if he did not find the pleasures of London rather different to his travels in Africa. He answered her pleasantly, describing some of the scenes he had witnessed and explaining that Africa was a huge country and there were many different aspects to it: from the high veldts to vast stretches of desert; from rich farmland to swamps and dense jungles.

"These festoons of lamps Miss Anne," he said with a twinkle, "are not dissimilar to the swinging vines of an African jungle. Imagine if you will that the coloured lights are but bright flowers, the sound of the fountains like the sound of swift streams and waterfalls, and the talk and laughter of the people not unlike the chatter and shriek of many monkeys. Thus you will see that there is very little difference between a jungle and a pleasure garden!"

Anne laughed very much at this, especially as at that moment a party of girls passed them, shrieking with laughter at some joke of their own.

"Very like chattering monkeys indeed," said Mr Vauney, with mock gravity.

Anne later informed Serena that she thought her dear friend a most amusing and interesting man and that she was sure they would deal extremely well together.

Fascinating as the visit had been, the ladies soon began to think of leaving and as carriages had been ordered to await them at the land-gate, they made their way past Neptune's fountain ("Exactly like a waterfall?" murmured Anne to Mr Vauney) and along the main colonnade to reach it. George Spalding now drew near to Anne and asked her in a low voice if she would consent to accompany Serena to take tea with his mother the following afternoon.

"I have a particular reason for wishing you to meet my mother Miss de Bourgh, which perhaps I will explain if you can agree to accept the invitation."

Anne was puzzled by this, but could think of no reason why she should refuse, especially as she knew Serena wished to renew her acquaintance with Lady Spalding. A time was agreed and the ladies were handed into their carriage which rolled away in the direction of Westminster Bridge.

Despite the lateness of the hour, Anne found herself unable to sleep. Sarah had drawn the heavy curtains close across the window, but not quite close enough to prevent a slender little moonbeam edging in and tempting Anne to get up and investigate its source. She slid out of bed, thrust her feet into slippers and pulling a shawl around her pulled back the heavy drapes to reveal a full moon flooding the room with silver light. Anne leaned against the casement and thought of Diana, the huntress, the Goddess of the Moon. The old Greek myths told how the Goddess rejoiced in her singleness of purpose, needing no man to pursue her, no husband to rule over her. But Anne was no Diana; she enjoyed the company of both men and women, she liked to dance and she welcomed the sensible conversations of men such as Mr Vauney and her uncle Sir Thomas. But there were occasions, such as tonight, when she would find herself withdrawing into herself, because she found attention from certain quarters becoming too close, or too persistent. As George Spalding had himself commented, she had perfected the art of the delicate refusal. Would it always be so? Was she destined to walk alone, like Diana, who delighted in her own silver beauty and was unwilling to share it? There had been one with whom Anne would gladly have shared her life, but he was lost to her and she had since refused to think of him. Nonetheless, when she left the window, her fingers sought the comforting smoothness of the little carved bird she kept in the Chinese box beside her bed.

*

Lady Spalding regarded her eldest son with a small crease of anxiety between her brows. She had not seen him for a number of years and her first thought was that the excited boy who had left to take up a diplomatic post with Sir William Hamilton in Naples, determined to make a name for himself and repair the family fortunes, had returned a disillusioned man. Her next thought was how like his father he had become. Or rather like the sixth earl as he had once been: handsome, laughing, charming and with just that touch of rakishness which would appeal to just such the young impressionable girl doing her first Season that she had indeed been. Except that George laughed but seldom, and already was possessed of an air of hardness, of disappointment. How, thought his mother, had his experiences abroad shaped him? He had close association with the Neapolitan court, whose queen was the sister of the unfortunate Marie Antoinette; he had been in company with the beautiful Emma, a courtesan who had once been the mistress, but was now the wife of Sir William, and also, if rumour were to be believed, the mistress of Admiral Nelson. All this surely not the kind of company where a young man with such a father could be expected to behave with integrity and propriety. Yet, reports seem to suggest that he done so! But Lady Spalding knew her sons: the younger was an open book, all could read him; the elder was secretive and had learned to keep his heart well hidden. Which meant she had no means of knowing if such a heart remained untouched.

Had she known it, he was neither so untouched nor so unsullied. The beauteous Emma had ensnared him, dazzled him and amused herself with him, but had allowed prudence to dictate that an impoverished young Earl was a poorer prospect than the older, infinitely richer and besotted Sir William. A young husband, she thought to herself, would be watchful, possessive and jealous; an old one less mindful if his lovely wife strayed just a little from the marital bed. Thus George was firmly dismissed from Emma's affections, if indeed he had ever held a place within them. He carried the bitterness of the rejection well hidden and resolved that on his return to England he would seek out and marry any well-born woman with a reasonable fortune for whom he might form a degree of respect even thought he could never hold her in affection. His choice, deliberate and calculating, fell upon Anne de Bourgh, whom he knew by repute and met at Lady Cecilia Gould's ball. With the arrogance of his forebears, it did not occur to him that the lady might not fall in with his wishes.

Lady Spalding regarded her eldest son over the breakfast cups on the morning after Vauxhall and wondered what his thoughts were. She resolved to ask Serena Pope's opinion, which she knew could always be relied upon to be thoughtful and honest. Presiding over the tea-caddy that afternoon, she watched Miss Anne de Bourgh with interest and approval. She was aware of George's interest in the lady and as letters had passed regularly between Rosings Park and Tanglewood House, she was well aware of Anne's history. She beheld now an attractive and elegant young woman, with a ready smile and quiet confident manners. Lady Spalding's gaze then travelled from Anne to George, and she received a shock. It was the look on her son's face as he watched Miss de Bourgh. It was not however a look of admiration, of love - that would not have surprised her ladyship at all - it was a look of calculation, almost one would say cunning, as though he were estimating the price he might be expected to pay for a piece of prized horseflesh. It was gone in an instant as Anne turned towards him, and was replaced by a smile of practised charm. Lady Spalding decided she had imagined the whole and turned back to Serena to answer her question about Tanglewood School.

Lord George engaged Anne in conversation, talking of the situation of Spalding House and his plans to re-furbish the whole in order to set about making a life for himself in London.

"I was hoping I might elicit your opinion Miss de Bourgh on furnishings and fitments. The place is sadly old-fashioned, indeed decidedly antique. My mother does not feel she could take up the task of bringing the house up to modern tastes, but I hoped I might interest you in such a project. I understand that you do not, at present, have a London house to which you could repair for the Season?"

The implications behind these remarks Anne found to be disturbing and she was conscious once more of a wish to withdraw. She said however, with a smile:

"You must excuse me, Lord Spalding, from attempting an opinion on so grand a programme as you envisage here. My own London house, as you may indeed know, is let and although my aunt, Lady Cecilia Gould, was so kind as to prevail upon me to do this one Season, which I have enjoyed, yet my feelings are such that I would not want to repeat the experience too often."

"You are too modest, Ma'am," George persisted, "but maybe I can persuade you to lend an ear to my schemes and ideas every now and then. I feel sure that were it known that your good offices had been employed on my behalf, my credit in the polite world would rise considerably."

"I think," Anne returned, by now really uncomfortable with the apparent earnestness which accompanied his words, "that your credit stands high enough without intervention from me. I am sure that everywhere you go, you are well spoken of."

"As to that—" Lord George began, but he was interrupted at that moment by the entry of the butler, who intimated discreetly to Lady Spalding that an urgent message awaited her.

*

Robert Brightwell had finally arrived in London after a frustrating and wearisome journey. He set out equipped with letters: two from Will, one being for their master Mr William Smith and one for his mother Lady Spalding, and a further letter from Mrs Castleton for Miss de Bourgh. His first task was to seek out Mr Smith and to apprise him of the situation at Rosings Park; Robert had set the men to work on the lock and the river bed under the foremanship of one Josiah Cobb, a trustworthy member, Mrs Castleton had informed him, of the small Methodist community in Hunsford. But Mr Smith would need to come himself to oversee the project as a whole while Will was laid up in his bed. Robert travelled first to Norfolk where Mr Smith was last known to be working, only to find he had moved to supervise the final stages of work on the London canal. This at least meant Robert could deliver all three of his letters together; he had feared to learn that Mr Smith had travelled to York, or Wales or the Midshires. To London therefore, Robert turned his steps.

The journey, though tedious, gave him plenty of time for reflections, and the chief of these was what he now knew of Miss Anne de Bourgh. He found he still retained a clear memory of her from their childhood days, indeed, although he had tried to close his mind against his happier memories, because they had only accentuated the pain of his later experiences, they had remained clearly etched in some comer of his brain. And they contained an image of a laughing girl, with chestnut hair that glinted red in the sunlight and eyes the colour of the summer sky. She wore a dress as white as the daisies, with a yellow sash, and she danced with his sisters in a green meadow. Martha, Margaret and Anne; the three little Graces, his father had said, and his mother had replied in her softly lilting voice:

"Three little imps of mischief. Would you look at them dancing there in a fairy ring? They belong to the Little People, I'm thinking."

Now Margaret lay under a green mound in a Northamptonshire churchyard and Martha had become companion and help in Mrs Prudence Barton's household. And Anne de Bourgh?

From every side Robert had heard reports of her: how like her father she was; how good a Mistress of a great estate; how unlike her mother. Yet he had been only too eager to link them together in his mind and attribute to the daughter the attitudes and behaviour of the mother. He had not thought; he had not truly reflected how impossible it was that Miss Anne could have been implicated in all the misfortunes which befell his family and which in his anger he had laid at Lady Catherine's door. Indeed how could she have been? How could she have known? She had been but a child of nine, ten summers, just a little younger than himself. What had he been thinking? With shame he remembered how he had spurned her hospitality, rejected her offer of a warm and welcoming friendship with bitter words that rose now in his memory with a taste of bile.

Robert reflected too on the last class meeting he had attended; the last that Mr Castleton had conducted. The subject had been forgiveness. One Obadiah Cobb, cousin to Josiah, had confessed to losing his temper (a condition to which he was prone) and had spoken harsh words to his long-suffering wife, who, he said now, did not deserve them.

"Do you desire forgiveness from the Lord, Obadiah Cobb?" had demanded Mr Castleton.

"I do. I do."

"Are you in love and charity with your neighbour?"

"Indeed I am."

"Are you in charity with your neighbour Dick Stone, who you say stole two hens from you?"

Obadiah got up from his knees.

"That ol' varmint said 'e never did steal 'un. 'E never has confessed, not to this day. But I know full well 'e did take my 'ens, and best layers they were too!"

"Then you have not forgiven him?"

"No I 'aven'. Nor never shall." And Obadiah glowered round on the assembled company.

"Then how can you expect God to forgive you? What does it say in the very words of the Lord's Prayer? Forgive us … as we forgive others."

With a groan, Obadiah sank back on to his knees.

"I do then, I do forgive 'un Lord, tho' 'e be a proper varmint an' a fibster, I do forgive ol' Dick Stone. If Thou wilt forgive me, Lord for bein' such a curmudgeon!"

Robert smiled at the memory of that meeting, but Mr Castleton's words remained. "As we forgive, so we shall be forgiven. Not only those who have wronged us, but the wrong we know to be inside our own selves. Without this forgiveness of sins done against us, the pardoning grace Jesus Christ holds out to each one of us cannot be accepted. Without that acceptance, we cannot move towards God's Heavenly Kingdom."

The coach wheels rumbled over the cobbles of the London streets with a rhythm which said; *"As we forgive, as we forgive …Well,"* thought Robert to himself, *"so be it."* He made a resolve that, should an opportunity arise, he would go down on his knees before God and to Miss Anne de Bourgh and ask her pardon, not only for what he had said, but also for what he had thought.

He reached his destination; finally managed to locate Mr William Smith; inform him of events and pass on Will's letter. He had next to find Spalding House, and here Mr Smith was able to direct him. He was received by the butler, and informed that Lady Spalding was entertaining visitors to tea, but when he explained the nature of his errand and proffered Will's letter, he was set to cool his heels in the hall while the butler intimated that this would be conveyed immediately to her ladyship.

Lady Spalding retrieved her younger son's letter from the salver, and excusing herself to her guests, carried it to the window before breaking the seal and perusing its contents. Her exclamation of dismay caused consternation among the others, and both Anne and Serena immediately said that perhaps they should take their leave.

"No, no," said Lady Spalding, "Miss de Bourgh, this also concerns you."

"Concerns me?" Anne asked in amazement.

"Will writes that he has sustained an injury while working on the canal at Rosings Park, but that"—she consulted the letter,

'It will all be explained by the bearer of this note, who has been the best of good fellows to me. He carries a further note for Miss de Bourgh containing, I regret to say, news of a much more serious nature'.

She turned to the butler.

"Harding, is the man who brought this letter still in the house?"

"I instructed him to wait in the hall, madam."

"Have the goodness to ask him to step up."

The butler bowed, and within a few minutes, ushered Mr Robert Brightwell into the room.

***

**

*

Chapter Eight

"I know that you could neither be happy nor respectable unless you truly esteemed your husband, unless you looked up to him as a superior. Your lively talents would place you in the greatest danger in an unequal marriage .... My child, let me not have the grief of seeing you unable to respect your partner in life."

Mr Bennet to Elizabeth
Jane Austen: Pride and Prejudice (1797 / 1813)

As Robert Brightwell entered the room, prepared to make his bow to Lady Spalding, he came under the scrutiny of four pairs of eyes. Conscious of his appearance which was dusty with much travel, he began to apologise, but that Lady Spalding came forward to greet him with kindness and with warmth in her look, to thank him for his friendship towards her younger son. She then introduced Lord George, who accorded him a polite welcome, and Serena Pope, who extended her hand with a friendly gesture saying:

"We know each other too well, ma'am, to have the need of a formal introduction. How do you do, Mr Brightwell?"

Robert managed a courteous reply before turning to Anne.

Their eyes met, and time and the world stood still for them both. Each forgot there were any other persons in the room. Lady Spalding, observing them, immediately wished them well in her heart; Serena thought to herself: of course, I should have known how it would be; Lord George muttered under his breath: sits the wind in that quarter? Then came a stir, the tiny clatter of a teacup, which brought the two bemused persons back to their surroundings; Robert made his bow and Anne said, with but the faintest tremor in her voice:

"I believe you have a letter for me, Mr Brightwell?" As Robert handed Anne the letter—"From Mrs Castleton, Ma'am."—there came, simultaneously, into both their minds the memory of their last meeting in the hall at Rosings Park: a cold December day, Mrs Castleton fussing slightly with her shawl; the clatter of the carriage being brought round; Anne's invitation to dinner, and Robert's reply:

'I would rather not be beholden to you, nor indeed to receive anything other from your family than can be considered recompense for my work ...'

Anne, remembering, turned pale; Robert, remembering, flushed darkly. His was greater discomfort as he realised that this was no moment for that which he had resolved upon: to lay before Anne de Bourgh his awareness of the error into which he had fallen. He bit his lip and murmured:

"Forgive me Miss Anne."

A few inadequate words which she could only take to mean he wished to be forgiven for being the bearer of bad tidings. She excused herself to her hostess and carried the letter to the window to read it.

The afternoon resumed its polite social course. Lady Spalding called for more tea and another cup, and Robert was invited to provide more details of the sorry tales of Will's accident and Mr Castleton's fatal one over the teacups. In spite of the obvious distress this caused, matters then had to move on to practical things: it became obvious that Robert must return to Rosings Park as soon as possible, and that Lady Spalding should accompany him. Anne felt she could not abandon her obligations to her Aunt and Uncle in too hasty a manner, but promised she would return to Rosings within a fortnight. In the meantime, she offered the hospitality of her house to Lady Spalding; her good Mrs Rowlings would, she felt sure, receive them cordially. But, she turned to Robert, perhaps if Mr Brightwell would return with her and Serena to Gould House, she could furnish him with a letter to carry to the housekeeper, apprising her of the situation. She could not of course take it upon herself to offer him lodging with the Goulds, but no doubt when her aunt, Lady Cecilia knew of the position, she would at the very least invite him to dinner. At this, Lady Spalding hastened to offer the hospitality of Spalding House, and Robert found himself in the surprising and rather embarrassing position of dinner in two grand houses, for neither of which he felt he was adequately prepared, nor could be adequately dressed. He stammered his thanks, and was inclined to refuse both offers as being the most diplomatic action, when Lord George Spalding came to his rescue.

"You need not worry about sitting down with us, my good sir. We shall be dining alone, whereas I imagine Sir Thomas and Lady Cecilia may well have dinner guests. If necessary I can lend you such articles as may be needful, and it would be as well to be on hand here, if you wish to make an early start on your journey tomorrow."

Such a practical solution could not but be accepted with gratitude, and thus all was arranged.

The journey back to Gould House was accomplished with Serena taking upon herself the burden of the conversation; neither Anne nor Robert finding they had much to say. Anne speedily wrote two letters: one to Mrs Castleton and one to Mrs Rowlings, and as she gave them to Robert she was moved to say:

"I am so grateful to you, Mr Brightwell, for undertaking such a journey to bring us the news, but you must be anxious about your work on the canal."

"I am hoping, ma'am, that I have left all in order for things to continue in my absence, and although Mr Will Spalding is laid up in his bed, he is able to issue orders and receive reports on the progress of the work. Mr William Smith hopes to return to Kent in a while to continue to oversee the final stages of the project. I hope that you will find there has not been too much delay."

"You have done all you can and more, Mr Brightwell," and Anne held out her hand. Robert took it, and almost without thinking, raised it to his lips. Colouring up once more, he then hurried from the room, and so did not see Anne lift her hand to her cheek and hold it there.

*

It was not to be supposed that Lord George Spalding would give up his pursuit of Anne de Bourgh easily. Whatever he had read into the look that had passed between her and the young engineer, he did not consider that anything could come of it. It was perfectly natural, he thought, that the young man would become enamoured of such a mistress as Miss Anne, and that she would recognise such devotion as her natural right. But the more he reflected on the matter, the more he became convinced that any offer he might make would far outweigh any feelings Robert Brightwell had, perhaps unwittingly, displayed and that she may hold towards him. George had after all, a title to offer and a place in society to which she was eminently suited. She would grace the position of Countess of Rettingborough as well as his mother had done, and he resolved not to place her in any danger of having to undergo such humiliation as his mother had suffered under his father. Only one woman could tempt him away from his marital duties, and she was lost to him forever. The memory of Emma Hamilton would haunt him always; no other woman would ever match her in his heart, but perhaps in time he could come to esteem his wife as far as he was able. He would certainly hold her in respect, and what more could any woman reasonably ask of marriage? Thus, George felt perfectly able to sit down to dinner with one he considered to be hardly a rival for Anne's affections, so much more did he feel he had to offer. And what after all, could one whose birth could not but be lowly have any right to expect? All the same, he felt it could not but serve his interests were he to give a hint to Mr Brightwell where his best interests lay: viz: to remove himself from Miss de Bourgh's notice and leave the way clear for his lordship's greater claim. This he did, discreetly, after dinner over the port.

Robert Brightwell needed no such hint. Conscious as he was of his need to vindicate himself before Miss Anne de Bourgh and to reassure her he had abandoned his prejudice toward her family, he nonetheless steadfastly closed his mind against the possibility of any further or closer friendship than that she had once offered and he had spurned. That he loved her, he now had no doubt at all. What he read into her look and manner on their sudden and surprising meeting, he would not let himself think. They had been childhood friends; however, what had been permitted to children under the aegis of an easy-going baronet like Sir Lewis, would not be permitted between the grown-up daughter

196

of that baronet and an engineer's apprentice. True, his mother had been the youngest child of an impoverished Irish peer, and his father the son of a gentleman farmer, but the marriage had been viewed with disfavour by both families and they had been compelled to make their own way in the world. They had succeeded, and had brought up their children with grace, good manners and a willingness to work, but none of this could raise them in the eyes of society. And circumstances—and Lady Catherine de Bourgh's hostility—had lowered them yet further. Robert bowed to the inevitable, if Will Spalding as the younger son of an earl felt he could not aspire to address Miss Anne de Bourgh, then what did his older brother think humble Mr Brightwell could do? He turned to Lord George.

"My lord, I have the greatest respect and admiration for Miss de Bourgh. I feel sure she would grace your house with her presence. May I say I wish you well?"

*

Sir Thomas and Lady Cecilia, on hearing the sad news from Rosings, were all concern, although Lady Cecilia could not quite see the necessity for Anne's leaving so soon. Surely, she said, all things can be managed by the staff at the house and by the bailiff of the estate …

"But I have lost my good bailiff, Aunt," Anne interrupted to remind her, "and although things will certainly go on for a while without him, no doubt any number of things may arise which he would manage, but which I must undertake until I can find a replacement. I must also pay my respects as soon as may be to his widow and ensure she has all she needs for her future comfort."

Cecilia indeed saw the necessity for this, but could not help bewailing the fact that Anne's first season was to be cut short just as a large number of parties and events were beginning to get under way.

"And I had such of hopes of you becoming established creditably, my dear Anne, there being so many eligible young bachelors on the scene…"

Anne shook her head at this and half laughing, exclaimed:

"Indeed there are, Ma'am, and many more not so suitable. But I have indeed enjoyed my season, short as it has been and I am more than obliged to you for all you have done on my behalf. I fully intend to return to London for cousin Kit's wedding, so let us say au revoir, dear Aunt for the present."

Anne found she had much to do in the weeks in which she had resolved to bring her London season to a premature end. She visited the Fortescues and found, to her surprise and delight that her Uncle Percy was with them. It seemed that the mills of British Justice grind but slowly, but they did indeed grind to some purpose. Due to the efforts of Mr Coke, the case of the Honourable Percy Trethallen de Bourgh was brought before His Majesty, who, perhaps remembering his own incarceration during his spell of - the King would not admit the word 'madness' even to himself, calling it 'illness'—felt that eighteen years in prison was enough for any crime short of murder, and signed his release, with immediate effect. Mr Coke carried the Royal Pardon with all speed to Newgate, and Percy was borne off to the Fortescue's. Here, Mr Fortescue set about making him a suit of clothes necessary for a man about to re-make his way in society, and Mrs Fortescue set about building him up in order to fit them. Anne expressed her joy at her uncle's release:

"It is strange to consider the workings of Providence, Uncle," she said. "At one time, you told me, you wished to become secondary to Mr Castleton, and I had thought to ask you to consider taking up such a task. But due to his unfortunate and untimely death, it is the position of bailiff at Rosings which now needs to be filled. Do you feel you could accept the post?"

Not often did the Honourable Percy find himself lost for words, but he was speechless now.

"I will leave you to think on it," Anne continued. "You need to rest and recover strength of both mind and body. But if, when you feel able, you would come to Rosings and let the beauty of the park and the estate in summer help you recover your spirits, then perhaps, you will also feel able to decide what to do."

Collecting his thoughts and finding his voice at last enabled Percy to thank his niece and assure her he would give her kind offer due consideration. Grateful as he was to the Fortescues for all they had done, and were continuing to do for him, the thought of Kent, of Rosings Park, of his home, acted on his spirits like the balm of Gilead.

On returning to Gould House, Anne found Lord George had called and was sitting with her Aunt Cecilia. He had come, he informed her, to offer to accompany her back to Rosings. Anne's first instincts was to refuse this offer, but two things gave her pause. Lady Cecilia had been the interested recipient of Lord Spalding's confidences with regard to his seeking to pay his addresses to Anne, and she was delighted to think she had been the instrument of bringing them together at Kit's Ball. All her work and effort on Anne's behalf would not now be wasted if such an eligible match could be brought about. She urged Anne to accept his lordship's kind offer.

The second thought which came to Anne was that she could scarcely refuse Lord George's wish to visit his mother and brother. She therefore summoned all her effort to accept with gratitude. But that she was not all pleased, she admitted, almost crossly to her companion later.

"I know he was a pupil of yours, my dear Serena, and he is everything one could wish for in a gentleman, but…" she paused.

"I knew there would be a 'but'. What is your objection to him?"

"I hardly know. Except I think he is paying me far too much attention, and yet—yet I feel his heart is not in it."

"That is an interesting observation. Is it not true, however, that your heart is not in it either?"

"Indeed, you are right. And if neither party is heart-whole, what chance is there of happiness in a friendship, let alone anything more? Oh, Serena, I wish it were Mr Vauney who was to accompany us!"

"Ah so do I, my dear. But he has his work and obligations here in his teaching and his lectures to the Royal Society. Perhaps though, if you offer him an invitation, he might visit us at Rosings during the Long Vacation?"

"Yes, do invite him by all means. I would like nothing better and he would be such a lively addition to our dinners. You would also have the time and leisure to get to know one another!"

To her astonishment, Serena blushed at this, but the look of joy in her eyes told Anne that she too would like nothing better.

*

Mrs Rawlings was delighted that Rosings came once more to be filled with inhabitants, as this enabled her to exercise her housekeeping skills to the fullest extent. She chivvied the maids and the house-boys; encouraged Cook in her efforts; inspected the footmen, and spent hours with Roberts discussing the necessary arrangements. The Earl and the Dowager Countess of Rettingborough were installed in the West Wing; Mr William Spalding exercised his efforts at walking in his old apartments in the East Wing, aided by Mr Robert Brightwell, and where they were joined in due course by Mr William Smith, and Mr Percy took up his abode in the Muniments Tower, where, he told Anne, he had always wanted to reside.

Anne was delighted to be home. She took the opportunity to ride out every day on her beloved Firefly, who had welcomed her with obvious affection. If her rides took her more often than not to view the workings of the canal, John Groom thought nothing of it. Her manner towards Mr Smith and Mr Brightwell was always of the most correct.

She tried also to maintain a cool distance from Lord George Spalding, but alas, was not always successful in this. He pursued her with a gentle persistence and although his manners were impeccable, his attentions were such as to come to the notice of Percy de Bourgh. He came upon his niece in the book-room, where she had sought refuge with the excuse that she needed to consult her father's agricultural pamphlets. Never one to abandon the direct approach Percy asked Anne bluntly what she intended to do with regard to his Lordship's suit.

"I do not want it, Uncle," Anne said with spirit, "If he comes to the point of making me an offer, I shall have to refuse him, but I can find no good reason for doing so, except that the thought of marriage with him fills me with repugnance!"

Percy raised his eyebrows.

"Well, well. Now why I wonder should that be? Have you not considered his position? His title?"

"I care nothing for his position, nor his title. I should be sorry if my refusal disappoints his mother, because I like and respect Lady Spalding, but it must be so. I cannot marry him, Uncle."

"Then, my dear, I shall bestir myself on your behalf"

Anne looked at him in wonderment.

"How will you do that?"

"I do not know as yet, but I feel sure I shall hit upon the very thing: Leave it to me, Niece, and I promise you all will be well."

Anne was not at all satisfied with this and pressed him to explain further, but he would say no more.

Whatever Percy had in mind did not prevent matters coming to a head that very afternoon. The weather had turned warm again after several days of showers and in the cool of the day, Anne had gone into the Rose Garden to gather blooms for her own and Serena's sitting rooms. Here Lord George came upon her, and lost no time in declaring himself, even going so far as to go down on one knee. Anne's first practical thought was that he would spoil his beautiful pale pantaloons and she adjured him to get up as the ground was still damp. But George persisted, and was ardent in his pressing his offer. Anne was searching for words with which to refuse him, when Percy de Bourgh came strolling round the comer of the house. George rose to his feet with surprising dignity and stood his ground, expecting Percy to make his bow and his excuses and leave them. Percy however did no such thing. And responded at once to Anne's look of entreaty.

"Dear me," he said, "It seems I have stumbled upon a scene of romance."

"Sir," began George, but Percy held up a hand.

"I take it you are seeking my niece's hand in marriage? Well, you will find I have something to say to that."

"I cannot think that it is your concern, Sir. Surely you are not Miss Anne's guardian? Or indeed the head of the family? She is indeed her own mistress and therefore must be allowed to speak her own mind," and he turned back to Anne.

"She can indeed," Percy went on. "But there are things about this family that you need to know if you wish to marry into it. And I am the one who can best furnish you with such information. Permit me, Niece, to talk with his lordship in private if you will."

Anne hastily picked up her basket of roses and went swiftly into the house.

"Now," said Percy smoothly, "I know something of your family's history, Lord Spalding. I have spent the past years reading any number of newspapers and periodicals, and I know of your father, and of your own efforts to rescue the family name and fortune. All this is very commendable. But I would beg you to consider whether your purpose would be served were it known you sought to ally yourself with a family which contained a jailbird? Myself," he added.

George gave a harsh laugh.

"Surely, my own family contains worse than that? And at closer quarters than your relations with Miss de Bourgh?"

"Just so. But you have not fully considered, dear sir. All your diplomatic efforts under Sir William Hamilton would come to nothing if you married my niece. What would the polite world think? That you could not do better than to link yourself with this family which has just such a disreputable member as myself in its midst? And that therefore there must be some truth in the rumour concerning your amiable relationship with Sir William's beautiful wife …?"

George uttered an oath.

"Leave Lady Hamilton out of this discussion if you please!"

"Ah! Just so. We will leave her out. But you may well find that Society is not so willing to leave her out. You cannot afford any rumour to upset the careful position which you have worked so hard to build up, and on which I congratulate you. Think hard and long Lord Spalding. I bid you good day."

And Percy bowed and strolled away.

***
**
*

Epilogue

"Why hast Thou cast our lot
In the same age and place?
And why together brought
To see each other's face?
To join with loving sympathy
And mix our friendly souls in Thee?"
Charles Wesley (1749)

    Anne, angry at herself, wondered what she could have done to prevent matters coming to just such a head as she had feared. She was not at all sure that Uncle Percy would succeed in whatever he had in mind, and she paced her sitting room in agitation. A glance at the little French clock on the mantle-piece told her the time was growing late; in an hour or so she would have to dress for dinner. How would she face Lord George and Lady Spalding after this? Thoughts of pleading a migraine came to her, only to be rejected as unworthy. No, she would act as she had always done, with the dignity of her position. She began to arrange her roses and try to calm her mind.

    What was it that prevented her from accepting Lord George? As she had said to Serena, he was everything one could wish for in a gentleman, but that his heart was not hers. He did not love her, of that she was sure. How she was sure of this she did not know, but she did know her own heart did not, could not, belong to him. She had already bestowed it elsewhere. She remembered leaning on the windowsill at Pemberley one evening last summer and thinking she was in the happy position of being able to choose any man of birth and breeding she wished. Suddenly she knew what she had to do. Her heart had made its choice; all that was needed now was to discover whether it was the right choice. A clatter in the stable yard, heard clearly as the windows were open to the warm air, told Anne that Mr Smith and Mr Brightwell had returned from their work.

    "Why not now?" thought Anne. *"Why not here?"*

    She hastily made her way to the stables.

    Robert Brightwell was rubbing down his horse with a wisp of straw and whistling like an ostler. Anne laughed to herself; how did know how to do that? Her shadow fell across the doorway and Robert looked up in surprise.

    "Miss de Bourgh?"

"Mr Brightwell," she returned rather breathlessly, "I have come … have come to ask something of you, which …which you may not want … not want to hear …"

"Miss de Bourgh, there is something which I have wanted for a long time to tell you, or rather to ask you. I have not had the opportunity, nor the courage, but I wanted to say…to ask if you would forgive my words to you last December, when you invited me to dinner and I refused. Whatever you wish to ask of me, and I would understand if you wished me to be gone from here."

"No!" cried Anne, "Not that! Please, anything but that!" She recollected herself. "Mr Brightwell, you have no need to beg my forgiveness. I have become aware of at least some of the things you have suffered under my family, and it is surely my task to ask forgiveness of you. I simply wanted to say … to tell you …"

Robert threw away the wisp of straw he had been using, and took Anne's hands in his own.

"I am dirty from my work, I am sorry. But you are obviously in some distress, Miss de Bourgh, and I would do anything in my power to help you. What is it you want to say?"

"That I have received an offer from Lord George Spalding."

Robert made to draw his hands away, but Anne clung to them.

"And I wanted to tell you that I can never accept him, not indeed anyone because there is only you. Since our days together as children there is no-one else I want in my life as friend, lover…or indeed as husband, but you. Only you, my dear Robert."

*

What is there left to tell? As in all the best stories, the two lovers found each other after each had undergone trials, tribulations and misunderstandings, the bitters and the sweets of love. That summer was warm and bright, walking and riding the lanes of Rosings Park, they each told their tale; each asked and freely gave pardon; together reached an understanding that their childhood friendship had indeed blossomed into mature and lasting love. If there were any members of Anne's family so disobliging as to cavill at her choice of life partner, she had only this to say:

"What family do I have to disoblige? What other considerations should there be than those of inclination, respect, liking, love? He is my equal in intellect and interest; indeed my superior in knowledge and learning. In manners and courtesy he is more the gentleman than some others I have encountered who consider themselves to have a greater claim to birth and breeding."

But if certain members of Anne's family found themselves unwilling at first to accept such an alliance, there were others who, together with a number of friends, rejoiced at Anne's and Robert's good fortune. Especially those who themselves had found mutual respect, liking and love in their life partners. Elizabeth and Fitzwilliam Darcy lost no time in writing to Anne to express their delight in her happiness. Charlotte Collins, invited to Rosings to celebrate her betrothal to Mr Stevens, said in her quiet way that she was pleased Anne was not to fall into marriage as a necessity or as society dictated, but that she had had the courage to follow the wishes of her own heart. Glad too were those whose fortunes, linked in the web of this story, improved as the year wore on: Percy de Bourgh took up his duties as bailiff of Rosings Estate; Hannah Brightwell, with her little son Lewis was prevailed upon to come back to Kent, where Anne and Robert installed her in the Dower House, as befitted the mother of the new Master of Rosings Park, while the Fortescues found their business going from strength to strength, due in some part to Anne's patronage and even more to their own industry and skill.

*

September of the year 1801 was as warm and golden as the last. The harvest was brought in and proved to be better than in previous years. In Hunsford and among the friends and family of the de Bourghs, September became known as the month of weddings. Kit Gould was united with her baronet in a truly splendid ceremony at St George's in London; Mr Stevens wed his Charlotte; Serena Pope married Mr Vauney and Anne and Robert de Bourgh celebrated their marriage in a quiet manner in the little church in Hunsford which, like so many of its kind, had seen its plentiful share of both sorrows and gladness.

***
**
*